CHARMED
NIGHTS

THE WITCHES OF HOLLOW COVE
BOOK THREE

KIM RICHARDSON

FABLEPRINT

FablePrint

Charmed Nights, The Witches of Hollow Cove, Book Three

Cover by Kim Richardson
Printed in the United States of America

ISBN-13: 9798582353034
[1. Supernatural—Fiction. 2. Demonology—Fiction. 3. Magic—Fiction].

CHARMED NIGHTS

THE WITCHES OF HOLLOW COVE
BOOK THREE

KIM RICHARDSON

CHAPTER

1

I stood in the entryway of Davenport House, my eyes tracing the wood grain from the front door. It gave the place a rich, organic glow, and my heart thumped on superspeed. My aunts and Iris stood a few paces behind me, their nervous energy intensifying my nerves until I felt as though I might jump out of my skin and leave it in a pile on the floor like a heap of discarded clothes.

Today was October 31. It was Samhain, or Halloween as the humans called it, a celebration of the end of summer and the beginning of a new magical year. We prepared a huge feast and honored our dead—witch or animal familiars who'd passed—and took our celebration through the streets of Hollow Cove. The festivities ended with a massive bonfire on Sandy Beach, where we sang and danced until the early morning hours.

It was by far my favorite witchy celebration, yet my heart was not in the celebrating mood.

Today was Samhain, but it was also my first day of the Merlin witch trials.

Oh, goodie.

Two months had passed since I received my summons, if you will, from the Witch Trials Training Division Director, Greta Trickle. In her short letter, Greta had stated that if I didn't attend the trials my Merlin license would be revoked.

How very kind of her.

According to the lengthy telephone conversation my Aunt Dolores had had with Greta after reading my letter, my Merlin license had been suspended. Greta had written to the North American Board of Merlins, the department that administers the licenses, and had managed—no doubt by exaggerating the circumstances in which I had received mine—to convince the board to suspend my license until I satisfactorily completed the witch trials.

So here I was, two months later, fully energized and ready to begin my newest adventure. Yeah, not really. Truth was, I was nervous as hell.

According to my little black book of ley lines, *The Ley Lines of North America*, I was going to have to transfer lines after the fifth stop and take another ley line west to High Peak Wilderness, New York—wherever that was. Jumping different ley lines wasn't the reason I was shaking.

The unknown had my legs doing a little jig—possibly a tap dance.

For nearly two months my aunts had done their best to coach and prepare me for what I might expect. Like clockwork, they'd been quizzing and testing me: Ruth on potions, Dolores on ley lines and power words, and Beverly on enchantments and glamours. It never stopped. Even Iris chipped in. She tested me on my demon summoning skills and Dark curses and hexes. Though the aunts kept telling her that wasn't in the trials, she just pretended she didn't hear them and taught me anyway.

And I wanted to learn. All of it. Knowledge was power, and the more magical knowledge I had, the better off I would be. Or so I hoped.

But the truth was, it had been more than thirty years since my aunts had navigated the witch trials, and a lot could change and happen in that amount of time. Which meant, anything they coached me on might not be valid anymore.

I could have responded to Greta with a nice drawing of my middle finger, but seeing how important it was to my aunts that I become a Merlin like them, I decided to keep that drawing lying on my desk. It might come in handy for someone else… like Gilbert.

Being a Merlin meant something. It meant respect in our paranormal communities. It meant holding a position that could actually make a difference and help our people. I wanted to be part of that. For the first time in my life, I felt I had a true purpose, like I was meant to become a Merlin.

So, I'd made a promise to myself. I *would* pass the witch trials and get my Merlin license back, no matter what.

"It's fifteen to nine. You should go," instructed my Aunt Dolores. She stood with a hand on her hip while she gestured with the other, reminding me of a schoolteacher. At five-ten, her deep frown and cynical eyes would have many men scurrying away. Her long gray hair was loose and fell down her back, giving her a softer edge. But you'd be a fool if you thought her soft, just before she knocked you down with one of her spells. "You don't want to be late on your first day," she said. "Being late would be *catastrophic*."

"The only late that's catastrophic is when you're pregnant," said Beverly, swinging her hips and tossing her blonde hair back. "Or when you have to choose between two men. Or three. Or four men. *That's* catastrophic. This isn't."

I gave a nervous laugh. "I won't be late," I answered, wondering if I'd just answered Beverly or Dolores. Letting out a sigh, I adjusted the strap of my messenger bag on my shoulder. I'd stuffed it with only the essentials: my ever-faithful *The Witch's Handbook, Volume Three*, my little black book of *The Ley Lines of North America*, a couple of power bars, one carrot muffin, my wallet, and my phone.

Speaking of phones, I grabbed it and glanced at it one last time, my heart dancing as I glanced at the screen. No missed calls. No new texts.

Deflated, I dropped my phone back into my bag. Marcus had been MIA for nearly two months. He'd been called on urgent business up in Pennsylvania to help with some crisis the same night we were supposed to have our very first date. He'd texted me that evening before he left.

Marcus*: I'm leaving for Pennsylvania tonight. It's urgent. Give you the details later. I'll be back in a couple of weeks. Sorry about dinner. I'll make it up to you. Promise. Call you when I get back.*

I'd texted him back.

You better. And added a smiling emoji.

That was the last text I'd gotten from him. It was the last anything I'd gotten from him. And that was nearly two months ago.

I'd remained hopeful as the weeks went by but nothing. I'd resisted the urge to call him the first two weeks. I didn't want to be *that* woman who kept her man on a tight leash. Marcus wasn't my man. We hadn't even been on a first date. He wasn't my anything. But after a month of not hearing from him, I decided to call.

It went straight to his voicemail.

Marcus never called or texted me back. I'd really wanted that dinner, damn it. But if he was ghosting me, he was going to get an earful the next time I saw him.

The fact that he didn't call back or text to let me know his trip was going to take a little longer than expected… hurt. I'll admit it. I was falling for the guy, the chief of Hollow Cove. That kiss had been extraordinary, causing my brain cells to explode on impact.

But the fact the guy didn't call back spoke volumes about said guy.

It said I wasn't important enough to him to merit one damn phone call.

My pulse sped faster at the thought, and I hated how it made me feel. I felt stupid for letting my guard down and allowing him in, and I was angry as hell.

I forced those gloomy thoughts away. I couldn't lose my cool or get distracted. I had to focus on what was more important and pressing, like passing the witch trials.

I'd need my whole brain for that—and then some.

My nerves skyrocketed the longer I stood there staring at the door. I glanced over my shoulder to Iris. She gave me a tight smile with her full lips, her dark eyes round with excitement. The thirty-two-year-old Dark witch had settled amazingly well into Davenport House with the rest of us. One look at her pretty, pixie-like face, silky black hair, and perfect little body, you'd never guess that only two months ago she roamed around Hollow Cove as a goat. That douchebag Adan had put the curse on her to keep her quiet. But with Adan six feet under, the curse had lifted. Iris was a witch again.

I thought she might have preferred to return home to her family, but she'd decided to stay with us. We'd become quite close, like sisters, really. Being an only child, I'd always wanted a sister, someone I could rely on since my mother and father (mostly my father) had been MIA most of my childhood.

Ruth handed me a small brown paper bag, pulling me out of my thoughts. "Here. I made you a lunch in case you get hungry. With all that traveling, you might get hungry. And if

7

you're hungry, all you have to do is eat what's in the bag."

"I think she gets it, Einstein," grumbled Dolores with a smile.

I didn't have the heart to tell her I'd already packed some snacks. "Thank you, Ruth. That's very thoughtful." I snatched up the brown paper bag and dropped it in my messenger bag, not wanting my aunts or Iris to see my shaking hands. It was the only thing I carried. Hauling luggage around would have been awkward. Since I was able to use the ley lines, I could come home after the trials. Thank the cauldron for that. I did *not* want to stay in a hotel with a bunch of strangers as my blood pressure was already hitting a record high.

Ruth took my hand and squeezed it in hers. "You'll do fine. Just be yourself," she encouraged, seemingly having noticed my unease and nervousness no matter how hard I tried to hide it. She smiled, the corners of her blue eyes wrinkling and holding a mixture of wonder and excitement. Her white hair was piled on top of her head in a messy bun held by two pencils.

"That's the problem," I mumbled. "Whenever I'm myself, crap happens."

Ruth laughed. "Me too. It's part of being a Davenport witch. It's our charm."

"Like hell it is. Crap is not *my* charm," huffed Beverly, her usual sultry tone high with nerves. She winked at me and added, "My curves are."

"You ready?" asked Dolores, the tension carrying through in her voice.

"No." But what choice did I have? Either jump the ley line or lose my Merlin license. I let out a shaky breath. "Well. Guess I'll be going now."

"Knock 'em dead," said Dolores, inclining her head by way of dismissal.

I beamed. "If you say so."

Dolores rolled her eyes. "You know what I mean. Though I wouldn't mind picking out a casket for Greta. A black one… with little red worms would do marvelous."

Iris stepped forward. "I wish I could come with you," said the Dark witch, her black hair swaying against her chin.

"Me too." I'll admit, having Iris with me might have helped some of my jitters. But I was a grown woman. I could do this. I *had* to do this on my own.

I dipped my head. "See you in a bit."

Steeling myself, I focused my will and reached out to tap the ley line. A vast, roaring current of magical energy radiated out and hit me. I felt the ley line's magic in my mind, flowing by with a power that vibrated up through the soles of my boots. It charged by like an enormous rushing, crushing river.

I took a deep breath and then thrust my thoughts down into that power. Into the ley line.

And then I reached out, grabbed the door handle, pulled open the door—and jumped.

CHAPTER
2

High Peak Wilderness was *exactly* how it sounded—a giant wilderness of pine, oak, ash, maple, fir, and spruce trees with rolling hills, vast lakes, and glimmering ponds.

After transferring ley lines west, I'd jumped out on the tenth stop (the closest to High Peak Wilderness, New York, that I could find) and found myself deep in a forest.

I stood on a hill, where red and orange leaves carpeted the ground at my feet, getting a view of my surroundings. A gentle, cool breeze lifted the hair from my face and set the leaves in the trees rustling. The remaining leaves on the trees were an explosion of color in deep reds, oranges, and yellows. But they wouldn't stay. With a strong wind, they'd all fall to the ground.

In the summer, this place was probably tick central, not to mention the swarm of mosquitoes and horseflies just waiting to make a meal out of you. However, the cold weather took care of that—thank the cauldron.

The rich smells of wet earth, leaves, and the balsam firs' spicy scent was intoxicating. I loved the fall, but I wasn't here for sightseeing, even if it was beautiful. A weekend here with Marcus would have been great, and my heart squeezed at the thought of me and him in a cozy hot tub in some log cabin, away from everyone. Just the two of us… naked in the steaming hot tub…

I shook my head, not wanting the chief to invade my mind, not while I was in an unknown territory. Hot flashes simply would not do. Though they were keeping me warm.

My gaze fell on a packed dirt road that wound down through the evergreen trees and reached a giant, log-like castle. The four-story mountain house rested on the edges of the lower mountain. I thought Davenport House was huge, but this place was ten times bigger.

The crunch of tires on gravel reached me and I looked over my shoulder to see three Greyhound buses, two dark SUVs, and a black sedan driving along the dirt road toward the log castle.

I checked my phone. "I've got five minutes to reach that castle or my ass is toast." I looked around one last time, expecting to see some other witches stepping out of the ley line, but it was just me standing there with a couple of angry squirrels giving me hell for stepping into their territory.

Seeing as no other witch used the ley lines as a means of transport, I decided to keep it to myself for now. The less they knew about me, the better.

My heart skipping with both dread and excitement, I followed the line of vehicles down the dirt road at a fast pace. When I reached the front courtyard, everyone was already out of the buses and cars and milling about. No one looked my way as I neared the group.

I slowed my pace so I could get a better look at who I was facing, the witches who were here to get their Merlin license like me.

At first, I'd expected to see young adults, just fresh out of their teens, and feared I'd be the oldest one here. I wasn't. The throng of faces ranged from fresh out of high school to those who looked like they could have been my aunts. Some witches had a confused, deer-in-the-headlights kind of look. Yeah, like looking at a mirror.

Okay, not so nervous anymore, but it was clear these witches probably grew up with magic all around them. Unlike me. I'd gotten glimpses over the years, but still, I had a lot of catching up to do.

The witches—an assortment of about a hundred with mixed ages, sexes, and ethnicities—all marched up to the front doors that swung open on their own to let them in, just like Davenport House. Maybe this place was just as magical.

The witches were all as different as they came, but they shared that same, wide-eyed, nervous, first-day-on-the-job kind of expression. I probably looked just as freaked out as they did. Nah. Probably more.

I hunkered near a parked car, pretending to look for something in my bag, as I peeked over to the witches moving through the massive entryway. I didn't want to be among the first idiots to walk into the massive mountain house, not knowing where to go or what to do. I'd look like a big ole fool. So, I stayed behind until the last witch, a short, older male with thick glasses and mousy brown hair surrounding a balding spot on the top of his head, climbed up the wide steps and hurried through the giant, wooden double doors.

I rushed forward and sneaked in behind him.

Just as I crossed the threshold, I felt it.

Magic.

And yet, it wasn't like the soft, warm ripples of energy that washed through me whenever I stepped into Davenport House, the kind of energy that sent tingling jolts over my skin. No. This was way more sinister.

A cold, hard pulse started from the top of my head and jerked all the way to my toes, hammering its way into every cell of my body. It did not feel good at all.

The best way I could describe it was like going through a customs full-body x-ray machine at the airport. I felt as though some invisible force was scanning me to see if I carried anything illegal or dangerous on my person.

"That was interesting," I said, making the older witch in front of me turn around.

"Groovy, isn't it," he said, his voice small and mousy, just like his appearance.

"Not the word I'd use." More like a violation of my body parts.

"It's a magic scanner. The MS 295 model. Top of its class. It makes sure you're not hiding any illegal curses and hex bags with you." He pushed up his glasses with his index finger. "Wow. You're tall."

I stared at the little witch. "Is there anyone stupid enough to bring curses and hex bags with them?"

He grinned. "Yes. Loads of times. Well, only last year a witch went through the witch scanner with a hex bag—older model—and managed to get a foot from the director before the old witch felt the hex bag and immobilized him. She's had over two hundred attempts on her life in the last twenty years."

"Really?" Though I was not surprised someone wanted to off Greta. I was just surprised it hadn't worked yet.

I stepped further away from the threshold and felt that horrid thrumming pulse ease until it disappeared. "You were here last year?" I looked past him to the last cluster of witches who disappeared through another large opening to the left of the entryway.

"Yes," he said and exhaled. The tension in his voice pulled my eyes back to him. Distress flashed across his features. "This will be my thirteenth time trying out for my Merlin license." He rubbed the back of his neck as the rim of his ears turned red. "Lucky number thirteen, right?" He laughed. The anxiety in his voice was so thick, I could practically feel it brushing against my face.

A knot formed in my gut. Either this witch was a severe underachiever, or the trials were excruciatingly difficult. I just stared at him again, my eyes moving from his leather worn shoes and plain khaki pants to his washed-out green shirt. He looked more like a struggling, part-time teacher than an accomplished witch.

"What happens if you don't pass them this year? Will you be able to take them again?" It was strangely comforting to know that if I failed, I could always take them again, kind of like a driver's license test. But thirteen times seemed a bit extreme. Not to mention that my aunts would be mortified if I failed, seeing as they had already elevated me to Merlin. They expected me to pass. Failing was not an option.

The witch's face turned beet red. "Unfortunately, this will be my last time," he said, shifting from foot to foot. "If I don't pass this time around… that's it. I'm finished. I won't be eligible for another go. Thirteen is where they draw the line."

He looked so pathetic and sad I wanted to go over and hug him, but that would be totally inappropriate. I wasn't much of a hugger, though I felt sorry for the guy. From the angst that twisted his features, I knew this was the most important thing in his life right now. Maybe he had family members waiting on him too.

I forced my face into a smile. "I'm sure you'll do fine. I mean… you've got twelve years of experience," I told him, wondering if he might be able to give me some tips. "That's got to be good for something. Right?"

The witched shrugged. "I don't know. Maybe. I'm Willis by the way." He stuck out his hand.

I shook it. "Tessa."

Willis's face brightened. "Hey… you think we can sit together? I don't know anyone here."

The sound of voices carried over and I pulled my head up toward the opening where I'd seen the last of the witches disappear. I recognized that voice. It was Greta's.

I stiffened, my pulse jackhammering. "Shit. They've started."

Securing my bag on my shoulder, I shot past Willis.

"Hey! Wait!" he called, but I didn't look back as I hurried through the doors and into what looked to be a large theater-like room housing rows of gray seats with red and yellow runes and sigils etched into the fabric. A stage sat at the far end.

I ducked into a back row and sat. I didn't want to be rude to Willis, but I wasn't here to make friends. Luckily, the older witch walked right past me and down the aisle to one of the front rows and sat. The scent of earth and pine needles sifted through the air. The magic from the hundred or so witches thrummed in the air and through me. Wow. I didn't think I'd ever been in a place surrounded by so many witches. It was like a radio had been turned on inside my head, flipping through the different channels so I heard hundreds of voices—

magic—all at once. I couldn't be certain, but it felt like all White magic.

My eyes moved to the front stage and settled on Greta. Her pale skin drooped down along her face, her dark eyes barely visible under the layers of wrinkles. Her white hair was cut so short she was nearly bald. She might look like a hundred-year-old witch, but she stood tall and proud and strong. The last time I'd seen her, she'd worn a gown of white silk. Today, a smart, dark skirt suit wrapped her thin frame and was paired with flat shoes. She looked like an experienced lawyer. Not so sure I liked this look better.

"…new and some familiar faces among you," Greta was saying, her voice magically magnified without a microphone. Her dark eyes moved along the rows of witches and settled on me. I stilled as the older witch frowned. She clearly wasn't happy to see me, like she hadn't expected me to show up.

Greta chewed on her lip for a minute, looking back and forth between some other witches. "For those of you who are unaware of what the witch trials entail, though I would imagine the most intelligent of this group would have done your research."

Research? "Are you freaking kidding me?" I whispered, and Greta's dark eyes snapped to me like she'd heard me.

Oh, crap.

"Merlins are our world's most respected and celebrated professionals in the witch community," continued the old witch. "Being a Merlin commands respect. Merlins are admired. Held in the highest esteem. Your peers will look up to you, want to be you. It's not something to be taken lightly." She hesitated, as though waiting to get everyone's full attention before continuing. "Only ten percent of you will pass," she added with a slight smirk, and a cacophony of disapproval and panicked voices rose around the theater like an angry gust of wind. "Because… the witch trials select only the best. And only the best witches can be Merlins."

I looked over to Willis and saw his head drop. My stomach fell somewhere around my toes.

Greta paced the stage, surprisingly fast and steady for someone her age. "The trials consist of three major concentrations." She lifted her hand and gestured with her fingers. "Defensive Magic, Operational Skills, and Case Exercises. Three separate trials will test each concentration. This program provides Merlins with specialized training in intelligence analysis, the study of magical intelligence." Greta's gaze flew over the rows of witches. "My program is the best. And *only* the best… will make it."

"You've already said that," I mumbled, a bad feeling knotting in my stomach.

"As such," continued Greta, "your first trial will begin on December first, at 8 a.m. sharp." I noticed Willis jotting down this information on a pad of paper. A strange, wicked smile spread over the folds of wrinkles on her face. "Fail two of the trials… and you fail *all* the trials," she said, her voice filled with twisted delight, as though she took pleasure in the failure of others.

"Lovely," I grumbled and swallowed. My aunts had forgotten to mention that part. My nerves anxiously started a Ping-Pong match inside my chest. This was worse than I had expected. Much worse. The only good thing was apparently I had a month to prepare for the first trial. That worked for me. I had thirty days to get my act together. I just hoped it was enough.

"You'll have a six-day break between each trial," Greta went on. "Each trial will be conducted by its selected arbitrator." She looked down to the left of the stage. "Marina. Silas. Please join me."

Two people got up from the front row and joined her on the stage, a woman and a man. The woman I immediately recognized. That strange, eerie smile that seemed to pull up more on the left of her face and blonde hair could only belong to one of the witches from the New York Merlin group I'd met along with Greta at the Night Festival. Though I'd never known her name until now.

She wore tight jeans and a short leather jacket with studs. The right side of her head was shaved to the scalp, and she let her other side flow loosely with a strand of golden braids in sort of an eighties punk vibe. I was digging it, though she was creepy.

The man called Silas had me holding my breath, and not in a good way.

He was tall, maybe six-three, thin and wolfish, with a dark goatee and long black ponytail. Half of his face was hidden in tattoos of magical runes and sigils. He was dressed in all black, and I could see some more tattoos peeking from under his shirt and around his neck. He looked to be in his mid-thirties. He wasn't handsome, more brutish like an ogre.

When he crossed his arms over his chest, I caught a glimpse of his hands. Dark markings that were too far away to decipher covered them until I couldn't even see evidence of his natural skin. He smiled nastily at the reaction he was getting from everyone, and a little chill went through me. Definitely not the type of guy you brought home to meet your family— or maybe you did. If you were into tats.

"These are your arbitrators." Greta's voice bellowed around me. "Marina will be mediating the first trial, Silas the second. And I will be evaluating the last. Do not think because you've made it to the final trial that it will be easy. Make no mistake. The last trial will be the hardest." Greta's face took on a harder cast. "Let me be clear. Even if you succeed in the first two trials… if you fail the last trial—you *fail* the witch trials. Fail the last trial, and you're finished."

"Figures, the old hag would get the last trial," I whispered, though it came out louder than I'd anticipated. *Whoops.*

Greta's eyes searched the rows of witches and settled on me. "Tessa Davenport. Stand up."

Oh… crapola.

My heart slammed in my chest as heads turned in my direction, trying to determine who Greta was talking to. I thought about flattening myself to the ground, but the old witch had already seen me.

I stood up slowly, aware of everyone's attention on me, and I tried to keep my trembling body still as I kept my focus on Greta. If they saw me shaking, I was finished.

Greta's expression was hard, though the amusement was evident on her face. "Did you have something to add? Please speak up so we can all hear what a Davenport witch has to say. Yes, that's right. We have among us a celebrity." Gasps and low, vicious murmurs ran through the theater.

Thanks a lot, you old cow. "I have nothing to add. Please continue," I said, my voice surprisingly strong amid the shaking in my legs.

"Of course, you don't," continued Greta, "because you know all about the trials. Don't you, Tessa? Because you Davenport witches think you're above everyone else. You think you can do whatever you please and change the rules as you see fit."

Marina snickered, her eyes widening in delight at my humiliation. Hated her.

"We don't," I countered, imagining her head exploding. "I don't."

Greta's low, mocking laugh grew in depth but then faded with a bitter sound. "You see, dear witches. Tessa Davenport believed she was above the rules, believed that she was *better* than all of you."

I gritted my teeth. "I never said that."

"And do you know what she did?" continued Greta, as though I never spoke. "She elevated herself to a *Merlin*."

Gasps rushed around me, and I swore I saw a few witches curse me.

Well, this was going way better than I had hoped. I was all fuzzy inside.

"All without doing the trials," finished Greta. "She thought she could get away with it, but she didn't. I made sure of that." She pinned me with her eyes. "In other words, you cheated. And by cheating, you cheated everyone here."

Way to go, Grandma. Now everyone thought I'd cheated. Just by catching a few glares, it was obvious they hated me. Hell, I would hate me too if it were true, but it wasn't.

I caught Willis's eyes, and I could see the hurt and anger flashing there. He thought I'd cheated too. This was just getting better and better.

My face burned with hot anger. "I didn't cheat," I said, my voice rising. "I didn't even know about these stupid trials until two months ago." *Oops.* Shouldn't have said that.

Greta's features turned hard. "These… *stupid* trials, you say?"

"I didn't mean it like that. You *were* attacking me. The words just flew out—"

"You think these trials are a joke? You think everyone here is a joke?"

Oh, boy. "I don't think that. Of course not." My pulse hammered. This old witch wanted me to burn. That part was clear.

Greta watched me for a moment. "Why are you here, Tessa Davenport, if you think these trials are a joke?"

"I don't think that." I frowned, my hatred for her dripping through my voice. "I'm here to get my Merlin license. Just like everyone else."

Greta laughed softly. "But you don't think you're like everyone else here. Do you, Tessa Davenport? You think you're something special. Like your aunts."

"I get it," I told her, willing her to shut her face, or I was about to go up there and do it myself.

"Do you?" she mocked. "Well, we shall see. Won't we?"

A shiver rose through me, and I stifled it. "What's that supposed to mean?"

Greta looked to the crowd and said, "The first trial will take place here at Montevalley Castle in one month from now, on December 1. Fail to be here, and you fail the trial. Fail two trials, or fail the last trial, and you'll have to wait another year to apply again," she concluded, her eyes settling on me. "Since you already think yourself qualified as a Merlin, these trials should be a piece of cake. I look forward to seeing these gifts with my own eyes."

At that, a consensus of laughter sounded through the crowd of witches.

I had no idea what to expect, but on account of Greta's evil satisfaction, I knew it would be bad. Really bad.

Not only did Greta despise me, so did the entire Merlins in training. I hadn't come here to make friends, but now it looked like I had my pick of enemies.

It was obvious Greta had it in for me. My aunts had elevated me to the Merlin status without advising her. And this... Well, this was her payback.

Oh, goodie. This was going to be fun.

CHAPTER
3

I sat on a flat rock on the beach, surrounded by golden sand, watching the waves hit the shore while letting the serene scene take some of the edge off. The cold winds brushed against my face, my ears whistling with their music. The sun was right above me, a lonely, brilliant disk in a vast blue sky, not a cloud in sight. Without the afternoon sun, I would probably have been a witch-sicle.

Sandy Beach was completely deserted except for a man walking his golden retriever. It was too cold to go swimming, and the sand was too icy to go barefoot, which I'd learned after dipping my toes in it. I just liked to watch the waves crashing against the shore and then receding. Something was strangely calming about that. A spray of the waves speckled my face. I didn't care. I didn't even wipe it off.

My butt was numb from sitting on the cold rock. I wasn't sure how long I sat here, though it felt like hours. I found I couldn't move. Once my butt settled on that rock, it was glued to it.

I'd decided to skip the ley line stop to Davenport house and jumped out somewhere right after it, which turned out to be smack on the boardwalk next to Sandy Beach. I realized, afterward, this was probably the same spot Adan had used for his escape.

The truth was, I couldn't face my aunts right now. My head still thrummed with anger at Greta, at the vile accusations that spewed from that witch's mouth. I'd been shocked at first, but my familiar friend—Mr. Anger—had soon taken over.

I needed a little quiet time to calm my nerves and wrap my head around what had just happened. The last thing I wanted was to alarm my aunts. I didn't want them to know just how *disastrous* my first day had been.

It had been a complete disaster of epic proportions and then some.

I'd been really looking forward to celebrating Samhain tonight with my aunts and Iris, but these trials were already taking their toll on me. I wasn't in the proper mindset for a celebration of any kind.

Thinking back, I'd been excited and nervous at the prospect of joining such an elite group of witches. The idea of the witch trials had had my heart doing jumping jacks, yes. But now… now I was left with a dull throb of anger that grew like an infected sore. Worse, I knew from Greta's expression and those of the other arbitrators that they were going to make my trials hell—literally.

It was very clear she wanted me to fail. They all did. She would go above and beyond to make these witch trials the hardest, most complicated, and most dangerous ever.

She wanted to break me. To scare me. To make me give up.

I wouldn't.

She could try to intimidate me, but she'd be wasting her time. I wasn't a child anymore. In fact, I'd practically raised myself, with my mother being away all the time. With my birthday coming up in December, I'd be thirty. Thirty was shedding the skin of your twenties, the years of apologizing constantly because you were afraid to hurt other people's feelings.

Screw that.

I had thick, thirty-year-old skin now. No one was going to mess with me. I was tough, and I had a pair of thirty-year-old lady balls. The more Greta wanted me to fail, the more it drove me to do better.

That old bitch didn't know who she was messing with.

"You're on, Greta," I growled.

My gaze traveled over the beach and fell on a couple walking hand in hand. Gray eyes framed by thick lashes, a square jaw, and full lips that should be illegal on any man flashed in my mind's eye.

I let out a sigh. Thinking of Marcus wasn't going to help. Though, it would have been nice to talk to him about these trials. I didn't know why he was ghosting me, but it sucked. I'd admit it. I just wished I knew why.

A bell sounded from my phone. I yanked it out of my bag and glanced at the screen. It was a text message from Iris.

Iris: *You home yet? Hope you kicked ass today. When you get this, please come to 1313 Shifter Lane. They found a body.*

"Excellent," I said, which was totally inappropriate. A job would be a welcomed distraction. Even though I wasn't technically a Merlin anymore, my aunts were, and there were no laws against trying to help.

I texted her back.

On my way.

Shifter Lane was just a few blocks away from Sandy Beach. I slipped my phone back in my bag and took off at a jog, which was very slow and awkward in the sand. Still, I made it in less than seven minutes.

31

A large orange sign proclaimed BERNARD'S BAKERY. The red and yellow brick building was sandwiched between Witchy Beans Café and Practical Magick bookstore and directly across from Gilbert's Grocer & Gifts. A large bay window had newly baked pastries and breads. The smell of baked bread sifted in the air and my stomach growled. I hadn't had lunch yet. I never touched the snacks I'd packed or Ruth's bag. I didn't have the stomach to eat anything right now. If I tried, I had a feeling it would just come right back up.

Panting, with what I suspected was a cramp on my side, I walked up the driveway just as my aunts' Volvo station wagon pulled up at the curb. The brakes squealed loudly as my Aunt Dolores put the car in park and killed the engine.

Dolores waved at me as she slammed her car door with her hip. "And? How was it? Did they make you do any magic? Did you try the wind cyclone spell I taught you? Was Greta surprised at your brilliance?"

My stomach twisted. Somehow I felt like a failure, though I hadn't even started the trials yet. I hated that Greta had instilled this new fear in me.

I pulled my face into the best fake smile I could muster. "It was fine. All good." My throat contracted. "What happened here?"

Dolores eyed me for a moment, her features twisting in skepticism. "Someone is dead. It's why we're here."

"We don't know who it is yet," said Beverly as she made her way around the car to stand next to her tall sister with Ruth and Iris following behind her.

Ruth's face exploded into delight at the sight of me. "Tessa! Oh, thank the cauldron. I was worried about you all day. Boy, I was a nervous wreck. I made a fruitcake without the fruit! So? How did it go?"

"I bet it was awesome," said Iris, giving me a thumbs up. "You kicked ass. Didn't you?"

My aunts and Iris all watched me expectantly like I was supposed to tell them this amazing news of how I performed miraculous spells as all the other witches oohed and ahhed at my brilliance. They'd elevated me to Merlin. They'd expected great things from me. They had no idea Greta was going to do everything in her power to watch me fail.

"Today was more of an orientation. A meet-and-greet," I replied as heat rushed to my face, hoping my sudden blush wouldn't give me away. "Everything's fine. It's fine. I'm fine. It's all fine."

Eyebrows high, Dolores said flatly, "I take it you're trying to tell us it *went fine*?"

"Yup."

Beverly stared at me suspiciously. She leaned in and whispered, "You look like you were caught sleeping with someone's husband." She smiled and added. "I invented that look. But you, my dear, need to work on your act a little if you expect us to believe you."

I opened my mouth in defense but then closed it. What good would it do to try and convince them? Absolutely nothing.

My aunts rocked into motion and made for the entrance of the bakery.

Angry and unsure, I headed toward the front door as Iris fell into step next to me. I could feel her eyes on me, but she didn't say anything. And I was grateful for it.

Bells chimed as Dolores pushed the front door open and we all followed her inside. The scent of baked breads and pastries was a lot stronger inside the shop, and it was warm, like the ovens were on, baking new and delicious pastries filled with fruit and chocolate and calories—yum.

I swept my gaze around the store. The shop was small with a table in the middle packed with wicker baskets stuffed with breadsticks and an assortment of cheeses. The walls were lined with wooden shelves packed with homemade jams. A large glass counter was at the opposite wall, where a display of cakes, cupcakes, donuts, cookies, more and more pastries sat, waiting to be eaten—waiting for *me* to eat them.

Behind the counter was a tight opening through which I could spy several stainless-steel ovens.

And in the middle of the room lay a man.

He looked to be in his late sixties, with a belly as large as if he were pregnant and a head full of gray and white hair. He lay on his side, and his eyes were open, bulging, and red with busted veins like he'd suffocated.

His green apron gave him away. He either worked here, or the dead guy was the owner, Bernard.

"Oh, thank the cauldron!" A plump woman in her early sixties came bursting out of the back door, smelling of cigarette smoke and rose perfume. Her flowing, horizontally striped yellow and black dress made her look like a giant bumblebee.

"I'm beside myself!" she shrieked, shaking her head and nearly sending her bejeweled glasses flying off her nose. "I came in for my usual order of strawberry turnovers and found Bernard lying there. He's dead! Dead! Look at him!" she howled, making my ears ring. The witch had some serious lungs.

"Calm down, Martha," ordered Dolores as she stepped toward the body. "We can see the witch isn't breathing."

"He's a witch?" I asked, looking down at the body but not getting any witch vibes. I sent out my senses, looking for any familiar magical energies, but felt nothing.

"He was," replied Ruth, sadness drawing her face into lines. "His gift wasn't like yours. No. His gift was with this shop, you know? Making pastries. It's where his magic shined. He loved it. Always gave me some extra Nutella twists with my orders." Her eyes widened. "Did you ever try his magic brownies?"

I smiled and shook my head. "No. But they do sound delicious." And maybe even illegal.

The sound of bells rang again, and I turned to see a short, pudgy man with gray hair and a bow tie standing in the doorway, his brown eyes bulging as he stared at the dead witch.

"Is that Bernard?" he questioned. "What happened to him? He looks dead… is he dead? Oh, my god! He's dead! Bernard's dead!" shrilled the little man as he stepped into the shop.

And so the circus begins.

"Get out, Gilbert," commanded Dolores, and then she turned her eyes on us. "We need to keep that door closed and locked."

Beverly unbuttoned the first three buttons from her blue silk blouse. "I've got this." She sashayed her way back to the front of the store, pushing out her chest with her black bra visible as she showed off the girls. "Out, Gilbert," she said pushing the shifter out the door. He looked utterly uncomfortable at the display of cleavage Beverly was showing. "This is Merlin business. Not nosey, tiny little men's business."

Gilbert backed away from Beverly. "But— but—what happened? Did you call…"

The rest of what Gilbert was saying was lost as Beverly slammed the door in his face and locked it.

She whirled around smiling. "Don't think I've ever done this before," she said, sounding surprised.

"What?" I asked.

"Thrown a man out." Her perfect face screwed up in a frown as she thought about it. "Gilbert doesn't count. My record is still untarnished," she added happily and made her way back to the dead witch.

"You think this was a heart attack?" questioned Ruth, sounding solemn and drawing my attention back to her. "He'd been complaining about his weight. He was a little out of breath the last time I saw him."

"Could be. He *was* overweight," concluded Dolores. "Heart attacks are common for men his age who don't exercise and eat all the wrong things."

Iris moved next to the body and knelt as she started sniffing his head and chest like a sniffer dog at the airport. Guess we didn't get all the animal out of her.

Dolores pressed her hands to her hips. "His wife doesn't know." She exhaled. "I hate this part. I've never been a good comforter. They always seem to cry more when I'm finished."

"That's because you scare them," said Beverly. "Bad news comes better from a petite, and delicate woman rather than a six-foot sasquatch with a broomstick." She won a dangerous glare from Dolores.

"I'll do it." Ruth moved behind the glass counter. "I'll call Patricia and tell her what happened." She picked up a phone next to a stack of papers and started dialing.

"So, how did it go with the witch trials, hon?" Martha appeared next to me, making me jump. I'd forgotten she was here.

I frowned at the large witch. "How did you know about the trials?"

Martha cocked a hip, her smile devious. "Darling, nothing happens in this town without my knowing about it," she said, as though that was supposed to mean something to me. "So? How was it?"

I thought about making the point that the witch trials were nowhere near Hollow Cove but decided against it. "Well. It went fine," I said again, sounding like a broken record.

Martha raised a manicured brow. "That bad, huh?"

Dolores's eyes snapped to me, and I moved away from Martha. This was not the time to bring up how horrible my first day had been.

"Well," sighed Dolores. "There's no evidence of any foul play here. Looks like Bernard died of natural causes, but we won't know for sure until the medical examiner performs an autopsy. And with Marcus still away, it is left to us to do the cleanup. It's our responsibility."

"Don't look at me," said Beverly, tossing her hair and looking like she just stepped out of a beauty salon. Wiggling her fingers, she said, "I don't touch dead flesh with these manicured hands."

Dolores rolled her eyes. "We all know what *flesh* you touch with those hands," she said, making Beverly giggle like she'd complimented her. Dolores turned and looked at me. "Tessa. You'll have to take Bernard's body to the morgue, and make sure to tell Grace who he is."

My mouth fell open. "Me? You want me to clean this up?"

"Yes."

"To bag Bernard and take him away?" God, that sounded awful.

"Yes."

"But I've never done this before."

"Today's your lucky day." Dolores cocked a brow. "I won't lie... this is one of the most unpleasant parts of being a Merlin. But you need to suck it up. With Marcus still away, it becomes our job. We can't just leave him here to stink up the entire town."

"Stage three rigor mortis is when the body's soft tissue decomposes and fluids are released through orifices as organs become liquefied," interjected Iris. "No matter how many times you bathe, that smell never leaves you."

"We still don't know when Marcus will be back," Dolores was saying, eyeing Iris strangely. "You need the experience. And with everything being fine with the trials, this shouldn't be a problem. Right? Right, Tessa?"

"Right," I ground out, knowing she was trying to get back at me for not telling them what really happened on my first day at the witch trials.

"Marcus has been gone an awfully long time," said Beverly, her brows low. "Strange that we haven't had a word from him. He usually always checks in with us. Tessa? Have you heard from him at all?"

I avoided my aunt's gaze. "No. Not since he left." It was no secret he'd ghosted me. But I didn't want to bring it up again. It stung enough as it was.

Beverly made a sound in her throat. "It's so unlike him to disappear like that without keeping in touch. I hope nothing's happened to him."

My gaze snapped back to her. "You think something's happened?" He'd better be dead lying in a ditch somewhere. Otherwise, he was going to get an earful when he got back. Still, the thought of Marcus being hurt didn't sit well with me. Not well at all. What if after all this time Marcus hadn't ghosted me but just couldn't call me back because he was injured?

Beverly shrugged. "I'm sure he's fine. Don't you worry. You'll see him soon enough."

I had no answer to that. My lips were glued together, and I had a strange, heavy dread growing in the pit of my stomach.

"Then it's settled." Dolores straightened. "There's nothing else we can do here. An autopsy will tell us the cause of death. You can get a gurney from the Hollow Cove Security Agency. Grace will help you."

"I'll help you too, Tessa." Iris stood. She winked and said, "You know me. I love dabbling in death."

I gave her a tight smile. "Thanks." My gaze went to the body again. "Wait. Where's the morgue?"

"Basement level of the Hollow Cove Security Agency's building," replied Dolores.

"Right." I had no idea Marcus's building doubled as a morgue. My day was just getting worse and worse. And now I was charged with moving corpses around town. Excellent.

I pulled my eyes from the body and they settled on Ruth. She was standing next to the counter, looking down at something, her eyes wide with horror. Then her gaze snapped to the dead witch. She was looking at Bernard with such dread and overwhelming fear that every other thought in my head vanished.

"What's the matter, Ruth?" I questioned, seeing my aunt's face pale, and my chest tightened.

She glanced at me. Her lips moved but no words came out.

"Ruth? What is it?" demanded Dolores, stepping over the body.

I moved to the counter. "Did you find something?"

Ruth looked down at the counter and picked up an empty vial next to a half-drunk mug that could have been coffee. She lifted it to the light, and a small amount of cream-colored liquid remained at the bottom. "This is gingerweed. I made it for him for his indigestion."

I felt the blood leave my body and heard the intake of breaths from behind me. A wisp of panic unfolded like a leaf inside my chest. "What exactly are you saying, Ruth?" I asked, though I had already made the connection.

Ruth gave me a feeble smile. Her expression grew haunted as big fat tears spilled down her face. "I did this. I killed him."

CHAPTER
4

Hauling a dead body was a lot harder than you might think. Especially a large, six-foot male, who looked like he ate his wife—and possibly his children.

Even with Iris's help, it took us at least a half-hour just to lift Bernard and drag his body over the gurney I'd acquired from the Hollow Cove Security Agency. Thank the cauldron it was one of those gurneys with a lift mechanism already built in it, otherwise we couldn't have rolled Bernard out, let alone madc it to the morgue.

Grace, Marcus's administrative assistant, wasn't too pleased at the sight of me, nor was she very optimistic about lending me the gurney so I could bring poor Bernard to the morgue. I guess she was still harboring some ill will from my ambush into Marcus's office a few months back.

"Where's your Merlin ID card?" Grace had asked, a winning smile wrinkling over her face, framed with short white hair. "Word is… you're not a Merlin anymore. Without proper ID, I can't authorize this." She'd given me a pointed look from behind the front desk.

"How about I authorize you with my foot up your ass," I'd snapped. Iris had applauded. I'd been so filled with anger and dread about my poor Aunt Ruth that my temper was off the charts.

"Tell me where to find the damned gurney, or you'll just have to go get Bernard's body yourself," I'd screamed at her. There might have been a little spit.

Meanwhile, Iris, my loyal sidekick, had been giving her the stink eye while pointing two fingers and throwing make-believe curses at Grace, though she didn't know that.

Grace's face had turned an ugly red, nearly purple. "I don't care who you are, or what surname you share. You can't speak to me like that."

"I already have," I told her. "He's starting to smell. In a few minutes, the entire town is going to smell like a giant sewer."

Apparently, that had been the right thing to say, as Grace finally agreed to tell us where to find a gurney.

Together, Iris and I pushed the sheet-draped gurney with Bernard's body on it down a hallway in the basement level of the Hollow Cove Security Agency and through a pair of double doors with the word MORGUE painted in large, black letters on the right one.

Cool air hit me as we entered a large lab-like room. It stank of disinfectant and the sweetish odor of dead flesh.

"Smells like roses," I choked, trying to breathe through my mouth and finding it harder than I thought.

Iris took in a deep breath. "Nothing like the smell of bleach to clear out your nasal passages. Am I right?"

Yup, Iris was a strange one.

Plain white walls with matching boring white tiles surrounded us, all lit with fluorescent lights from above. The morgue was equipped with stainless counters topped with medical tools and devices. It had a cold, dreary feeling, and I couldn't wait to get the hell out.

Heart thumping, we pushed the gurney to the middle of the room, next to a stainless-steel autopsy table. A rolling medical cart stood beside it, covered with gleaming, sharp medical tools that looked like they belonged to a butcher.

I swept my gaze across the room, to the metal refrigerator doors on the opposite wall, wondering how many more cadavers were still in there. I did not want to know.

Though I'd never been in a morgue before, it looked exactly how I imagined it would—thanks to all the police dramas I'd watched over the years.

Yanking my bag around to my front, I flipped the flap open and pulled out two Ziploc bags. One had Bernard's empty cup, and the other had the vial that contained Ruth's gingerweed tonic. Her fingerprints were probably all over it too, but it didn't matter. My aunt had nothing to hide.

I dropped the bags on the stainless-steel autopsy table, with a slip of paper stating Bernard's name and next of kin, wanting nothing more than to leave.

Iris inhaled deeply, looking around the room. "God I love the smell of morgues. All that death and missing souls gives me goosebumps. You know what I mean?"

"You're insane. You know that?" I laughed, staring at the pretty, pixie-like witch who'd crossed the room and was now pulling out one of the refrigerator doors.

"Uh… should you be doing that?"

Iris shrugged. "I don't know why people are so afraid of dying. It's just a transition to another place." Disappointment flashed across her face at the empty slab of stainless steel.

I eyed the Dark witch. "You believe there's an afterlife? A place where we all go after our batteries run out? Up or down... the light or the darkness?" I'd never given it much thought. I knew angels and demons existed, so why not a heaven and hell? Or a Horizon and Netherworld as we paranormals liked to call them. Same difference.

Iris shut the door, her eyes widening. "Of course, I do. Don't you? I'm not saying if you lived a good life you go to some version of Horizon and if you cheated on your wife you'll end up in the Netherworld to be tortured for eternity by demons... because the Netherworld is a realm of demons and devils. Did you know human soul trafficking is huge in the Netherworld? I mean big, really big."

I stared at her. "I had no idea." Again, I was happy to have Iris around. She was a walking Netherworld Wikipedia.

"Well," continued the Dark witch, happy to have an audience. "I believe souls go somewhere after we die. And it's not so black and white either." Iris walked over and pulled the sheet off of Bernard's face. "Take him. Where do you think Bernard is now? His soul? His body is dead, but his soul... I'd like to think his soul is somewhere safe."

I looked at the dead witch's face. "I don't know. I've never died and come back—but if I ever do, I'll let you know. Promise," I said with a smile. "But maybe you're right. Maybe his soul is somewhere safe."

I felt bad for Bernard, and knowing he had a wife made me feel terrible. He probably had kids too, and grandkids. But seeing as Ruth believed she had something to do with his death made me feel worse. No. Not Ruth. Never Ruth.

But what if I was wrong…

"Now what?" Iris stood with her hands on her hips, looking at ease and in her element in the cold, stale morgue.

"I'll make the arrangements and call the medical examiner." I didn't think Grace would be as helpful as my Aunt Dolores had thought. "Let him know there's a body here. He'll need to know what to look for." I swallowed hard. "You know… see if Ruth's potion really did cause his death." My words choked off. My gut twisted until I thought I might puke.

Forget about celebrating Samhain tonight. I had to help Ruth. I had to help clear her name and make her realize she had nothing to do with this.

I looked at Iris. "Ruth didn't do this."

Iris squeezed my arm. "I know she didn't. He probably just died of natural causes, like Dolores said."

My lips curved down into a frown. "I wish Marcus was here. Not because of me… but because he would know how to do all this," I stammered, feeling like an idiot.

Iris eyed me from under her thick lashes. "No word yet? No sexy texts? No naked pictures?" She moved her eyebrows suggestively.

I laughed. "No. None of those. Nothing. I think… I think he ghosted me. Or maybe during our time apart, he realized I wasn't dateable."

"Not dateable?" Iris moved so fast I barely had time to register her movement as she appeared in front of me, a finger pointing to my face. "Don't even go there," she threatened. "You are *so* dateable. *You* are date-e-licious."

"How'd you do that?" She'd moved like a vamp. Maybe all that time she spent with Ronin was rubbing off of her—literally.

"Marcus is really into you," she continued as though she didn't hear me. "I saw how he looks at you. Like he wants to rip off all your clothes."

"Well, if it's just sex he wants, he's wasting his time."

Iris sighed. "He is really into you, Tessa. If he hasn't called or texted, I'm sure he has a pretty good reason. He's a mature, very virile dude. Anymore virile, and he'd be a caveman. He's going to call. Trust me."

I gave a silent nod. I couldn't think of all the reasons why Marcus hadn't called yet. I had to focus on my Aunt Ruth. Just the memory of the fear on her face had my stomach twisting again.

"Well," I exhaled, "we won't know for sure until the doctor runs his tests."

"Don't worry. It'll all get resolved." Iris pulled the sheet over Bernard's head and turned to face me. "What we need is to haul our butts to Wicked Witch & Handsome Devil Pub and get some alcohol in us. I want details on your first day. What d'you say?"

"Sure. Why the hell not. Let's get out of here." Telling Iris about my disaster was a hell of a lot less painful than telling my aunts.

We left Bernard and took the stairs back up to the first floor. I did not want to be here when Bernard's wife showed up. Knowing Martha, that witch blabbed. By now the entire town knew Ruth thought she'd killed the town baker. Wonderful.

With that in mind, I hurried up the stairs. When we reached the platform, I could make out voices through the door. One was Grace's, but I didn't recognize the other.

"What now?" came Iris's voice next to me on the platform.

"No idea."

I pulled open the door and we both hit the hallway, marching back towards the front desk.

Next to Grace stood a fit, leggy and lean woman dressed in black with flat boots. Reddish hair curled down past her mid-back in a riotous cascade, complementing her flawless skin, high cheekbones, and lush lips. She didn't have much makeup on, but she didn't need it. Her face held an ageless beauty, her large green eyes framed with black lashes. I'd never seen her before.

"You think that's his wife?" whispered Iris.

"If she is, he's a lucky man," I whispered back, making her laugh.

At the sound of our approach, the woman turned and looked at us. She wasn't just pretty. She was freaking gorgeous. Eyes alight, she stared at us for a few seconds, enough to satisfy her curiosity, and then turned her attention back to Grace.

"Where's the suspect now…" said the stranger as she glanced down at a piece of paper. "… uh… a Ruth Davenport? Do you know where I can find her?"

I jerked as my heart sped. "Excuse me. What the hell is going on here?" I demanded, my voice dangerously loud and dripping with angst as I stomped my way over, actually stomped.

The stranger eyed me for a long moment. "Ruth Davenport. You know her?"

"Yeah. She's my aunt." I glared at Grace who sat back and crossed her arms, a stupid, knowing look on her stupid face.

The stranger blinked at me. "Then you can tell me where she lives," she commanded, her voice like a whip but not giving me a clue as to who she was.

"Why?" I crossed my arms over my chest just as Iris brushed up against me. "What do you want from her?"

The woman stared at me without blinking, which was really creepy. "She killed someone," she answered, her voice coated with amusement. "She's a murderer."

My heart pounded, and I felt as if I was at a cliff's edge ready to fall. "What? Wait just a minute here." I put myself in front of this woman with my hands on my hips. "My aunt didn't do this. You've got it all wrong." I had no idea who this stranger was, but I hated her already.

She looked at me, her eyebrows high on her face as though somehow she was superior. "I've already gotten a confession."

"She's confused." I was going to slap her. I just knew it. "Gossip about what happened isn't going to help anyone or this town. Leave this alone and stay away from my family. It's none of your business." That's it. I was going to kick her in the throat.

Her face was expressionless. "I don't do gossip. I stick to facts."

"Here's a fact," I growled, seeing Iris rock forward on her feet close enough to the strange woman, take a sniff, and rock back. "There's no way my aunt would do something like that. Tell her, Grace," I said, looking at the vile woman behind the desk.

Grace pursed her lips. "Ruth is a kind soul and a friend. She wouldn't poison Bernard on purpose."

The stranger snapped the folder she was holding. "Well, that's really not up to you to decide."

My brows fell around the bridge of my nose. "Who the hell are you?"

She met my gaze and gave me an icy smile. "I'm the new chief."

CHAPTER

5

"**A** new chief? We have a new chief? How the hell did this happen!" My voice rose around the kitchen. "We already have a chief and his name is *Marcus*."

I wasn't sure why I was being so overprotective of him. The guy was pretending like I didn't exist. Still, Marcus had shown me just how good a man and shifter he was. He'd been there for me, fought alongside me, and had carried me home after the battle with Samara—a.k.a. evil bitch sorceress. I couldn't just forget that. He might not be into me, but he didn't deserve to be cast aside like that.

"Marcus has been gone for nearly two months, Tess," said Ronin. "And the dude hasn't given us a sign of life. What'd you expect?" Ronin had showed up ten minutes after Iris and I had made it back home. We'd cursed all the way, making up new curse words that fit this new chief. It was a *long* list.

I clenched my teeth. "Not this." Damn. I had *not* been expecting those words out of her mouth. And judging by the sly smile she'd given me right after, she'd seen it too.

Guilt hit hard, making me feel ill. I'd been so shocked and upset by the news of this new chief that I'd forgotten all about Ruth.

Ruth had disappeared upstairs when I came home with Iris after I'd blabbed about the new chief. Well, demanded some answers was more like it. That had been an hour ago. Ruth had not come back down.

"The Hollow Cove Security Agency has certain protocols to follow," said my Aunt Dolores, pouring herself another cup of coffee. "Hollow Cove's never been without a chief before." She turned around with the cup in her hands and leaned against the counter. "With Marcus missing, they had to send a replacement. It's how it works."

My lips parted. "A replacement. Are you serious? You're all acting like he's dead. He's not." Fear spindled through me at the thought that maybe Marcus *was* dead. No, I was just being an overdramatic fool. Marcus was a brutally strong and powerful shifter. He was practically King Kong. Nothing could hurt him… right?

Dolores glared at me. "I'm not the one responsible for this. I'm just stating the facts. There's a new chief. There it is. You need to deal with it." After Dolores took a sip of her coffee, she asked, "Did you call the medical examiner?"

"Yes," I sighed. "Told him everything. He's probably there already. Working on Bernard." I rubbed my finger along the wood grain across the kitchen tabletop, not wanting to say the question that I had to ask—but finding I couldn't help myself. "What happens if he finds that Ruth's tonic killed him?" Ruth would never harm another soul on purpose, but there was a slight chance her tonic might have accidentally killed the baker.

Silence soaked in, broken by the ticking of the refrigerator.

"Then we will deal with it," answered Beverly finally, as she shifted in her chair next to me. "Bernard could have had a severe allergic reaction to Ruth's gingerweed… or he still might have died of a heart attack." She sounded as though she was trying to convince herself, even if her fear was obvious. "We just don't know until we hear from the medical examiner."

My gaze went to Dolores, waiting for her to add something, but my aunt's face was torn with emotions running across her tight features. Panic stirred in the back of her eyes as she leaned against the counter, staring at her mug. She was afraid. Afraid Ruth might be blamed for this.

My emotions warred between dread and anger. The only good thing about this mess was that my aunts were so preoccupied with what was happening to Ruth that none of them even thought of asking me more about how the witch trials had gone. Just the thought brought on another wave of guilt. I wasn't perfect. Right now, the trials were the least of my problems.

My jaw clenched as I hit my palm with a sharp snap on the table. "Argh! You should have seen her, thinking she's all that. Thinking she's the boss of everyone. We don't need her. We can function well enough without this stranger."

"Adira," corrected Ronin, and I heard the distant ring of the phone in the hallway.

"What?" I growled, nearly spitting at Ronin sitting across from me.

Ronin leaned back in his chair, casual and relaxed with his hands laced behind his head, like the vampire he was. "Her name is Adira. The new chief."

I glared at him. "She's been here like… what… two minutes? And you already know her name?" Knowing Ronin, he probably knew a lot more too about this Adira. And I would make him tell me later.

"Don't go all Tess-zilla on me," said the half-vampire. "I know things. I'm knowledgeable. It's part of my charm."

"Vampires." Iris rolled her eyes, but a smile tweaked her lips as she took a sip of her coffee.

The fact that a name was now attached to the stranger made it worse. More permanent somehow.

A click sounded from the hallway as the phone was picked up followed by Ruth's muffled voice as she answered it.

"Well, I don't care what her name is." I shifted in my seat, trying to hear who Ruth was talking to, but her words were too low, and I couldn't make out a thing. "She better not get too comfortable because Marcus is coming back." *He better.*

The fact that the Hollow Cove Security Agency had sent out a replacement meant something was definitely wrong. Either they couldn't get in touch with Marcus or they were in contact, but something had happened to him. Did the Hollow Cove Security Agency know something we didn't? Was Marcus in trouble?

I needed answers. And Adira was going to give them to me. Either that, or I was going to make her.

The sound of shoes hitting the hardwood floors pulled my attention up from my mug.

Ruth walked into the kitchen and grabbed her jacket and purse from the wooden peg rack on the wall next to the back door.

Panic jerked me to my feet. "Where are you going?"

Ruth's sad eyes met mine. "The chief asked me to come to the office. She said she wanted to sit and talk about what happened. I said I would."

Adira had been on the phone with Ruth. "She's *not* the chief," I said, making my way around the table to stand next to Ruth. "She's not."

"She is now." Dolores set her mug in the sink and whirled around. "Better go and get all this sorted out. The longer we wait, the worse it'll get."

Anger flashed through me, fed by the memory of Adira's smug smile at my aunt's expense. Something was off about her, and I just couldn't put my finger on it. Or perhaps I was just looking for ways to hate her because she'd basically stolen Marcus's position.

Ruth stared at me, her face returning to a numb state. "I… have to go…" she stammered, looking frightened and small.

I reached out and pulled her into a hug. "It'll be all right," I said into her fluff of white hair, not knowing what else I could say. A sudden overwhelming urge to protect Ruth welled in me. My Aunt Ruth was the kindest, sweetest, and most loving person I'd ever met. Seeing her like this, sad and demoralized, had my heart shattering in pieces.

I had to do something. I had to help my aunt.

"I'm coming with you," I said, as I let her go and stepped back. "I have a few things I forgot to discuss with this new chief." Like how I was going to accidentally curse her hair on fire.

"You're staying here," ordered Dolores. She gave me a pointed look at the frown on my face. "You're too angry right now and we need to speak to this new chief without having to worry about an outburst from you. The last thing we need is this Adira to lock Ruth up because of something you might say."

"I *can* control myself," I said, making Ronin snort. "What?" I narrowed my eyes at the half-vampire. "You think I can't?"

Ronin raised his hands in surrender. "It's just… when you're upset, you tend to act before you think. Your emotions make you a tad bit impulsive. Remember what you did to Marcus the very first night you met him?"

"I made him fly," I said, remembering how I'd hit him with a slam of my magic without even uttering a single word. "I gave him free flying lessons. So what? That's water under the bridge. I've forgiven him for his poor choice of words about my mommy dearest."

Ronin raked a hand through his hair, smoothing it. "We don't know anything about her. That could be dangerous. You don't want to piss her off."

I stiffened. "She's not the boss of me. I might not be a Merlin anymore, but she can't tell me what to do." Or could she? I had no idea.

"It'll be fine, Tessa," said Ruth. "I've already confessed."

"You didn't kill him," I protested. I felt my face go blank as I saw her raw and stripped down to the pain in her soul.

Ruth shook her head, her eyes filling with tears. "But I don't know. I can't be sure. Maybe I did." She sniffed. "It's best that I tell her everything I know." She wiped her eyes. "I was stupid and careless. I'll never do another potion ever again."

"Don't say that," argued Dolores, her expression troubled. "You don't know your potion killed him."

"But I do." Ruth's face was twisted in pain. Her bright blue eyes fixed on her sister, and the hurt in her was obvious. "He used it. He trusted me and I killed him."

Ruth walked out the back door before I could counter with something witty or just a few comforting words.

I shook my head. "This is wrong. It's all wrong."

"What does this new chief look like?" Beverly stood with a hand on her hip. "Fat? Old and wrinkled? Bad dye job? Is she overly botoxed? Too many fillers? Does she have sausage lips or is she more of the duckbill sort?"

"She's hot," said Iris with a shrug. "Really hot."

Beverly frowned. "Damn. I need to change." She hurried out of the kitchen and I heard her kitten heels hitting the stairs to the second floor. It sounded like she was running.

"Don't wait up if we're not back for tonight." Dolores pulled her jacket off the wooden peg rack on the wall. "Samhain is an important part of our culture. At least one Davenport witch has to celebrate it. If not, there'll be hell to pay tomorrow," she said, buttoning her jacket. "Martha will crucify us. She'll never shut up about it."

I crossed my arms over my chest, dread pulling my head down. "I don't really feel like celebrating." I had more ominous and murderous thoughts at the moment.

Dolores pointed her keys at me. "You stop that right now. You hear me?" My aunt narrowed her eyes. "This is just a setback. It'll all get cleared up. You'll see. We're Davenport witches, for cauldron's sake. Nothing's going to happen. So, stop worrying. I'll give you the details when we get back."

I watched as my Aunt Dolores shut the door behind her. Somehow I wasn't so optimistic.

"I'm ready!" came Beverly's voice behind me.

I turned my head and stared at my aunt, who'd ditched her casual jeans and opted for a pair of black tights that could have been painted on, a low black cami that revealed she was braless, and a short black leather jacket. Her blonde hair was up in a messy bun with a few strands framing her face that looked like she'd just spent hours putting on makeup. There's no way she could have pulled this off without magic.

Beverly cocked her hip and beamed. "Does this make me look like a sex-starved slut in need of a man to bed?"

"It does," I answered with a smile, knowing it was the precise answer she wanted to hear.

Beverly's plump lips pulled into a dazzling smile. "Thank you, darling. See you later." Beverly strutted her way out the door in her red pumps, looking like a million bucks.

My smile faded. Tonight was my favorite witchy celebration, and I'd really been looking forward to it. But now, there was no room for celebrating. Not after seeing the pain on Ruth's face.

And I had the horrible feeling things were about to get a hell of a lot worse.

CHAPTER

6

What does a witch do when her witchy aunts haven't come back from the chief's office, and she was told to stay put?

She goes to find them, of course.

It's not like I'd *promised* to stay at home. And I didn't trust something about Adira. I didn't know her. A little voice inside told me she wouldn't believe Ruth's innocence, and my gut also told me Adira had something to prove. She needed to show everyone she had the stuff to be a chief, which meant she was about to go all queen bitch.

And Ruth was her first victim.

I rushed down Shifter Lane. The sun had set an hour ago, which meant the festivities had already begun.

What looked like a giant circus had invaded Hollow Cove.

Standing torches lined the streets for a hundred yards in either direction, filling the streets with a yellow and orange glow. Leaves of orange, yellow, and red carpeted the sidewalks and streets, covering the asphalt completely, as though it never existed. Gazebos and tents were stockpiled with tables covered in food, where a few paranormals manned their grills and singed their meats. Dozens of male paranormals crowded around, talking loudly, laughing, and arguing about some football game.

Music drifted from several different locations, the beats rolling into one another. Lanterns and carved pumpkins with large, toothy grins and wide eyes decorated porches and walkways while dozens of kids—all wearing costumes from Spiderman to Olaf and of course the familiar pointy hat witch— opened their bags to accept candy and took off running to the next house with equal amounts of enthusiasm. More kids ran in packs all over the streets, excited cries and giggles propelling them faster.

I smiled. It was a mix of the traditional Samhain with a modern Halloween flair. There was something for everyone.

Paranormals crowded the streets of Hollow Cove in a blur of color and motion, talk and costume, like some Medieval painting. Most witches sported Medieval-like gowns while other half-breeds decided to go more modern in their zombie costumes and dead flesh makeup.

I scanned the crowd and spotted Ronin and Iris. Both their faces were carefully painted with blood and rot, their clothes torn and stained with dirt and more blood. Zombies. I laughed as I stared at the zombie couple. I laughed harder when I realized they were walking in a slow, zombie-like jerky manner, hands out in front of them, while some kids ran around them screaming in delight.

"You guys are *really* into this," I mumbled to myself, laughing. At least they were enjoying Samhain. I thought about going over to say hi but decided against it. I needed to find Ruth.

I crossed the street to the bland, gray brick building with the sign HOLLOW COVE SECURITY AGENCY. My chest tightened as my eyes moved to the left side entrance, remembering that kiss Marcus had planted on me. It had been a hot-flash, rip-off-your-panties kind of kiss. It had been *that* good.

Yup, I was hot for the chief. *Hot for a guy who doesn't call you back.* Yeah, that was stupid.

Pushing those thoughts away for later—because, let's face it, I was going to think about it again—I pulled open the front glass door and made my way inside. I blinked into the harsh white lights inside the building's entrance. The scent of freshly brewed coffee hit me as I arrived at the front desk across the lobby, where it opened up into a larger space.

"No, Grace, huh?" I said, leaning on the desk, having expected to see the old woman. Her chair sat empty.

I looked around. The place was deserted. With Adira believing in her claim that she was the new chief, I'd expected to see a few of her deputy cronies. Yet I could sense the presence of people…

That's when I heard the sounds of erratic conversation.

I was both relieved and anxious that my aunts were still here. They'd been here for hours. Either they were having a grand conversation, or it was worse than I thought.

Voices trailed from the door to the right of the front desk—Marcus's office.

She was using Marcus's office?

With my heart pounding like my veins were pumping caffeine, I pushed off the desk and made for the door—and froze.

The last time I was here, the name MARCUS DURAND had been stenciled on the window of the door. Now the name read ADIRA CREEK with the words CHIEF OFFICER written under it.

Oh, hell, no.

I stared at the door, my anger triggering my magic until I felt it crawl around and over my skin like another layer.

Would you knock? No. I didn't think so.

I burst through the door in a storm of curses, wild hair, and angry eyes. The last time I was here, I'd sneaked in with Ronin to find some info on Marvelous Myrtle. The space looked exactly the same, except for the three witches who sat across from Adira.

Dolores, Beverly, and Ruth all stared at me with their mouths hanging open in a shared expression of disbelief, like I'd just crashed their tea party. Okay, maybe I did.

My eyes found Adira and they narrowed. "What the hell do you think you're doing?" I growled before I could stop myself. "That's Marcus's chair. This is Marcus's office. And these are his things. That's his stapler. And his pens. That's his mug. Don't you go touching his mug." I sounded insane, but it was too late.

Sitting behind Marcus's desk, Adira gave me a cold smile. "This is *my* office. And my ass is sitting in *my* chair. And as I recall, you weren't invited."

I charged forward until my thigh bumped against Marcus's desk. "I don't see your name on it. Ha-ha!" Yup, I was definitely losing it. What the hell was wrong with me? Why did I even care?

"Tessa, I told you to stay home." Dolores stood from her chair, looking pale with her brows knitted together at the bridge of her nose. "We have this under control. You should go."

"Really?" I turned to face her. "Did you see what she did to his door? She took his name down. His freaking *name*. Like she owns the place."

"I do own the place," came Adira's voice, and I wanted to bitch slap the laughter I heard in it.

I turned back around slowly, my magic prickling at my fingertips. "What did you say?" I asked, my voice dangerously low.

Adira's smile was truly evil, but she didn't say anything. By the tone of her voice, I could tell she was enjoying making me angry.

"Please, Tessa," pleaded Beverly, her usual confident smile replaced by what looked like fear. "Don't make this worse."

I took a breath at the sound of worry in Beverly's voice. "What do you mean *worse*? What's happened? I can tell something's happened. What? What is it?"

70

My gaze found Ruth. Her eyes were red like she'd been crying—a lot. She sat in her chair, her hands hidden beneath her jacket on her lap, and wouldn't look at me.

Dolores was still standing, watching me like she was about to tackle me at any moment. Yet I could see the fear and tension lingering at the edges of her eyes.

My aunts looked trapped. They looked like… like they'd lost. But lost what?

I turned my gaze on Adira, tension pulling me stiff. "Did you threaten them? What the hell did you do?"

"Tessa," warned Dolores, her voice high.

Adira interlaced her long fingers on the desk. "My job."

My magic pounded inside my core until it became a tight-knit grenade of energy, ready to explode. "What the hell does that mean?"

Adira's posture emanated menace. Her face was an icy display of determined anger, sharp like a dagger, and her confidence annoyed me on so many levels. She believed herself above me, above us. I hated people like her. She wasn't a witch. I was certain of that. But she *was* something—something dangerous, even primeval.

But it had been decided that from now on I had crazy big lady balls.

I leaned over the desk, my face twisting in a snarl. Hell, I nearly showed her my teeth.

"What did you threaten them with?" Anger swept through me like a racing hot river. If she thought she could attack my law-abiding aunts and intimidate them without me getting involved, she was a moron. I didn't care about rules, but I *loved* to break them. Just as I loved to ride the edge of my emotions.

It seemed the angrier I got, the wider the smile grew on Adira's face. She wanted me to screw up. I wanted to bitch slap her. Twice. Okay, maybe three times. All right, four.

"Tessa, stop. It's okay. I've already confessed," said Ruth, and I pulled my eyes away from Adira to look at my aunt. "There's nothing else you can do."

"Yes. We're almost done here," added Beverly, though her voice shook with a small tremor. "Everyone's out celebrating. You should be out there with them. You're young. You should be out there having fun. We'll join you shortly."

Pulse fast, my eyes shifted from Beverly to Ruth to Dolores. "You're not telling me something. It's written all over your faces. What is it? What did she threaten you with? What are you not telling me?"

"You should go, Tessa." Ruth shifted in her chair, and her jacket slipped to the floor. She reached down and grabbed it, and I registered the metal bracelets wrapped around her two wrists. Only those were no ordinary bracelets.

I felt the blood leave my face. The bracelets were iron cuffs.

They looked just like the cuffs used by the human police, but these were used to dull or even oppress a witch's magic or prevent any practitioner from using magic. If you had the cuffs on, you couldn't do magic. Yet the ones around Ruth's wrists were different. For one thing, they weren't tied together in the middle with a chain link. These were separate on each wrist. They may look different, by there was no mistaking the slight pulse of energy emitting from them.

Adira had banned my Aunt Ruth from using magic.

"You cuffed my aunt? You psychotic bitch!" I howled, out of my mind with anger. I felt my hair lift off my shoulders and float around my head.

Adira's body stiffened as her eyes went black.

And then something inside me snapped.

Fury electrified me, and I tapped into the elements around me.

"Tessa! No!" screamed Dolores, but I barely heard her. All I cared about was ripping that bitch in half. Nobody treated my Aunt Ruth like that. Nobody.

A torrent of energy swarmed out to find me, and I thrust out my hands and yelled, "Inflitus!"

A burst of kinetic force shot out of my palms—

A blur of red and black moved before my eyes.

The kinetic force slammed into the wall behind the empty chair in an explosion of wood and drywall.

I stared at the gaping hole. But there was no Adira.

By the time I'd felt the presence behind me, it was already too late.

My arms were pulled back with a sudden painful thrust, just as I felt cold metal slip over my wrists.

Oh.

Shit.

Adira had cuffed me too.

CHAPTER

7

"**Y**ou cuffed me? You bitch!" I snarled, struggling with my restraints.

Hands pushed me forward and I stumbled into the desk. I was suddenly acutely aware of the cuffs around my wrists, and that sobered me right up. I'd never been cuffed by human handcuffs before, let alone magical ones.

Instinctively, I sent out my senses, tapped into the elements around me—and nothing. Nada. Zero. Zilch. Nothing responded. It was a strange feeling. The elements were there—I could even feel the ley lines—but I couldn't *reach* them.

"Take them off!" I wrestled with my cuffs, trying to pull my arms free and feeling like a caged animal. That's it. The bitch was going to die now.

Marcus's blue ballpoint pen rested on the edge of the desk. I leaned over and snatched it up with my fingers. With my thumb, I managed to hike it up my sleeve. I never knew when it might come in handy.

"What is the matter with you?" Dolores bellowed next to me.

I looked over, my mouth ready to come up with an excuse, but Dolores was glaring at Adira. Not me.

Adira placed her hands on her hips, looking smug. "She just tried to kill me. I had every right to put her magic out."

"Clearly, she made a mistake," pressed Dolores. "She's an emotional being. Seeing her aunt handcuffed drew out some strong emotions. She's not herself."

I cocked a brow. "Thanks."

This was not how things were supposed to go down. But I had just tried to kill the new chief. *Oops*. I was losing my temper way too easily these days. It had to stop, or I would get myself or someone I cared about killed.

I had managed to screw things up royally. How was I supposed to help Ruth now? *Nice going, Tessa.*

Beverly shot to her feet and began to pace the room, rubbing her temples. "This is bad. This is bad. This is very, very bad."

"Your vocabulary is improving by leaps and bounds," commented Dolores, her dark eyes hard.

Beverly planted herself in front of Dolores. "Oh, shut up. At least she had the balls to try what we'd all been thinking—"

There was a sharp clap as Beverly's head snapped to the side. A large red handprint appeared on her cheek.

"Control yourself," said Dolores, her cheeks just as red as the handprint on her sister's face.

Beverly's lips pressed into a thin line. "You slapped me!" Her eyes narrowed dangerously. "You good for nothin' tree—"

Smack!

Dolores's head snapped back at the force of Beverly's hand.

Oh, dear.

The sound of flesh hitting flesh exploded around us as the two sisters kept slapping each other.

"Guys. Stop." I hobbled forward, which was a strange thing with my hands tied with iron cuffs behind my back. "Don't do this. Please. This is my fault." The last thing I needed was to start a fight between my aunts.

Dolores rubbed the side of her cheek. "That was a lot of power for someone with such a small chest."

Beverly looked smug. "I've never had any complaints."

My gaze shot to Adira, who leaned on the bookcase, watching the exchange with a sick sort of pleasure. I breathed through my nose, trying to control my thrashing heart. But the longer I stared at Adira, the angrier I got, and the faster my heart pounded.

Once Beverly moved away from Dolores, my gaze shifted to Ruth. She wouldn't look at me, her face pained. I noticed she had covered her wrists with her jacket again.

I swallowed hard. "Mine are different." I couldn't pry my arms apart; my cuffs were tied together in the middle with a chain link. I yanked on my wrists, and my arms burned from trying to work them at a strange angle. I looked at Adira again. "Why are mine different." I didn't expect her to answer, but it was worth a shot.

Adira smiled like I had asked her an important question. "You've got the usual counter-magic cuffs." She pushed off the bookcase. "We use those on dangerous criminals about to be locked up… sometimes forever."

I glowered. "Nice." She was really asking for it. I felt very much obliged to give it to her.

Adira watched me for a long moment. "The ones around your Aunt Ruth are partials."

"Partials?"

"She gets to stay in her home," answered Adira, her face showing no emotion. "She can go about her business in town, but she can't do magic. Not until her court date."

"Her court date?" I realized I was repeating Adira like an idiot. And when I saw the tight look on my aunts' faces, I knew they had been discussing the very thing before I barged in. My shoulders sagged. It must have been a horrible thing to have seen your sister cuffed like a criminal. With Dolores's permanent scowl since I came in, I was sure she'd done everything in her power to persuade Adira not to charge Ruth. But it hadn't worked.

Ruth was innocent. If she'd poisoned Bernard, it wasn't intentional. The system would recognize it had been an accident. I hoped.

"Are we talking about the White Witch Court?" Hope kindled inside me. If Ruth had to face a board of high witches, she'd have a fighting chance. They would understand and side with her. I was sure of it.

"You'd like that. Wouldn't you?" Adira pulled her face into a pout. "And have them slap her on the wrist for being a bad, bad witch?" Her face became harsh, and the little hope I had vanished. "Murder charges go all the way to the Gray Council. She goes through the proper channels. No exceptions. I don't care if you're one of the founding families in Hollow Cove or that you're the greatest witch that ever was. No one is above the law."

That sounded strangely like what Greta had said.

I frowned. The Gray Council was the elite governing body of half-breeds like us and angel-born. It consisted of one member from each half-breed court—vampires, faeries, werewolves, and witches—and included the leaders of the angel-born. This was bad. The very worst.

"When?" I asked, the longer it took, the worse it would be for Ruth.

"Once I file the paperwork and depending on the other cases before hers... you're looking at probably the first week of December."

"December!" I shouted. "She can't wait that long. This is crazy."

Dolores moved to face me. "If you don't calm down, I'm going to lock you up myself!"

I clamped my mouth shut. No point in getting my aunts to turn against me. I'd messed up enough for one evening.

My eyes found Ruth again and I saw her lips trembling. "But she can still do potions. Right?" Taking away her ability to do potions would be like taking away her air. She'd die without it. Or drop into a severe depression, which was worse.

The new chief flashed me a smile. "No magic of any kind. No tampering with spells, no mixing potions, no channeling talismans or wands. The laws are very clear."

An avalanche of uncontrollable fury ignited in me, and my heart pumped with adrenaline. "You're so dead."

"Tessa, shut up," cried Beverly. "I think we've had enough drama for one day."

I kept my eyes on the new chief and dipped my head low. "You might have taken my magic and the use of my hands… but I can still give you the headbutt of the century."

Adira laughed. The bitch actually laughed. "I'd love to see that, little witch."

"With pleasure." I made to move forward, but one look in Ruth's direction sobered me right up.

She was shaking like a leaf, looking so frail, fragile, and small as she sobbed. I was being an asshole. I needed to get my shit together.

I gave Adira my best smile. "Raincheck? I'd love to kick your ass, but looks like my hands are tied. Get it?"

Adira shrugged. "It's your funeral."

I gave her a hard stare, seeing that her eyes were deep green, like a dark forest green. Hadn't I seen her eyes go black a moment ago? Right before I made a fool out of myself?

"You're not a witch," I stated, my eyes never leaving her smiling face. "You wouldn't be speaking about witches with such disdain if you were. What are you? You moved fast… almost like…"

"A vampire," answered Adira, smiling without showing any teeth.

My insides churned. Damn. The new chief was a vamp. It explained her cruel beauty and her ability to be in one spot at one moment and then in a blink of an eye, somewhere else.

I'd missed her once, but I wouldn't miss twice.

It also came to me that Ronin, being half-vampire and nosy as hell, would have known she was a vampire when he'd sought her out. But he didn't tell me.

"Nice. A vampire. That's great." I sighed. "So. What's going to happen to me? You going to toss me off to your vamp pals so they can drink me dry? Lock me up in some coffin?" Yes, I was being a bit overdramatic. I was having a horrible day. I was entitled to a little bit of drama.

"I thought I'd let you go with a warning."

"You did?" That was unexpected.

Ruth turned her head and her wet eyes met mine, pleading for me not to keep pushing my luck. Immediately my tension dropped to my gut like lead.

"You gonna behave?" asked Adira, twirling the key to the magical cuffs in her fingers.

I flashed her my pearly whites. "How about you uncuff me and we'll find out, vamp."

"Tessa," growled Dolores. "For the love of the goddess, enough is enough. Please, for all our sakes. Just let her take them off. She's the chief, now. Do as she says."

I sighed, feeling slightly guilty. "Fine. I'll behave. I won't beat your ass tonight. Satisfied? Acting chief."

Adira grabbed my arm none too gently and pulled me around. "You should know," she said as I felt her hands on the iron cuffs. "Marcus is still on a job."

"How would you know?" There was a small click of metal and the weight of the cuffs around my wrists fell away. "No one's heard from him," I said, turning around and rubbing my wrists as I felt the magic returning to my core in a warm rush.

I felt something small slide down my right wrist. The blue ballpoint pen slipped from its hiding place, and I snatched it up before it fell, stuffing it in my pocket before Adira noticed anything.

"I have," answered Adira, and my chest tightened. "I just spoke to him this evening. Right before your aunts showed up." She moved to the desk and dropped the cuffs inside a top drawer.

My world shifted and I scrambled for balance. It also turned an ugly shade of red.

Marcus.

The man I'd been trying to reach for weeks, who never called me back, not even once, never returned my phone calls, and had me thinking the worst… was fine.

He was more than fine and he'd chosen to call Adira. Not me. Guess I didn't deserve a call back.

Well, then. Marcus could go screw himself.

CHAPTER

8

The weeks that followed weren't any better. In fact, things got worse.

Ruth barely left her bedroom. She took her meals in her room, and that's if she even ate anything. She seemed to wither away as the weeks went on. I knew she blamed herself for what happened to Bernard. And no matter how many times Dolores, Beverly, Iris, or I told her otherwise, it was as though she didn't hear us—or refused to.

For the last four weeks, I'd called Grace every single day to get an update on the coroner's report. And each time, she would reply, "I'm sorry. But I don't have any new information to give. The chief will call if she deems it necessary to tell you."

It didn't matter how loud I became or how many obscenities I shouted to Grace, she wouldn't give me anything. And I wasn't about to call Adira either. That vamp made my skin crawl.

And in those four weeks, the idea of Marcus came and went. I won't lie. I'd been livid after I left the chief's office. The fact that he'd called Adira sent fury into my core. Rage shook me, but it also left me feeling ill.

Marcus had called Adira but not me.

And still no news from him.

All rational thought fled from my head. The kiss, his careful protection, carrying me home—everything—was a lie. Either that, or I had some serious imagination issues. I'd been played a fool more than once in my love life, and I thought at my age—nearing thirty in a few weeks—I should have known better.

Apparently, I didn't.

Inside me, fury built and howled. I wanted to scream, to kick, to punch something—preferably Marcus's face. I had to settle for imagining his junk exploding instead.

Worse, Adira was making herself right at home in Marcus's old office and his hometown. She'd brought in her own team of four vamps—three males and one female. It was as though Marcus had never existed.

But I couldn't think of Marcus now. I had more urgent and pressing issues in my life, like my Aunt Ruth and the witch trials.

With a heavy heart, I watched my beloved Aunt Ruth wither away and spiral into a deep depression, knowing I could do nothing about it. I felt helpless. If only she could have been allowed to do some of her potions, it would have brought her some joy and kept her mind on other things while she waited for that damned court date.

Yup, we had a court date. December 7. Ruth was to appear before the Gray Council here in Hollow Cove. And without any news about what the medical examiner had uncovered, she was going in blindly. But she wouldn't be alone. I would be there. So would her sisters, and Iris and Ronin.

I didn't know how or when, but I *would* make this right somehow. I would.

Suffice to say my four weeks of training didn't go as well as I'd planned either. With this horrible mess about Ruth, I'd been left on my own to prepare for my very first witch trial, which was happening at this very moment.

My aunts had already done their best last month. It was up to me now. And I'd show them I was worth the name Davenport.

The morning of December first was a cold one as I marched back to High Peak Wilderness. An icy wind blew the leafless branches from trees of the dense forest that surrounded me for miles. The forest looked naked without its greenery, like it was missing something. A thin layer of ice covered a pond to my left as I treaded along the gravel path that led to the towering log mansion. Heavy gray clouds covered the sun, and the air smelled like snow. It was coming. A lot of it.

I might be a fool when it came to men, but I was no fool when it came to climate.

I'd dressed for the weather in the north. I'd put on my Merrell high winter boots and flexible black cargo pants over a pair of tights and packed on the layers of camis and sweaters under my North Face down-filled winter jacket. It was long enough to keep my ass warm but short enough to be flexible if I needed to be.

I had no idea where the trials would take place. If they were inside, I'd just take some layers off. I wasn't taking any chances.

Feeling cozy despite the cold winds, I made it to Montevalley Castle, the giant, log-like mansion. I nervously climbed the front steps and waited as the massive, double wood doors swung open for me.

Just as I stepped through the threshold, the same, cold, hard pulses rushed through my body from the castle's body scanner. Shaking away the odd feeling, I stepped into the grand foyer.

"Where's everybody?" I spun on the spot, listening for voices but only hearing the beating of my own heart slamming into my ears.

I pulled out my phone and checked the time. "Seven fifty-two. I'm early. So where is everyone?" Yes, I was talking to myself like a lunatic, but no one was here to hear me.

A feeling of dread started to climb up from my toes all the way to settle around the back of my neck. Did I get the date wrong? I'd remembered perfectly that Greta had said December first at 8 a.m. sharp.

Panic hit and I burst into motion. I ran to the side theater, where all the witches had assembled last month. I pushed through the swinging doors and blinked… into a dark and empty room.

"Shit. Shit. *Shit!*"

I ran back to the foyer, passed the grand staircase of polished wood that led to the upper levels, and dashed toward the right wing of the mansion into the large common room. The space was decorated with rustic furnishing, lots of wood, and big, comfortable couches and chairs surrounding a large stone fireplace.

The room was nice. Big. And freaking empty.

"This is not happening."

I stood in the large room and felt claustrophobic. Suddenly there wasn't enough air, not enough space. How could I have screwed this up? Dread choked me. A fist grabbed my heart and squeezed it tightly into a painful ball.

I'd failed, and I hadn't even begun.

I took the ball of guilt and fear that threatened to engulf me and stuffed it away, deep into the nooks of my mind. I needed to focus.

No, I hadn't screwed up the dates or the time. So why wasn't anyone here?

A shout from outside caught my attention.

It had come from the window across from me. With my heart in my throat, I dashed to the window and looked out.

About a hundred witches stood in the middle of a large open field roughly five hundred feet from the castle, all huddled around in a circle around a person. The person was the size of my thumb, but if I were to guess, that was Marina.

"Damn."

No time to wonder why this was happening. I sprinted back through the castle and out the front doors. My boots hit the gravel path, and I put on a burst of speed, running around the right side of the enormous building. I hit the field at a sprint, adrenaline pumping my thighs.

I'd made it to the first line of witches in under forty seconds. Not too shabby.

Out of breath, I leaned forward and took a few gulps of icy cold air.

"How nice of you to join us," said a voice.

I straightened, aware that the attention of all the gathered witches was on me. The group broke apart as a blonde witch with half her head shaved stepped toward me.

"Didn't think you'd make it," said Marina, a smile on her face. "You've already missed the written exam."

"What?" I panted, the cold air burning my lungs. "But, I'm here on time. It's two minutes to eight. Greta said 8 a.m. And I'm here. I'm on time."

The witches around me whispered at each other, and some of them laughed.

"What?" I growled.

Marina cocked her head and made a false pout. "You obviously didn't get the email," she said, and my heart seemed to implode.

"What email?" I asked, my mouth dry and my words pasty like my mouth was full of cotton balls. "I never got an email."

"Clearly," said Marina, and a handful of witches laughed openly. "An email was sent two weeks ago about the time change. Seven a.m. was the written exam. You didn't show."

I shook from adrenaline or anger, perhaps both. "But I *never got* this email. Someone forgot to send it to me. Check your files." I gave her a hard stare. "I didn't get one." I had the sinking feeling she'd done it on purpose. But she couldn't… could she?

Marina raised her head. Power bristled in her eyes. She looked royal, like some arrogant goddess. I had to give it to her. She knew how to put on a show.

"Everybody got one," she said. "You got one, but you didn't show. Because what? You think you don't need to? You think you're better than everyone here?"

My face warmed. Not this again. "No. I don't think that at all. I just didn't get the damn email."

"There are no do-overs here," expressed Marina. "The witch trials are serious. If you can't treat them as such and respect them, that's on you. And if you can't read your emails… well… that's not my problem. The written exam was part of the first trial. You'll just have to make do without it." She turned and walked back to a spot in the field.

Yup. She'd done it on purpose.

I clamped my jaw shut before I made things worse. Okay, so I missed the written exam. But I was still in the game, she'd just said so.

I felt eyes on me, and I spotted the witch Willis giving me a small smile before turning around with a note pad and pen in his freezing red fingers. The others all moved away from me like I was a walking plague.

"Listen up," called Marina. "There are no teams, no friendships here. You are each other's enemy because, well, only a handful of you will make it. So why bother? You are on your own. The trials are fierce and only the fierce will succeed. If you can't pass this trial… might as well give up because it'll only get harder from here." Her eyes cast around the waiting witches. "Depending on your scores from the written exam, your door will choose you. Good luck."

"Door? What door?" My stomach cramped as I looked around, but all I saw were rolling hills and acres of forest. Forget about asking anyone. It seemed like I'd missed a lot more than just the written test.

Marina's lips moved in a chant as Latin spilled from her mouth. A flash of sensation flickered over me as Marina drew in power. A lot of power.

Magic coursed into the words, and they reverberated with power, echoing from the surrounding forest and vibrating the ground where I stood. A powerful wind lifted, and I squinted through the debris of fallen leaves and dust as it formed into three giant funnels.

The wind died as leaves and debris fell back to the ground.

And there, standing in the middle of the open field were three doors.

CHAPTER
9

Everyone burst into motion, running at the three doors in a wild frenzy, like it was a race. All except for me.

Yeah, I'd totally missed out on the important stuff. And yeah, I had no idea what to do.

Once I got my legs to work, I followed the other witches and rushed over.

The three doors stood about ten feet apart in a flat patch of the field. No beams of any kind supported them, yet they remained upright. They were just… there.

The first door was painted white. The middle door was gray. And the last door was black.

The next thing that happened was really weird, but then, three doors had just magically popped into existence. Weird was my new normal.

I slowed down as I neared, watching the first witch—a young female with a face full of acne—stand before the doors. I held my breath as the white door suddenly opened.

She rushed through and the door shut behind her.

Okay, weird. But I could do weird.

Standing behind the crowd of witches, I bounced on my toes, trying to see what was beyond the door. But with everyone moving, I couldn't see.

Next, a handful of witches went through the gray door and then the black door. In about one minute, all the witches, including Willis—who'd marched through the gray door before it shut behind him, leaving me staring—had all gone through the doors.

I was the only one left.

Your door will choose you…

I took a step forward toward the white door and halted. I don't know why, but I looked behind me at Marina. She stared back at me with a winning smile, the kind a confident opponent gives when they're certain of the outcome.

"So, what's behind door number one?" I voiced in my gameshow host voice impersonation. I laughed. She didn't laugh back. "Door number two?" I tried again. "Guess you're not going to share what's behind door number three. Huh?" I asked, though I knew it was pointless.

Marina gave me a blank stare.

"Okay then. Screw this." I took a breath, trying to calm my nerves. "Three doors. Three possibilities. And my door will choose me." If the doors really were a reflection of the previous test, I was screwed.

I'd arrived late on my very first day and failed my written exam. How could things get worse? Because they could always get worse.

When in doubt, go with your gut.

And my gut said the black door.

With my heart trying to make a hole through my ribcage, I positioned myself in front of the black door and waited. It didn't open.

Instead, the gray door next to it swung open on its hinges.

"Was not expecting that." I cocked my head to the side and stared through the opening. I blinked into the same rolling hills and forest. No magical land. No secret chamber, just the same old field. It was just a doorframe standing in a field. Yet it wasn't.

"Okay. I have no idea what that means. But who cares. Right? Gray it is."

I stepped to the side and walked through—

My body was pulled forward, and I felt my feet leave solid ground. I'd been expecting it, so I didn't panic, and it was familiar somehow. Kind of similar to when I jumped a ley line. My breath was pushed out of my lungs, and I felt myself fall. A tingling washed through me as my lungs rebounded, filling with cool air.

A moment later, my boots hit solid ground and I straightened. My heart pounded as I readied myself with a power word on my lips.

I stood in the middle of a street, a small downtown core of sorts with small commercial buildings crammed together for lack of space. I was not in the field anymore.

After a few heartbeats, in the first ten seconds of looking around, the houses, the streets, even the leafless trees were familiar.

"What the hell?"

I was in Hollow Cove. My town. Only it wasn't.

The sky was pitch black, and brilliant stars shone from above. The moon was low and exceptionally large and bright.

I was standing in a different reality, another version of Hollow Cove—a made-up version, a fake version. Marina's version. Swell.

She was the architect of this fake world. I didn't know the witch. If I did, I would have had a glimpse into what to expect. For now, I only knew this was going to suck.

"This is part of the witch trials," I reminded myself. "They're just trying to freak you out."

Figuring I better start moving, I made my way down Marina's version of Shifter Lane, trying to uncover anything out of place—a lamppost, a bench, a street, or a store, but no. It was identical to my real town in the creepiest sort of way. But my real town had people in it. This place was deserted.

The moonlight lit the town in crystal clarity. I walked up the street, looking over my shoulder every few seconds with my senses on high alert, listening for the sudden scrape of a shoe or any telling sound of someone coming at me. Anyone or *anything* could come at me from everywhere at once.

I listened. I waited. I watched.

I was still furious at Marina for having purposely sabotaged my witch trials—'cause we all knew she did. But I didn't have any proof, nor did I expect Greta to believe me. They all wanted me to fail.

I walked in silence. No movement. No noise. No useful scents either. Nada. It was like that movie when the main character wakes up after a coma only to find they're the last person left on earth. Only this time, I was the actor.

"Hello?" I called out, not expecting to hear an answer, but I figured I'd give it a try anyway.

A heavy, creepy silence settled over the town.

"Hello," replied a voice.

I halted, and a jolt of adrenaline pulsed through me. I whipped around toward the sound of the voice—

And cursed.

The image hit me like a choking tide.

A person stood in the street. A person who looked and sounded just like me. She even wore the exact same clothes, all the way to the same messenger bag wrapped around my shoulder and the high ponytail. A clone. *My* clone.

I was in fake-Hollow Cove staring at fake-me.

Holy hell.

An eerie, cool frisson rolled across my skin and down my spine, all the way down to my legs until I felt it in every single inch of my body.

If Marina had wanted to unnerve me, she'd succeeded.

Whether all the witch trials were the same, I knew without a doubt what mine was. My first witch trial was that I had to *fight myself.*

Awesome.

I glanced at fake-me. "I'm supposed to fight you. Aren't I?"

Fake-me smiled. The expression was so wrong, yet so familiar. It was like those horror movies where the main character stares at themselves in the mirror with that split-second recognition that their reflection *isn't* them, but rather some demonic representation smiling back at them. Their movements are not entirely the same. Yikes.

"You are correct," answered fake-me, in my exact voice.

I shivered, goosebumps riddling my skin. "This is *so* wrong on *so* many levels," I answered, racking my brain for all the spells and power words I was going to use on myself.

Fake-me cocked a brow. "Oh, no. Not wrong. This is exactly what it should be."

I cocked my brow too. "What is that supposed to mean?"

Fake-me smiled at me the way I might have smiled at Marina after I'd headbutted her. "You'll never be a Merlin," she informed me, her tone mocking. "I'm here to make sure of that."

"Excellent." I grinned and cracked my knuckles. "Bring it on, fake-me."

If any word could describe the oddness and eeriness of having a conversation with oneself—well, it would be plastered on my forehead.

"You betcha." Fake-me matched my grin. "Inspiratione!" she cried.

My mouth fell open. "Hey. That's *my* new power word—"

Pain lanced through me as fractures of red energy hit, setting every cell in my body on fire and lifting me off the ground. I cried out in searing agony. I hit the ground hard and rolled, my heart thudding loudly and filling my ears with its rapid beat. My body jerked and thrashed as waves of pain washed through it.

Through my tears, I watched fake-me, her face cemented in a twisted amusement at the pain I suffered.

I too could play this game. It wasn't over yet, not by a longshot. If Marina thought I wouldn't fight myself, she was as stupid as that hairdo.

With most of the pain gone, I rolled to my feet, called forth the magic of the elements, and shouted a power word.

"Accendo!"

Twin fireballs hurled from my palms, flying straight and true, right at fake-me's head.

"Cataracta!" she shouted, and a curtain of water rose before her.

The fireballs hit the water and were extinguished into sizzling smoke.

"Okay," I said, fuming. "So, you've got some skill with magic. But I'm still the prettier one."

I planted my feet and cried, "Fulgur!"

A bolt of white-purple lightning blasted at fake-me's chest.

But my doppelganger sidestepped at the very last second. The lightning hit the pavement, sending up a shower of asphalt chunks.

Pissed, I tried again. "Inflitus!" I bellowed, tapping into the elements and sending a blast of kinetic force at her.

And again, fake-me spun and ducked out of the way, causing the blast to miss her by a hair.

What the hell? There's no way she could have moved like that, like she'd anticipated my spell, as though she *knew* what I was going to do even before I did. Freaky. And a little bit creepy.

Panting, I staggered as the magic took a chunk of my energy, my life force as payment. My gaze rolled over fake-me. She stood firm, strong, and focused, as though the use of power words didn't affect her. Of course, they wouldn't. She wasn't real, she wasn't made of flesh and blood. She was a magical representation of me. She had all my strengths and none of my weaknesses.

A blur of movement caught my attention, and the sound of a voice articulating a spell reached me.

Shit.

I threw myself sideways. But not fast enough.

Pain tore at me in a blinding torrent of agony as if I'd slashed open my stomach and ripped out a clump of my guts. Black marred my vision and I tasted blood. For a moment, I was blind and afraid to move. Pain would do that to a person. But then the pain subsided, as the aftershocks of agony rocked through me and vanished.

I didn't know which spell or power word fake-me used on me, but it hurt like a sonofabitch.

I blinked through my blurred vision, seeing fake-me standing in the middle of the street, waiting for me to get up so we could go at it again. She was cocky. She was bold. She thought she could beat me. She *was* me.

I wasn't beaten, though, and I was going to kick my fake-ass. Yeah, that sounded weird.

If she was me, following that logic, she would react the same way I would. Which was why she could anticipate my movements. With that in mind, I had to do something I *wouldn't* normally do. Be different. Think differently. So, what would the opposite of me do in a spell fight?

Absolutely nothing.

And so I stood, placed my hands on my hips, and waited.

Fake-me eyed me suspiciously, like I was a five-year-old kid caught in a lie. "What are you doing?"

I flashed her my best selfie smile. "What do you mean? I'm not *doing* anything."

Fake-me narrowed her eyes and I watched her face go as dark as the street. "Why aren't you attacking me?"

"Why aren't *you* attacking me?"

"I'm waiting for you," answered my doppelganger with a shrug.

"Well, I'm *waiting* for you too."

Fake-me cocked a hip. "I can do this all day."

"Same here, sister."

"You're pathetic."

I shrugged. "Well, in that case… if *I'm* pathetic, and if you're *my* doppelganger… it means you're pathetic too." I laughed.

Fake-me blinked, her expression a mix of sullen mistrust and anger. "You're an idiot."

"No, *you're* the idiot."

I was seriously losing my mind. But this was *so* much fun.

I dipped my head. "Here's a tip, since we're all about sharing right now. All insults you throw at me… well… you might as well be throwing them at yourself. 'Cause you're me."

Fake-me's face twisted into something truly ugly, distorting her cheekbones too high and her nose too small to look even remotely human before smoothing back to looking like little me. I could see the plans forming behind her dark eyes—my eyes.

Good. She was losing her cool. Just like I would. Time to crank it up a notch.

I cursed. "Damn. Is that what I look like when I'm mad? Gotta tell me—you—whatever, I look kinda stupid. Huh?"

Fake-me's eyes darkened until they looked almost black.

"Nothing to say?" I watched as I homed in my senses as fake-me took a breath, the power word on the verge of her lips.

"Evorto!" she shouted.

But I was already moving.

I put on a burst of speed—something Ronin would have been proud of—and pitched to the ground, rolled, and came up behind her.

"Shit. It worked," I breathed, surprised. I was even more awesome than I thought.

Fake-me shifted, her image rippling like it was made of water. But I was onto her.

With my newfound confidence, I drew in my will and shouted, "Accendo!"

Fake-me's shape solidified. Ruth stood in her place, her eyes wide and wet.

"Ruth?" I jerked. My fireballs zipped past Ruth's head, complete airballs as they hit Gilbert's grocery store's front windows, and the entire wall burst into flames.

In that split second, I'd known it wasn't Ruth, but my mind had just enough doubt to make me miss.

Ruth sneered and shouted, "Fulgur!"

"Fuck me."

I didn't have time to move. There was no point in moving. I blinked as the approaching fireballs' fire scorched my face before they exploded on my chest.

Searing pain screamed through my body, making me crumple to the ground in agony. Just when I thought I was going to burn alive, the pain stopped.

I blinked up at Marina's smiling face.

"Tessa Davenport," she said, a smile in her voice. "You have failed."

CHAPTER
10

"**Y**ou failed!" shrilled Ronin, leaning forward on my mother's old bedroom chair in what was now my bedroom.

"Shhh!" I ran to my bedroom door and slammed it shut. I recognized the muffled voices that came from the kitchen downstairs as Dolores and Beverly.

Keeping my back to my door, I spun around. "I don't want my aunts to hear. Especially not Ruth."

My thoughts flicked to Ruth, and my heart seemed to fall to my gut. After the trials, the first thing I did when I got home was to check up on Ruth. Her bedroom door was closed, and no matter how many times I knocked and called out, she wouldn't come to the door.

Ronin had showed up moments later, all excited and jittery about my trials. He'd brought a bottle of champagne to celebrate. An actual bottle and three glasses.

I'd taken the bottle from him. "Are you mad? It's eleven in the morning."

Ronin had flashed me one of his infamous, lazy, sexy smiles that had the females unlocking their knees for him. Though now all his attention was focused on Iris since she arrived in Hollow Cove.

"But somewhere it's past noon," he'd said. "Everyone knows noon's the acceptable time to get wasted."

He'd been all smiles then. Now, well, I didn't like the shock on his face. Nor the pity. Pity? Pity was for losers. I wasn't a loser.

Depression had replaced my embarrassment at the thought that I could be found out, that somehow Marina or Greta would have sent word of my failure to my aunts. So far they hadn't, but it didn't mean they wouldn't.

I'd been so certain, so sure I would ace these trials, and my overconfidence had bitten me in the ass—hard.

I was a fool, an overly self-assured jackass, and I'd paid dearly for it.

"Tessa's right." Iris shifted on my bed, her straight black hair grazing her jaw. Her eyes were sad as she fixed on a spot on the floor. "Ruth's in a dark place. I know. I've been there. I know it well."

I knew Iris was talking about the curse Adan had put on her, how scary it must have been for her to be trapped in a goat's body, alone and frightened, and not being able to communicate with anybody to help her. Not until she found me.

"How do I get her out?" The idea that Ruth was slowly being pulled down into this darkness didn't settle well with me. Depression was real, and I had no idea how to help.

"You don't," answered Iris. "Be there for her, but she needs to pull herself out. Out of the darkness. She needs to *want* to. Because anything you or we do won't help if she's not responsive. If she's not ready. And right now, she's not."

I didn't know if Iris was referring to when she'd been cursed as a goat, or if this was something else entirely. But I didn't press it.

We all knew Ruth was blaming herself for Bernard's death. She was taking it hard, too far, and it scared the crap out of me. My Aunt Ruth had always been the cheery one, the one with all the smiles, without a care in the world. Her love of animals and nature had always touched me deeply. Seeing her so broken and lost was terrifying. I was afraid I'd lose her forever if we didn't do something fast.

"Tess," declared Ronin, and I lifted my eyes to find him staring at me with a frown.

"What?" I shot back.

The half-vampire let out a sigh. "What do you mean you…" he said and then whispered, "… failed the trial? What the hell happened? You were really prepared. You prepared for an entire month. We barely saw you. You were either hitting the books or practicing your witchy things."

I raised a brow. "My *witchy* things? Why does that sound dirty coming out of your mouth?" I laughed.

Ronin gave me a hard stare. "Can't be right. You're a magic champ. You're the Muhammad Ali of witches. I've seen you do amazing witchy things. Hell, I was there when you did them."

"She's just messing with us. Right, Tessa?" added Iris with a pleading smile. "There's no way you didn't pass." She laughed softly. "You of all people. A badass witch could pass these old trials. Right? Right, Tessa?"

My gaze shifted between them, my only two friends in this town, if you left out my aunts. The fact that neither could believe I'd failed made me feel a hundred times worse—as though I'd failed them too.

My gut tightened as another wave of embarrassment hit. "Yeah, well. I didn't. I failed the first trial."

"No shit," answered Ronin. "So, what the hell happened over there?" I fixed my gaze on him with a threatening sharpness.

My humiliation was physical. I felt it everywhere, in my bones, my aches and pains. I had real-life experience. I'd battled demons. Evil sorceresses… and I still failed. I was a freaking Shadow witch.

And I failed.

I gave a mock laugh. "Well, you're not going to believe it, but Marina—the one with half her head shaved I told you about—made sure I failed the written test." I quickly told them about the email I never got and finally battling fake-me and losing.

"Basically," I let out a long breath as I pushed off the door and made my way to the middle of the room, "I got my assed kicked by me."

Ronin and Iris were silent for a long time.

Ronin finally broke the silence. "They can't fail you. She cheated. That Marina made sure you never got that email. She orchestrated the whole thing."

"You should report her," added Iris, her pale face dark with emotion.

"To who?" I shook my head, my anger flaring as I tried to rein it in.

"To the one in charge," replied Iris.

"Greta?" I laughed bitterly. "Greta is the trials' training division director. And it so happens that she hates my guts. She wanted me to fail. This is her payback for my aunts making me a Merlin. Trust me when I say she'll never believe my word over Marina's." My voice was low and controlled, but inside, I was seething.

I'm not going to pretend I'm perfect, or that I never cheated on a test or lied about stuff. Because *that* would be a lie. But having someone else cheat at my expense was just plain evil. That wasn't cheating. It was sabotage.

"It's done," I said, after a moment. "I failed the first test. And there's nothing I can do about it."

Iris's eyes flashed brightly, looking cross. "It's not fair. You never stood a chance."

I shrugged. "Life's not fair. Yada-yada-yada. But it's not over. I still have two trials left. And I'm not planning on failing them."

Marina might have sabotaged my first trial, but I was going to make damn sure I'd be on time for the next one. Hell, I might even sleep over, just to be sure I was there in the early morning.

Iris sat straight. "You think she'll try again? She'd be mad to try."

"I know she will." I knew it in my gut, my core. "That evil bitch is going to try to sabotage my other trials too. I just… I just don't know what she's going to pull next time."

"It won't be the same thing again," informed Ronin. "Unless she's really stupid."

I pressed my hands to my hips. "She's not stupid. It'll be something else."

The thought of the next trial had my intestines doing jump rope. A shudder in the middle of my gut started, a hollow ache. And it was getting worse.

"What a mess." I rubbed my eyes with my fingers, still feeling at odds with what happened this morning at the witch trials. "I can't think about the second trial right now. I need to be focusing on Ruth. She needs me. She needs us. The only way Ruth will ever get better is if we can find out what really happened to Bernard. Find out how he died. Then she can stop blaming herself, at least."

"I thought you said they weren't releasing that information until the trial," commented Ronin, real concern showing on his handsome face.

My lips pressed together in thought. "I did. Doesn't mean I can't find it by other means."

Ronin beamed as he leaned back in his chair and crossed his arms over his chest. "I like where you're going with this. This is you going all witchy again. Isn't it?"

"Ooh! Are we going after Adira?" Iris's dark eyes glinted in amusement in the light from the window. "You know… I've got a mean yeast infection curse with her name on it."

I laughed, feeling some of my tension letting go. "It does. Ruth's court date is on Monday, December seventh. Dolores told me. Which gives us six days to do our own investigation and find out what really happened to Bernard."

"And how do you suppose we do that?" asked Ronin.

"Easy," I shrugged, smiling. "We've done it before."

Ronin shot to his feet, his hand in the air. "Please tell me you're joking. Please tell me you're not planning on going in there. Trust me. You don't want to mess with Adira."

"You," I barked, pointing a finger at Ronin. "Why didn't you tell me Adira was a vampire in the first place? Could have saved me lots of embarrassment." I had never told Ronin or Iris about Adira handcuffing me. I thought it was best to leave that part out.

Ronin raised his hands. "I gave you her name," he answered, like that was explanation enough.

"I can help." From her jean pocket, Iris pulled a small leather bag. She dipped her fingers in it and pinched a long red hair. "I've cursed vampires before. Pretty simple when you have what you need."

I raised my brows, impressed. "I seriously don't know how and when you managed to get that," I said. "But you are one awesome Dark witch, Iris."

She beamed at me. "I know."

Ronin pulled his hair. "Have you two gone mental in the past hour? We're talking about vampires now. Full-fledged bloodsuckers. Predators. Not your neighborhood cuddly, shifter monkey. Vamps don't play by the rules. They play by *their* rules."

I shrugged. "Your point being?"

Ronin made a harsh bark of laughter. "They're *vampires*. You know… super strength, speed, and stealth. They drink blood. Have freakishly large teeth. Ring any bells?"

"I drank blood one time," said Iris, her eyes a little unfocused. "I was experimenting with a blood curse." She giggled. "It *really* didn't taste like I had imagined. I realized only after that I wasn't supposed to ingest the blood."

I looked at Iris, not knowing what to say to that. I chose to remain silent.

Ronin paced the room, rubbing the back of his neck. He stopped and looked at me. "Have you ever faced a clan of vampires before?"

"No. And I don't plan to." A plan was formulating in my mind. I knew what I had to do. "There are other ways to get that information," I met Ronin's eyes, "that doesn't include messing with Adira."

Ronin gave me a pointed look and crossed his arms over his chest. "How? How are you going to do that?"

"With Marcus," I answered, and Iris clapped excitedly, bounding on the edge of the bed.

Marcus might have ghosted me, but he loved my aunts—especially Ruth, who'd been supplying him with some blue liquid. It was important, whatever it was. I'm sure he wouldn't want that to go away. He would help.

"Marcus?" questioned Ronin. "But we don't know where he is." His tension eased, seemingly grateful that I wasn't planning on snooping around Adira's things.

I moved past Ronin to my desk and picked up the blue ballpoint pen I'd forgotten to return after Adira had cuffed me. "With this," I said, a smile curving my mouth.

The half-vampire laughed. "You're going to write him a love letter?"

My jaw clenched. "No, dumbass. *This*… this is *his* pen." I looked at my friends, my pulse thrashing with excitement at the notion of what I was about to do. "And I'm going to do a location spell to find him with it. Then," I added, my heart pounding, "I'm bringing his ass home."

CHAPTER
11

Both White and Dark witches had their own versions of locator or tracking spells. Iris's Dark witch version was excellent, but it required hours spent on pre-spells and aura-detecting spells—that's *if* I did it right—not to mention adding the compass link to Marcus's pen. Then I would need to add all the mix and link it to an amulet that would act like an actual compass, which would then lead the way.

I didn't have hours to mess around with spells. I needed to find Marcus like yesterday. The longer we wasted time working spells, the further away we would be at discovering what happened to Bernard, and the worse off my Aunt Ruth would be.

Six days sounded like a lot of time, but it really wasn't. Not when someone's life was at stake.

So, we opted for the White witch approach.

With my *Witch's Handbook* lying on the floor to my right, I leaned forward and flattened the map of Pennsylvania we found from a large hardcover book called *The Atlas of North America*, which we'd discovered in my aunts' library.

Iris knelt on the floor next to me. "Thank you for helping me," I told her. Though I'd never tried one myself, with Iris's help the locator spell was completed in record time. She was freaking amazing when it came to spells.

Iris's dark eyes lit up. "I'm just super psyched you're letting me handle White magic. It's like Christmas… only better, without the creepy fat guy in the beard and the red suit. But the elves and reindeer are a nice touch."

I laughed. "You're nuts."

Ronin made a strange sound in his throat and I pulled my eyes up to look at him.

"Why are you smiling like that?"

"There's nothing hotter than two women on their knees," answered Ronin.

Iris laughed, but I threw a chalk at his head. "That's gross."

"Ow," he laughed. "Just stating the obvious."

"Stop stating all together," I said. "I need to concentrate. Can't have you spilling your vampire mojo while I'm trying to work."

While Ronin chuckled, I leaned forward and placed Marcus's ballpoint pen on the map of Pennsylvania before leaning back, my gaze back on my spellbook. "Okay. I've placed the tangible piece of Marcus's property with his aura on the map." I let out a breath. "Next comes the spell."

Iris let out a squeal of delight and clapped her hands. "This is soooo much better than sex."

"Hey," called Ronin. "Nothin's better than sex… other than…say… lots and lots of sex."

Pulse picking up, I tucked a strand of hair behind my ear, took a small container the size of a saltshaker, twisted the top, and sprinkled some blue-colored powder over the map. It fell like makeup glitter, glimmering in the light as it settled and coated the map and the pen.

I took a slow breath. Touching my will to the elements, I ran my gaze over the spell and chanted in a clear voice, "Power of the elements, I summon thee. I seek your help in finding the one called Marcus who is hiding."

Power surged. I stiffened, and my breath hissed in through my nose. The outpouring of energy from the elements fused with my aura, and I almost fell as my equilibrium shifted. Gritting my teeth, a tingling sensation fluttered from my fingers to my toes.

Putting out a hand on the floor, I steadied myself as the incoming energy continued to build and pull with tremors that shook me like a fever.

A burst of dazzling light flashed before our eyes as magic tore through the room. On the map, Marcus's pen spun around on its axis in a blur.

"Is that supposed to happen?" Ronin was leaning behind me, his breath hot on the back of my neck.

I stared at the pen. "No idea."

"Ooooh! I'm getting the feels!" expressed Iris, her eyes wide with a huge smile plastered over her face. She looked like she'd just performed her darkest curse ever as she rubbed her arms.

With another flash of light, the blue dust lifted off the map, hovering over it like a cloud. I watched in amazement as the dust came together to form an arrow and moved to the top of the map. Then the dust compressed together into a single tiny ball the size of a pea—and fell flat on the map.

"Holy shit," I breathed.

"Holy poop on a stick," expressed Ronin.

I leaned forward. "The dot is covering an area called Allegheny National Forest. And look—right on the Allegheny Tionesta Creek Camping site."

"The chief's on a camping trip?" asked Ronin, his voice thick with disbelief. "All this time, the dude's been hiking and making campfires, eating s'mores, and singing Kumbaya?"

He did have a point. Frowning, I stared at the blue dot, thoughts of Marcus spiraling in my head. Emotions cascaded over me, things I did not want to feel and experience right now in front of my friends. I hated that he made me feel like that.

But I had big lady balls now, and this wasn't about me or my feelings.

"Camping or not," I said, as I stifled my feelings away and yanked out my book *The Ley Lines of North America* from my bag on the floor next to me. "I'm going to drag his butt back kicking and screaming. I really don't care at this point."

Iris let out a creepy laugh. "I love it when they kick and scream," she said, as a strange smile flickered over her. "Means it's working."

My eyes met Ronin's and he shrugged.

Moving on, moving on…

"Wish I could come with you." Iris folded her hands on her lap. "I want to help Ruth any way I can, but I'm not going to lie. I just really want to see Marcus kicking and screaming."

"Me too," I answered, touched that my new bestie wanted to come. "But I haven't mastered ley lines. Well, with me yes. But I have no idea how to bring others with me. It might not work. It might even kill you."

"But I'm a witch," protested Iris, her cheeks darkened with color. "It'll work. I know it will." Her face was hopeful as her hands clasped before her.

My chest tightened at what I saw on her face. "And you're my friend. I don't want anything to happen to you."

Iris looked down at the map. "Promise that one day you'll teach me. You'll let me ride a ley line with you?"

"Promise," I said as Iris looked back at me, a smile on her pretty pixie-like face. I flicked my gaze back down at my ley line book. "Got it. I'll have to transfer two ley lines, but there's a stop close to that campsite. I'll have to walk about a mile, but no big deal in the right boots." I snapped my book shut, shoved it in my bag, and leaped to my feet. "Speaking of boots. I've got to go."

"What?" Ronin spun on his feet. "Like right now?"

"Yup." I dashed into the bathroom and closed the door. I did not want to have the urge to pee while traveling via ley line. The idea of what my pee could do to a passerby while traveling at light speed was a pretty disturbing visual… and a funny one.

Once I was done, I rushed out of my bathroom, grabbed my winter coat from my bed along with my black wool tuque and matching mittens, wrapped a thick scarf around my neck, and dashed to the hallway. I stared at Ruth's closed door for a moment before heading towards the stairs in the hallway with Iris and Ronin running to catch up.

"Hey, Flash. Slow down. Don't you want to tell your aunts where you're going?" asked Ronin, climbing down the stairs behind me.

"No." A thrilling mix of excitement and duty washed over me. I was going to fix this thing with Ruth. Right now.

I ran down the hallway to the entryway and slipped my tall winter boots on. Once I had my coat zipped up and my hat pulled over my head, I turned to my friends. "Don't tell them anything until I get back," I warned, hearing Dolores's and Beverly's voices trailing from the kitchen. "Don't want to get their hopes up if it doesn't work. Got it?"

"It's going to work," encouraged Iris. "He'll come when he hears about Ruth. I know he will."

For some reason, I couldn't answer, but I hoped she was right.

Ronin stepped forward. "Don't worry. We'll keep the old bags in line till you get back."

Nodding, I let out a breath. "Be back soon."

I spun around and faced the front door. Excitement pounded in my veins at the prospect of the hunt, the thrill of the chase, and the promise of kicking Marcus's butt if he didn't follow me home.

Yeah. Good times.

With my pulse throbbing, I called up my will and reached out to tap the ley line. A blast of energy hit me, just as I felt it vibrating beneath Davenport House.

My fingers curled around the door handle, and I yanked it open and jumped.

CHAPTER

12

My boots crunched on the gravel on the dirt road. The air was cold, and when I exhaled my breath came out in a long, frosty plume. An icy wind slapped my face as I paced up a short rise in the road. But I was warm. Walking nonstop with determination for about a half-hour would do that to you.

I felt pumped. Energized. Ready for anything.

I crested the hill. Below, at the end of the winding road, was a large campsite. Thirty, possibly more, log cabins that could be considered large family houses were spaced out in vast sites, all surrounded by tall trees and shrubs. In the middle of the cabins sat a much larger building that resembled an inn or hotel. Allegheny Tionesta Creek Camping was quite beautiful. And if I wasn't so mad and in a hurry, I would have taken the time to look around and marvel at the beauty of this place. People milled about, none of them Marcus from what I could see.

I put on speed as I made the descent to the site, my thoughts on Ruth's face and how she looked so disheartened and frail aiding my way down.

I hadn't thought about what I was going to say to Marcus when I saw him. There hadn't been any time. He'd just have to deal with whatever was going to fly out of my mouth. It wouldn't be pretty, but I didn't care.

The topography flattened as I reached the campsite. Trails of smoke billowed from the chimneys of some of the cabins. The smell of wood burning filled my nose in a stark contrast to the cold, brisk air from before. My gaze darted to a pile of ashes the size of a small house. When I got closer, I spotted what looked like the remains of wooden chairs, a few big trees, a couch, and tables. Dark gray smoke drifted from the still-red ambers.

I walked around the great pile of ashes and saw five large trees that could have been oak or maple (impossible to tell without the leaves) lying on the ground nearby. Some were uprooted, and some were split in half as though hit by lightning or like a giant had taken his ax to them. As I neared the cabins, I noticed some had windows smashed, some were missing their front doors, and one's entire front porch and wooden posts had collapsed.

Weird. Either they were just hit by a giant storm with the help of a tornado, or something more sinister had happened here.

I turned my attention back to the log cabins. I had no idea which one was Marcus's. It's not like the spell provided an address—I would have to work on that—and the people I had seen moments before had all but disappeared. Since I couldn't ask anyone for his whereabouts, it looked like I was going to have to go through *all* the cabins.

But when I got closer, I realized I wouldn't have to.

A burgundy Jeep Grand Cherokee sat in the parking lot of cabin number two.

Marcus's Jeep.

My heart did a little jig. "You better be in bed dying," I growled as I marched toward the cabin in a very Dolores kind of way. When my gaze flicked to the smoke that was shooting out of the chimney, more anger rose, and I balled my hands into fists, well, into mitts.

"It's okay. It's fine. Ruth needs him. Not me," I reminded myself, more like trying to make myself believe it if I spoke it out loud. Ruth truly did need him. Me? Well, I'd get over this. Just like everything else in my life. Life had made me hard, and I was okay with that.

Time didn't heal all wounds. You just got better at dealing with them.

With my heart in my throat, I climbed up the steps to a wraparound porch where a pile of wood logs leaned against the wall next to the front door. Before I knew what I was doing, I knocked on the cabin's front door with my fist. Hard. Harder than necessary.

I stepped back and waited.

Nothing.

I knocked again.

And waited.

Still nothing. I thought about leaving. Maybe he wasn't in there? But his Jeep was parked right outside. Maybe he went for a hike? This was what people came here to do. Right? Even paranormals. Hike and becoming one with nature, blah blah blah.

I couldn't stay out here in the cold. Sooner or later I would become a witch popsicle, and I still had to manage my way back to the source of the ley line. If I couldn't move, I couldn't get home.

My gaze moved to the bigger inn-like cabin. "Maybe someone in there knows where he is."

Just as I turned around, a voice sounded through the door, unmistakably female, and throaty and sensual.

The air slipped out of me, and I couldn't seem to make my lungs move to pull more in. Marcus had left his town to do the nasty with some woman?

That's it. It was time to pull out the castration charm.

Anger, my familiar winning emotion, took hold of me. I faced the door as my breath hissed out again. In a quick motion, I grabbed the doorknob and turned it. Seeing it wasn't locked, I pushed in.

Moans and groans sounded around me like I'd just stumbled into a live porn movie.

A couple was having sex.

Scratch that. *Marcus* was having sex with some woman.

Betrayal bubbled up, making my stomach clench. My heart sank as I stood there, unable to move, trying to put my thoughts together into something that made sense. I felt like I was having an out-of-body experience, like I was seeing something happening through someone else's eyes.

Just as the heartache started, it ended abruptly. I was shaking—not from the cold but with anger.

Emotions poured over me, frightening in their rapidity: anger, betrayal, dismay. Still, I wasn't about to break down because of a man. Besides, Marcus and I weren't exclusive. In fact, we weren't anything.

I focused on why I made the trip. The one person who mattered here was Ruth.

Ruth needed Marcus, but he was too busy exchanging bodily fluids to care or even notice.

I stood on the threshold, staring like a Peeping Tom—or a serial killer. The intertwined couple hadn't heard me come in. No wonder, with all the noise she was making. The woman's back was to me, as she bounced up and down like a cowgirl at a rodeo.

I couldn't see Marcus's face, but I recognized that golden skin I'd seen and felt. The same strong arms that had held me were holding tightly on the woman's waist.

"Oh, yeah, baby," she moaned. "Don't stop. Don't stop."

That's it.

And the first thing out of my mouth was, "She's *faking*." I said it loud and clear. I think I might have even shouted it. Couldn't be sure.

The woman screamed at the top of her lungs and flung herself over and off the bed in a tangle of sheets, still screaming—she had some serious lungs—leaving her partner exposed and erect.

My eyes widened as my jaw fell open. Not because of the large, erect penis that was hard to miss, but because I stared at a not-so-handsome face topped with short brown hair, small beady eyes, and thick beard.

Oh dear.

"You're not Marcus," I said, my voice high as a nervous giggle bubbled up. Oh dear, oh dear, oh dear.

"Who the hell are you? What the hell do you want!" the dude bellowed, his face red and sweaty, not even bothering to cover up his manly rocket.

"Not Marcus," I said again, as another wave of giggles hit. Damn. I was losing it.

The woman glared at me from the floor next to the bed. "I *wasn't* faking."

Another giggle burst out of my mouth. "The fact that you had to clear that up suggests otherwise." Why was I even talking to her?

When I screw up, I screw up big.

Time to go.

I raised my hands in an apologetic gesture. "Sorry, wrong cabin." I laughed as I backed away in a half bow. "Carry on…" I added, somehow seeming appropriate.

"Tessa?" came a familiar voice behind me.

I spun around.

A broad-shouldered man with a tussle of black hair stood on the front porch. Gray eyes framed with dark eyelashes focused on me. He had a square jaw, a perfectly straight nose, and full, kissable lips.

Marcus.

CHAPTER
13

"Tessa? What are you doing here?" asked Marcus, as he rushed past me, and I caught a whiff of his musky scent and soap. "Sorry, Anthony," he apologized and shut the door, leaving us alone on the porch.

He wore a black winter down bomber jacket that hugged his trim waist above a pair of jeans that fit his thick, powerful thighs perfectly. His hair was longer, and it brushed his shoulders in thick black, luscious waves.

He looked great. More than great. I'd forgotten how handsome he was, or rather, what the effect of seeing him face to face did to me. Daydreams didn't do him justice. Not by a longshot.

"Well," I said, my face flaming, peeling my eyes away from him before I started drooling. I flicked my eyes to his Jeep. "Funny you should ask. It's not like I planned to be here, but I came anyway. You didn't give me any other choice."

"Wait? What?" asked Marcus, and I met his gaze. He shook his head. "What are you talking about? Why did you barge in on Anthony?" He laughed.

Yum. I could stand here all day listening to that laugh. I strained to sober up. "I thought Anthony was you."

He smiled at me, his thick eyebrows high. "What?"

"Never mind." My pulse was just a shade faster as I pretended to be interested in the porch's railing.

Marcus watched me for a moment, a thoughtful expression smoothing his features. His face transformed into a lazy grin. "You're upset," he purred and a wisp of his usual, confident self settled in his posture. "You are. You thought that was me in there." He leaned closer, his gray eyes rolled over my face. "You like me. *Really* like me. Admit it."

I rolled my eyes. "Please…"

"You looove me," he teased, his lips parted to show a glimpse of teeth as his smile widened.

Damn. Here he was all mountain-like, manly man—a tall, strong, virile specimen of male.

"Don't flatter yourself," I said, though my heart practically jumped with joy. I was in so much trouble. Would it be bad if I started clapping?

"You look great," said Marcus in a voice that sent tiny tingles fluttering in my belly with that damn uber-hot smile plastered on his face. I wanted to take that voice and make it into a cream so I could rub it all over my body.

"Stop."

"Stop what?" His smile widened, and another wave of tiny tingles erupted.

"Stop looking at me like that." *No. Please don't stop. Don't stop. Don't stop.*

Marcus shrugged. "Can't help it. You're so beautiful. Especially when you're mad. Your eyes darken. Did you know that? It's damn sexy." His knowing smile made him a bad boy chief mix—a dangerous and intoxicating mix.

I stood there on the landing, not remembering why I was here or why I should be angry with him.

A new smile hovered about Marcus as he watched mc. I was going to clobber him. Only, I started to shiver, so much so, that my lips were beginning to harden like frozen sausages as my teeth clattered. Guess my rush of adrenaline was over, now that I knew it wasn't Marcus with Rodeo Barbie.

"You're freezing." Marcus reached out and touched my right cheek with his hand. It was warm, and I didn't pull away.

"Mmmm, hmmm." The soft touch of his hand on my skin sent my blood humming. I didn't move.

Marcus moved his hand from my cheek and rubbed my arms with both hands. "Come. Let's get you warmed up. Carol makes an amazing vegan chili."

I didn't come here to swoon over Marcus and some chili, but I was about to go all Frosty the Snow Witch if I didn't get into a warm place in the next few seconds. A few minutes in a warm place with a hot meal wouldn't do any harm. Besides, I couldn't feel my lips anymore.

I let Marcus lead me down the stairs and towards that bigger log cabin. Once inside, I was hit by a rush of heat, like I'd just stepped into a sauna. The air was thick with the scent of chicken soup, chili, and burning wood. A large stone fireplace rose at the end of the room, a blazing fire roaring in it. A rocking chair, with a figure sitting in it, squeaked as it moved.

The place wasn't a huge space, but it was dressed like a restaurant or pub. A dozen small round tables with chairs were placed around the room. Two men sat at the closest table to us, and a woman and a man sat at the table near a window. They all looked up when we entered, their faces hard as they looked me over. But their gazes turned away as soon as they saw Marcus with me. What was that about?

I was still shivering, so Marcus put his hand on my lower back and steered me gently with him over to a bar-like counter made of polished wood.

He pulled a stool out for me. "Here. Sit. I'll get you something to eat."

I did what I was told, too cold to do anything else, and watched as Marcus moved down the bar and addressed an older lady whose wrinkled face stretched into a large grin at the sight of him.

Her hair was long and white, pulled back into a long braid, and she wore an apron over her plaid shirt. Her skin was tanned leather, covered in fine seams and wrinkles. She patted Marcus's hand, poured him a fresh cup of coffee, and disappeared through a door behind the bar.

"Here's some coffee. The chili is on the way," said Marcus as he placed the steaming cup on the bar in front of me, pulled out the stool next to mine, and sat.

I peeled off my mittens and wrapped my ice-cold fingers around the cup. The skin on my fingers burned as they touched the ceramic, but it felt nice all the same. Bringing the mug to my lips, I took a sip. Then another. And another. The bitter taste of coffee was divine, and I moaned as the hot liquid poured down my throat.

I instantly felt better.

Once my lips thawed, I asked, "What is this place?" I set the mug on the counter with my fingers still wrapped around it.

"It's a shifter colony," answered Marcus, his eyes still holding some of that laughter from before.

"It is?"

"Silverback gorillas," he said.

I flicked my gaze behind him to the couple sitting near the window. They were both watching me with identical frowns. "Is everyone here a shifter?"

"Yes. Wereapes," replied Marcus, and I moved my gaze back to him. "Most of them don't trust outsiders… non-shifters."

"So, Anthony is a wereape too, then?"

"Yes," said Marcus, his unwavering stare piercing. "And my cousin." He unzipped his jacket and dropped it on the empty stool next to him. Muscles bulged from under his snug black shirt, and I found myself unable to look away because part of me wanted to rip it off just to see what was underneath.

I breathed through my nose, trying to shut him out. He hadn't even tried to reach out to me in three months. It stung. But it was the truth. I was tired of hating him and wanting him. That was a full-time job on its own. Enough was enough.

"I had no idea there were shifter colonies like this one," I said, reeling in my feelings. "And you have family here, but you live in Hollow Cove?"

"My family's from the city. But some wereapes prefer to live away from the modern world. They prefer wide, open spaces, surrounded by nature. They don't want to have to deal with humans… or other paranormals."

"Like me." I nodded. "Well, it is really pretty here. Must be spectacular in the summer."

Marcus shifted on his stool, our thighs touching as he moved closer. "I'm glad to see you." His mesmerizing gray eyes had me feeling all kinds of things I shouldn't be feeling right now—like hot flashes.

I raised a brow. I wanted to say so many things to him right now, things I had been thinking about for the past three months. I opened my mouth to reply, just as the older lady came to the bar.

"Here you go, hon," she said, all smiles as she set down a bowl of steaming and intoxicating-smelling vegan chili.

"Thank you," I answered, sticking my nose above the bowl and taking a sniff. "Smells divine."

The older lady laughed. It was infectious, and I found myself laughing and relaxing for the first time since I came to this freezing campsite. I took a spoon and scooped a large portion of the chili into my mouth.

"Wow," I said, my mouth full. "This is good. You should package it up and sell this stuff." I put another spoonful of chili into my mouth.

"Thanks, Carol," said Marcus, as he and she then shared some secret glances.

Carol leaned her elbows on the bar. "This one came to fetch you. Didn't she? Hmmm. Must have walked for over an hour to be frozen like that," she speculated with a smile on her wrinkled face. "She's still young and in good, childbearing years."

I spit the chili from my mouth. "I'm sorry. What?"

Carol huffed a laugh and disappeared back into the kitchen area behind the bar.

"Tessa, why did you come here?" Marcus's question pulled my attention back to him. He dipped his head and stared into my eyes.

I watched him for a long moment, trying to stifle the bubble of betrayal and anger that threatened to pop. I failed.

"Why didn't you ever call me back?" I accused, my heart beating a little quicker, and I hated that. Hated that I'd let my emotions be the boss of me right now, but I couldn't help it.

"I couldn't," he answered casually, like it was a normal thing, like commenting on the amount of sugar he used in his coffee. "Cell phones don't work here up in the mountains. And there are no phones. No landlines. I would have called you if I could." Marcus leaned back. "I never thought I'd still be here, to be honest. Things got… crazy."

"Does it have anything to do with the pile of burning rubble outside?"

"It does," he answered. "Here, the wereapes are led by an alpha. Like a chief. The alpha is the strongest and takes care of his or her colony, their family."

"So, what's the problem?"

"Too many alphas."

"So little time," I laughed. "Sorry. Bad joke."

Marcus considered me a moment. "A younger male is challenging the alpha wereape. Another male. They've been at it for three months."

"Does it usually take this long?"

"No. Usually, the older alpha submits to the younger alpha. But Stan is a stubborn old brute. He doesn't want to submit. He thinks he can continue to be the alpha, but his body isn't like it used to be."

I swallowed more chili. "Who's stronger?"

"It's hard to tell. Both are massive. But there can only be one alpha per clan."

"Right."

We stared at each other, and the tiny space between us felt too hot.

I pulled my gaze away before I did something stupid—like jump him right there on the bar. Yeah, I needed help.

"You still haven't told me why you came," prodded Marcus as our eyes met again. His lips curved in the smile of a man liking what he saw. "I wish I could say you came because you missed me," he continued, "but your eyes say something else."

How perceptive. "It's Ruth," I said, my voice tight. "I came here to fetch you because of Ruth."

Marcus's eyebrows knitted in the middle. "Ruth? Has something happened to her? Is she okay?"

I shook my head, my insides twisting with dread. "Not really. She's been—"

The door to the inn burst open. A big, burly man with the biggest arms I'd ever seen came rushing in. He looked like an action figure.

"They're at it again," said the stranger, his focus on Marcus as he came up to the bar. "You've got to do something. They're going to kill each other."

Fun times.

CHAPTER
14

I'd seen Marcus hulk-out into his King Kong alter ego before, but it never ceased to amaze and excite me.

His shirt was gone the moment he jumped off the stool, just as he yanked off his jeans and pulled off his boots. His fit, golden-brown body was sculpted like a Roman statue, and muscles bulged on his naked frame.

Hot damn. How could I have forgotten how splendid he was naked?

But I didn't have time to marvel at his nakedness.

He went down on all fours, and I heard a horrible tearing sound along with the breaking of bones as his face and skin rippled and stretched until his body tripled in size. His jaw elongated, revealing carnivore teeth the size of my kitchen knives. And then, instead of a man, was a four-hundred-pound silverback gorilla.

He was glorious and frightening all at once. Is it weird that I got turned on?

Marcus the gorilla stood on all fours, his front hands resting on his knuckles. The muscles on his chest flexed, and the gorilla roared as he pounded his great big fists on the ground, sending tremors through the inn. I felt the trembling along the bar.

And then he was moving.

On all fours, the gorilla leaped away and dashed out the front door with the stranger running behind him.

"Looks like I won't be going home anytime soon." I jumped off my stool and ran after them. No way was I going to miss whatever was happening. Even if it did sound dangerous.

I rushed through the front door and leaped off the landing—

And walked into a gorilla fight.

A large ring of both gorilla and humanoid wereapes circled two massive gorillas who were using tree trunks as clubs.

"Holy crap," I muttered.

Both were silverback gorillas, both huge, with mouths full of teeth. The closer I got, I could see that one had a lot more gray fur along his back, head, and forearms while the other was nearly covered in black fur. I guessed the one with the gray fur was the older alpha male, Stan, fighting this new one who wanted to take his place.

It was hard to see which of the two was bigger, and it was even harder to see which of the two was strongest.

Stan, the older gorilla advanced, flexing and hefting his tree trunk. He smashed it against the side of the younger gorilla.

The younger gorilla fell to the side, but he was up in almost the same moment, smashing his tree trunk against Stan, who tumbled to the side. An ugly grimace skewed the younger gorilla's face as he dropped his tree and charged.

He hit Stan like a freight train hitting a cement wall, and the two fell to the ground in a blur of fists hitting flesh, snarls, hissing, teeth, and dark fur. Each gorilla pummeled themselves with their fists, breaking into a rabid frenzy of blows. The ground beneath my feet shuddered and quaked. Each crushing punch sent bile rising up my throat.

The air smelled of blood and sweat and animal.

It was the most brutal and primal fight I'd ever witnessed. Around me the crowd roared, enthused by the prospect of one of the gorillas' death. Some were in their beast form, but some remained in their human forms.

"This has been going on for too long," said a male wereape.

"Stan has to submit," said a female wereape next to him with long black hair and matching eyes. "He's been the alpha for eighty years. It's time for Fredrik."

"Tell that to Stan," said the other male wereape.

"Stan, Stan, he's our man. If he can't do it, no one can," I sang, realizing too late that my thoughts came out in verbal vomit from my mouth.

The female wereape turned around and glared at me, her eyes telling me this wasn't my place, and she wanted to pound my head in with her girly gorilla fists.

I raised my hands. "I'm leaving soon. Promise," I told her, and she turned her attention back on the fight.

Yes, I was leaving. But not without Marcus.

Marcus in his gorilla form walked slowly around the fighting wereapes like he was the referee in a boxing match, waiting to call the winner or to pull them apart if things got ugly.

Would the gorillas fight to the death? Was that what this was? If so, I didn't exactly feel like watching.

But I couldn't pull myself away either.

I was a witch, so I didn't know much about wereapes or werewolves or any of the were species for that matter. And I knew even less about how their alpha structures worked. And yet, I knew I was witnessing something extraordinary we witches weren't usually privy to.

I was getting a glimpse into a world most paranormals could only dream of.

I could appreciate how easily they could destroy trees and houses with that amount of brutal strength. And Marcus was here to make sure they didn't kill each other, to make sure they both stayed alive, no matter the outcome.

Marcus had never ghosted me. He was just trying to keep his kin from tearing out each other's jugulars. Because that's just the kind of man, wereape, and chief he was.

Stan dodged the younger alpha's next attack, but the edge of a clawed hand caught his thigh. Blood drenched the frost-covered ground in spatters of red. Stan spun, and shock slapped his beast's face. Clearly, Fredrik was faster.

Fredrik crouched, his eyes on Stan's bloodied thigh.

Stan's face rippled in anger as his eyebrows came together. A wild light danced in his deep eyes.

"Here it comes," I muttered, and again the same female wereape turned around, surprising me when she flipped me off.

O-o-o-okay. Time to keep my mouth shut. I pulled my jacket tightly around me as I watched, half freaking, half amazed at what was happening.

With a terrible bellow, Stan threw himself at the younger gorilla, arms swinging.

Without a pause, Fredrik charged.

They hit with a terrible ferocity, and I took a step back, though I didn't need to.

The younger gorilla twisted and kicked Stan to the ground. With his face deranged, he locked his hands into enormous fists and brought them down onto Stan's skull like a hammer. Bones crunched.

Yikes. I stood there, horrified as Fredrik kept pounding on poor old Stan.

"This isn't right," I said, my voice loud. But no one seemed to hear me, their attention on the fight.

And just when I thought the hammering would never end until Stan's head looked like a smashed cherry pie, Marcus roared and crashed his fist on the ground with surprising strength. In a flash, Marcus loomed over the younger alpha and stood on his two feet, his arms thrashing to his side.

Fredrik stopped pounding.

To my surprise, Marcus's beast form was larger than this younger one. He had at least a hundred pounds more muscle, and it was obvious if Marcus wanted he could pulverize both. Clearly, he could be their alpha if he wanted, but Marcus was chief of Hollow Cove. He was our alpha.

It made sense to me then why Marcus was here. He was the only one who could defeat both their stupid monkey asses.

The younger alpha grabbed Stan by the throat and jerked him to his feet.

That got everyone's attention in a hurry, given that all he had to do was squeeze and they'd have their new alpha.

But Marcus growled, staring down at the younger alpha with his gray eyes that screamed he'd be toast if he didn't let Stan go.

Finally, Fredrik relented, and with a thud, Stan fell back to the ground. Angry eyes stared up at the younger alpha, but then, very slowly, Stan lowered his eyes and bowed in submission to the new alpha.

And just like that, it was over.

"Looks like we've got our new alpha," said the female.

Excited, I started clapping and only realized my mistake at the looks of horror and anger from the surrounding clan members.

"My bad," I said and shoved my hands in my coat pockets.

The gorillas and wereapes talked amongst themselves as they dispersed from the fight, their faces happy and relieved. Guess this was a long time coming.

"Tessa."

I looked up to find Marcus in his human form heading my way, which was awesome, except for the naked part. Not that it wasn't awesome to see him naked—because it was all kinds of awesome—I just didn't want it to be with a group of wereapes as an audience.

Coils of steam rose around him from his sweat in the cold air, like he'd just stepped out of a hot, steaming shower.

It was hard *not* to look at perfection, it truly was—and a little annoying when the perfection was staring back at you with a lazy smile because he knew you liked what you saw—but I managed to avert my eyes just as the same big dude I'd seen in the inn handed Marcus a pair of sweats.

"Sorry about that. What were you saying about Ruth?"

I turned back around, glad and maybe even a little disappointed that he was wearing the sweats. "She's in trouble." I started to feel the cold air seep through my jacket. "Bernard's dead."

"The baker?"

"Yup. And Ruth's being blamed for it. She actually confessed."

"What?" A brief flash of panic crossed his face as he looked at me.

I let out a breath, and it came out in rolls of white mist. "She made a potion for him. And it was found at the scene. I don't know what it was—gingerweed, maybe—but she thinks it killed him."

Marcus was silent for a long time, and I could see the regret and frustration on his face. "Okay. I'll have a talk with Ruth, and I'm sure we can clear all this up."

"Not if Adira can help it."

"Adira? Why does that name sound familiar?"

"'Cause she's the new chief."

Marcus cursed. "Of course. The office would have sent in a replacement while I was gone."

I stared at him. "You didn't know? She said she spoke to you." That's the precise moment I remembered he'd said there were no phones here. The bitch vamp had lied to me.

"I never got a call from Adira, and I never called her."

"That lying coffin-loving whore."

"Coffin-loving?"

"She's a vampire."

Marcus met my gaze. "I'm never leaving Hollow Cove ever again."

I smiled. "So, are you coming back?"

"How did you get here, Tessa." Marcus looked around me. "Did you drive here?"

"I jumped a ley line."

"Right." Marcus smiled. "I'd love to show you around, but I think I better get back to Hollow Cove as soon as possible." He was silent and then, "Can you take the same ley line home?"

"Not the same," I answered. "I need the one going east, but I know where it is. It's not far from here."

Marcus nodded. "Good. Okay, then. See you tomorrow morning," he said, and then he was jogging toward his Jeep, barefoot and half-naked as though the cold December air didn't affect him.

"Tomorrow morning?" I called after him. "But Hollow Cove's miles away." I knew it was a ten-hour drive from here to Hollow Cove, and that's if he drove really fast without stopping.

"I'll drive all night if I have to," he said, looking over his shoulder. "I'll be there in the morning. See you tomorrow, Tessa."

I grinned. "See you tomorrow."

CHAPTER

15

I paced around the kitchen, my heartbeat matching my strides as I glanced at my phone every minute or so, just in case I'd missed a text from Marcus.

He'd texted me at 7:30 this morning.

Marcus: *I'm here at the office. I'm speaking to Adira at eight. Give you the details later.*

And I'd texted back.

Okay, great. Talk to you later.

Sleep had been a struggle with the pillow last night as my thoughts shifted from Marcus to Ruth and then back to Marcus.

The experience with the wereape clan had been extraordinary. Even the fight between the two alphas had been amazing, in a brutal, violent way. But those damn gray eyes and the way he'd looked at me kept me awake—like I was a piece of cheesecake he wanted to sink his teeth into.

Not going to lie, being desired by a finger-licking-hot guy like that did wonders to my ego.

And I'd been so wrong about him.

I'd been quick to judge and I'd let my mind run wild with scenarios and ideas of who he was and how he felt about me. Yes, I'd been wrong. But three months without hearing back was a long time. I was pretty sure anyone in my situation would have felt the same—that he wasn't interested.

"Will you sit down," barked Dolores, sitting at the kitchen table wearing a frown and a light gray turtleneck sweater. "You're going to give me an aneurism."

"Leave the poor girl alone," snapped Beverly as she poured herself a cup of coffee. She turned around, her back to the counter. She took a sip of her coffee and said, "It's not her fault. Her body has *needs*."

My mouth fell open. "I'm sorry, what?" Cauldron help me.

"God, I love living here." Iris laughed as she licked the raspberry jam on her toast. "It's like living a real-life sitcom. Or is that reality TV? Meh, same difference." She was dressed all in black sporting a perfect cat eye with liquid liner. She looked like a cute goth girl.

Beverly adjusted the neck of her lowcut pink cashmere sweater. "It's all that sexual energy you've got pent up inside, darling," she said to me, and I cringed. "I recognize it. That's how I get when I haven't had sex in three days." Her green eyes widened. "It's the hot, *sexual* flashes."

"It's not that," I said, mortified. Or was it? "I'm just anxious to hear back from Marcus. That's all."

"Precisely," pressed Beverly, her brilliant white teeth showing through her red lips. "Sexual frustration is an ugly beast. It growls and roars… it just wants out of its cage. And when it does… I come out fightin' like a wildcat. Grab the first available bachelor and make mad passionate love on the floor."

Dolores spat the coffee from her mouth. "I think I just got an STD while listening to that."

I moved to the table and pulled out the chair next to Ruth. "Can we talk about something else?" I let myself fall into the chair with a sigh. It was way too early to have this conversation with my aunts.

"Please don't. This is *so* much fun." Iris giggled and took a bite of her toast.

My gaze found Ruth. She was staring at her toast, not having taken a bite, nor did she take a sip of her coffee. She looked weak and lost, and I had the sudden overwhelming urge to protect her. Part of me wanted to wrap my arms around her, but I wasn't sure if that was something she wanted. The last thing I needed was to make things worse for her.

Ruth had been so excited when I came home yesterday. She'd come out of her room when I told her Marcus was on his way and that he would fix things. I'd seen a light shine in her eyes that I hadn't seen for weeks.

"Marcus is a good man," she'd said to me and had kept a tiny smile on her face all night.

But this morning it was as though I'd never seen that light. She was sullen, her face drawn with her eyes empty and haunted.

That's why I was pacing and why my heart was racing like I'd just jogged ten miles. It wasn't about sex, though the idea of sex with Marcus would probably release a lot of tension. This was about Ruth, and Marcus was going to help her. I knew he would.

"If you want my advice," said Beverly, and my gaze flicked to her, a carnal smile on her face. "You need to sleep with him."

She just wouldn't give up. "Okay. What happened to talking about something else?"

"That's what I said," encouraged Iris, a glint of devilry in her expression. She licked jam from her fingers. "She has to jump him before she explodes."

"I'm not going to explode."

Iris nodded. "Yeah. You are. You're like a ticking sex-bomb."

A laugh spurted out of Dolores and I glared at her. "What?" she shrugged. "That was kind of funny."

"You know," continued Beverly, "at your age, I was having lots and lots of sex." She lifted her chin. "I guess that's the curse of being so *devastatingly* beautiful."

"Or you were working as a hooker," interjected Dolores. "Didn't you have a t-shirt in the eighties that said OPEN FOR BUSINESS?"

Beverly beamed. "I did." She giggled proudly. "I really did."

My eyebrows jumped to my hairline. "Way too much sharing."

Beverly dismissed me with a wave of her hand. "There's no such thing as too much sharing, darling. And someone your age should be having sex. Lots of sex."

I shivered. "I feel so dirty right now, and I haven't done a thing."

"Listen to me," said Beverly. "You need to ride that train and see if the rails and the wheels are all working *satisfactorily*," she said, her eyebrows moving suggestively. "Trust me, you don't want anything to be broken on that train. A broken train can't go nowhere."

I shook my head, letting out a long sigh. "Why is this happening to me?"

"Darling," said Beverly, clearly not giving up, like I was some charity sexless case. "It's all well that you are fantasizing about his abilities in the sack. Fantasizing is healthy. But you might be severely disappointed if you continue to fantasize without having the real thing. You need to hop on that train."

"You think the chief's train won't be a smooth ride?" I said, shocked at the words spilling out of my mouth.

"Might be a bumpy ride," said Beverly.

I doubted that. Something about the way Marcus moved told me he would be a very good lover. Call it my witchy intuition. Still, I wasn't going to have this conversation with my aunts, especially not until I jumped into bed with him.

A knock sounded from the front door and saved me from further sexless humiliation.

"Come in!" we all shouted at the same time.

"House. Open the door for Marcus," instructed Dolores. How she knew it was him was a mystery to me.

I jumped to my feet as the squeaking sound of the front door opening was followed by the unmistakable sound of heavy boots hitting the hardwood floors. My heart throbbed at the idea of seeing Marcus again. My pulse quickened with the memory of the hot chief's kiss high in my thoughts.

Not to mention that he'd driven all day and night just to get here this morning and save Ruth. I just wished I'd been there when he told Adira off and to pack her things. *Oh, well. Can't have it all.*

I moved to stand next to Ruth. "Marcus is here," I told her and gently squeezed her shoulder, though she did not look up. "Everything will be fine now."

Boots scraped the floor and I pulled my eyes up to find Marcus walking into the kitchen.

Though I'd seen him only a few hours earlier, he looked just as handsome as ever. I'd never get tired of looking at that face, and he didn't look a bit tired. Must have been a wereape thing.

He had on the same black winter coat, open to reveal a white T-shirt and jeans. His gray eyes met mine, the glint in his eyes going right to my core. A tiny smile curled the corners of his lips before his gaze went to my aunts and Iris.

"Ladies," he said and stopped short of the kitchen table, looking all chief-like and sexy as hell.

Dolores pushed her cup of coffee to the side and interlaced her fingers on the table. Her face had a severe cast, like a school teacher about to give someone detention for disrupting the class. "You've been gone so long... I'd forgotten what you looked like." Dolores's tone was light, but the meaning behind her words was sharp.

I resisted the urge to laugh because that would have been awkward. But then a soft laugh escaped from Iris, thus saving me the trip.

"I would have come back earlier if I could," said the chief, shoving his hands in his pockets. "I never planned on being away for so long. Things got… complicated. If I'd known…" His eyes darted over to Ruth, and I didn't understand what I saw on his face.

"Don't the people in this town matter to you anymore?" accused Dolores, her gaze cold and hard, looking like she wanted nothing better than to curse him.

Marcus looked taken aback. "Of course, they do. This is my town. Every single person in my town means something to me."

Dolores made a disapproving sound in her throat. She narrowed her eyes. "You need a haircut," she said, making Iris laugh out loud and smack the table with an open hand.

"I rather like it," purred Beverly, her eyes twinkling. "Makes me want to run my fingers through it."

Okay. Enough of that. "So, how did it go with Adira?"

"Is the vamp bitch gone?" inquired Beverly as she poured herself another cup of coffee.

She turned around and said, "I don't like having her around here."

"What's the matter, Beverly?" said Dolores, a mock smile on her face. "Don't like the competition?"

Beverly glared at her sister as a flicker of annoyance flashed across her pretty face, but she said nothing.

Marcus looked at her. "No. Adira is still here."

"But not for long. Right?" I asked, and his eyes jerked to mine. "You sent her on her way. She's packing right now and leaving and never coming back. Am I right?"

"Not exactly." Marcus took a breath. "Adira is staying… until Ruth's court date."

"Wait. What?" I cried, adrenaline making my head hurt. "You *didn't* send her packing? After what she did to Ruth!" My lack of sleep was catching up to me, and so were the deep emotions I felt for Ruth.

Marcus said nothing, his posture shifting into an uneasy acceptance as we all stared at him. His face was strained with emotion, and I saw then just how exhausted he was. I didn't think it was just from the drive.

My pulse hammered. "Look at her," I said, pointing to my Aunt Ruth who had never strayed her eyes from her uneaten toast. "Look at her wrists. Adira cuffed her. The bitch cuffed her, Marcus. You have to do something." I clenched my jaw. "Please, take them off."

Pain glazed Marcus's eyes, his face unfurling with emotions under his dark hair. "I can't."

"Take them *off*," I said again incredulously, hearing my voice shake.

A sigh came from Marcus. "I *can't* take them off. Not until *after* the court date."

The ground shifted at his words. "The court date? Are you serious? I thought you were going to take care of all that. I thought you were going to dismiss the charges. What the hell, Marcus?"

The chief opened his mouth as if to answer but then closed it again.

"Marcus?" Beverly's face paled. "This is Ruth we're talking about. She's known you since you were a child. Treated you like her own son."

Marcus's gray eyes shifted to Ruth. "I know that. Don't you know I know that?" He was silent, but I could see a dark storm brewing behind his eyes.

"Marcus." Dolores's voice was edged with barely controlled fury. "Are you saying these false charges against Ruth are staying? Is that what you're telling us? You won't remove them?"

Marcus went ashen. He looked at Dolores and said, "I know this is not what you were expecting."

"Ya think?" interrupted Dolores, giving him a poisonous look. "I was expecting more from you."

Marcus's eyes widened at the slight. "Certain regulations are set in place when there's a murder," said the chief, his face tight. "In order to dismiss a case or to try and reverse the conviction on the grounds of a bad arrest isn't that simple. Charges were filed, and we need to follow through with them. I can't just erase them."

My chest tightened in anger as my world all started to fall apart. He wasn't going to help. He was going to let Ruth take the fall...

"Take them off of her," I repeated, feeling the loss of control and the tingling of my magic as it responded to my emotions. I couldn't believe he would do this. To Ruth. To me.

Marcus shook his head. "I can't."

"You can't? Or you won't?" I trembled, seeing a tight ball of energy in my gut, screaming for me to release it on Marcus's ass.

"Tessa, this is not helping," warned Dolores, but I barely heard her.

I got into Marcus's face. "My aunt didn't do this, and you know it!" I shouted. "Take the cuffs off," I ground out, my throat tight and my anger high. "Or I will." I had no idea if that was possible, but in my life, the impossible was usually very possible.

"I'll help you," volunteered Iris, giving Marcus the stink eye and looking like she was about to spew a couple of curses. I thought I'd join her.

Marcus ran his fingers over his jaw, his shoulders tight with tension. "You can't take them off." He let out a breath through his nose. "If you try, it'll kill her."

"What?" Iris, Dolores, Beverly, and I all cried together.

My lips parted as a lump of fear settled heavily in my belly. My eyes fell to Ruth who looked dazed, like her mind was somewhere else, as though she hadn't heard a single word of the conversation.

"Cauldron help us." Dolores smacked the table with her fist. "What is the meaning of this? Are you telling me that if we tamper with these… these *things*… it could kill Ruth?"

"Yes, according to Adira," replied Marcus, his voice tight. It carried the softness of an apology.

"Holy shit," Iris breathed, her mouth hanging open. "Adira's psychotic."

I gasped and my stomach dropped. His words rang in my ears, chilling me. Son of a bitch…

My anger flamed back. "That vampire bitch. She put those on Ruth and never told us what they could do if we tried to remove them? What kind of chief does that?" Yup. I was going to find her, and then I was going to kill her.

The tips of Marcus's ears turned red. He moved next to Ruth. "Ruth? May I take a look at your wrists?"

For the first time this morning, Ruth slowly turned her head and looked up at Marcus.

"Oh! Hi, Marcus," she said, brightly, as though she'd only just realized he was here. "When did you get back? I would have prepared you some of those lobster rolls you love so much... but I've been feeling under the weather lately. Must be a stomach bug going around."

Beverly burst into tears, and I blinked fast to keep my own waterworks at bay.

This was so wrong—so, so wrong.

Marcus's jaw clenched. "Thank you, Ruth. But I'm not hungry. Can I take a look at your wrists?" he asked again, his voice gentle, soft, like I'd never heard it before.

"Oh, sure." Ruth smiled and gave him her wrist. "I won't be able to make your medicine anymore. I can't do potions anymore. That's what Adira said. The new chief. Have you met her?"

My heart squeezed at the emotion in her voice. I wanted to kill Adira. I wanted to cut off her head and stick it on a spike.

"I have," answered Marcus. "It's okay, Ruth. I have enough left of my medicine. You don't worry about that."

I knew they were talking about that blue potion she'd been supplying him with for months, but I really didn't care what it was right now.

Marcus took Ruth's wrist gently in his hand, turning it slowly, before setting it back down. "Thank you, Ruth." She smiled at him and then turned back to her toast, that same distant expression crossing her face once again.

"I've never used these before," said the chief, looking at Dolores and Beverly. "I'm not familiar with them. I would never have put these on Ruth. On any of you."

"It's twisted. It's barbaric is what it is," I said coldly. "She has no proof that Ruth killed Bernard, but she treats her like a criminal." I took a calming breath. "You need to fix this. If you care anything for her, for this family, you'll get these charges dismissed."

"You think I wanted this to happen?" he said in a harsh tone, a shattered look of disbelief in his eyes.

"Doesn't look like you want to do anything to stop it," I countered pinning him with my glare.

"Ruth confessed." Marcus met my eyes. "She confessed. There's nothing I can do."

"Dude, you suck," said Iris as she took a bite of her cold toast. "Total douchebag."

"She can unconfess," I yelled, no idea if that was a thing, but it was worth trying.

Marcus began to pace the kitchen. "It doesn't work like that."

"Then explain it to me." Frustrated, I groaned. "I don't understand. You're the chief! Damn it. Aren't you still the chief? Or am I missing something here?"

He stopped and stared at me. "I am."

"And Adira is also chief?"

"Yes."

I threw my hands in the air. "Great. We've got two chiefs."

Marcus's expression grew remote and guarded. "Adira was the arresting chief," he said. "She has to stay until the court—"

"Shut up! Just shut up!" I snapped, my magic and fury pounding through me.

Marcus took one look at Ruth and dread flashed in his eyes. He rubbed his hands on his face.

I stared at him hard, wishing I'd never gone to fetch him. "So, that's it. You won't help."

"There's nothing I can do. I'm sorry," he said in a voice void of emotion.

"Get out!" I cried, the words ripping at my soul, shredding it. My gut said everything about this was wrong, but my gut could no longer be trusted.

Marcus reached for me. "Tessa—"

"Just get the hell out!"

The chief's expression hardened and he watched me for a long moment.

And then that gorgeous man I was falling for but now despised turned around, disappeared down the hall, and went out the front door.

CHAPTER
16

My butt was numb.

Not from falling on the ground or from sitting on a cold surface outside for an hour, but from sitting on a hard chair inside until my buttock muscles stiffened, tingled, ached, and then finally went completely dull like I'd just shot myself with an anesthetic needle.

With my back to the wall, my right knee bounced up and down for the past hour and a half as I stared at the large black metal door to the conference room, waiting to see Ruth's smiling face as she walked out.

Today was December seventh, and the Gray Council had arrived and set up their court proceedings in the Hollow Cove Security Agency's conference room.

As it turned out, I was not allowed to attend the proceedings. Only Dolores and Beverly could attend since they'd been witnesses to Ruth's gingerweed making.

Speaking of gingerweed, for the past two days I'd been in the kitchen, trying to remake Ruth's tonic she'd given Bernard. Potions weren't my forte, and I'd managed to mess up thirty different tonics. Ruth wouldn't help. I'd asked her at the beginning of my experimenting, but she'd just smiled at me and continued staring out the window in her bedroom.

The idea was to remake the potion and test it. See if it was as dangerous as everyone thought it was since I couldn't get my hands on the real thing.

Even Dolores, Beverly, and Iris jumped to my aid. We'd finally gotten the potion to work, but the color was wrong. At the baker's shop, the color had been a light cream, and this one, no matter how many times we tried—always came out orange.

I shifted over to my left, putting more weight on that butt cheek to try and get some blood flow, and caught Iris staring at me on the next chair.

"What?" I said. "I've got numbbutt."

Ronin laughed. "Numbbutt. I like it. Sounds like nun butts." The half-vampire sat in the chair to my left. He'd come to show some moral support. Cauldron knew I needed it, and so did Ruth. We all did.

"Maybe we should go for a walk?" Iris shifted slightly to her left, signs that she too was experiencing numbbutt.

I thought about it for a moment. "No. I want to be here when Ruth comes out." Which was true. No matter the outcome, or my degree of numbbutt, I needed to be here.

"Have you spoken to Marcus?" asked Iris, and I looked up to find Grace staring at us from her desk across the hallway. I glared at her and kept glaring until she looked away. I did not need her to eavesdrop right now.

I sighed. "You mean, have I spoken to the jackass since I threw him out?"

"Yeah."

"No. And I don't plan to either." A flicker of anger rose in me at the memory of what happened five days ago. I had been an idiot to think Marcus would save Ruth. I'd put all my faith in him, and I'd been confident he would.

He was in there right now, in the conference room with the rest of them while we sat here fearing the worst, my imagination getting the better of me.

Again, I was an idiot. Every time I thought about the chief, I felt a deep, throbbing ache in

171

my chest like someone had landed a side kick in my abdomen. I hated how he made me feel whenever he was around me, like I couldn't control my emotions. Like I was weak.

But I wasn't weak. And so far, I had grown some serious lady balls in the past few weeks. I didn't need him.

Ronin let out a long sigh through his nose. "You can't blame the guy for this."

Angry, I turned in my seat to glare at him directly, narrowing my eyes at the half-vamp. "Are you freaking kidding me right now?"

"Ease down, broomstick," he said, a small smile on his face that I wanted to slap off. "I'm just saying what happened to Ruth wasn't his fault. He wasn't even here. And from what you've told me, he did try."

"Not hard enough." I shook my head. "He didn't try to remove the charges."

"I'm sure he did," answered Ronin. "But if he couldn't… it means he couldn't find any grounds for a dismissal. There was nothing he could do about it."

My stomach clenched. "I don't believe that," I said. "There's always something you can do. He's the chief. If the chief can't remove charges, what good is it to have a chief? Might as well tell him to pack up and leave."

Ronin leaned his head back against the wall and ran a hand over his hair to make sure it was lying flat. "I've known Marcus longer than you, Tess, and believe me, he loves Ruth. I know he did everything he could."

"Well, it wasn't enough," I said bitterly. "Not nearly enough. I expected a hell of a lot more coming from him."

"He did drive all day and night to get here for Ruth," said Iris.

I glared at her.

Iris shrugged. "Just saying."

"Don't."

"It means he cares."

I rubbed my sweaty hands on my thighs, my blood pressure skyrocketing the longer we sat here without any news.

News. "Grace?" I called out. "Do you know how long it's going to be?"

Grace looked up at me from whatever she was doing. A glimmer of annoyance crossed her face, like I'd just interrupted her crossword puzzle. She pressed her thin lips tightly and glanced back down at her desk.

"Thanks," I called back. God, that woman was infuriating.

This situation was going from bad to worse, and there was nothing I could do. Ruth had still been in her depressed state as I watched her walk into the conference room. My heart broke at the pain that flickered in her eyes.

I let out a frustrated breath and pushed to my feet. Moving to the conference room's door, I placed my ear to it and listened. Nothing. Not even a murmur. They'd spelled the room with a sound barrier spell like the one Marvelous Myrtle had done when I was in her tent to keep Ronin from hearing what was going on inside.

Knowing it was pointless, I moved away and let myself fall back into my chair.

"Any luck?" inquired Ronin.

"Nothing. The room's been spelled with a counter-hearing spell."

"Bummer."

"I just wish I knew what was going on in there," I said, exasperated. "The not knowing part is the worst."

"I know." Ronin leaned forward and said, "Tess, your face is really red. You need to calm down or you'll give yourself a heart attack."

"How am I supposed to calm down when Ruth's life is at stake? I can't. I don't know how."

"Well, sex is the best stress reliever I know," said the vamp. "It can even cure chronic hiccups."

"He got that from me," interjected Iris.

I let out a laugh. "Well, I'm not suffering from hiccups."

Ronin laughed. "No. But you do need to relax." He nudged my messenger bag on the floor with his foot. "You got a vibrator in that bag?"

I choked on my own spit. I stared at the vampire, not knowing what to say.

Iris burst out laughing, winning a deep scowl from Grace.

"What?" Ronin flashed me a smile. "An orgasm right now will lower your blood pressure. Just saying."

I knew my friend was just trying to make me laugh to ease the tension. "You're insane."

"You love me," said Ronin happily and put his hands behind his head as he leaned against the wall.

I moved my gaze over my friends, my heart slowing as it swelled with gratitude that I wasn't going through this alone. By myself, I probably would have had a heart attack or a stroke. I didn't want to lose Ruth, not when I'd only just started to get to know her better. I loved my aunt fiercely. There was nothing I wouldn't do for her. Nothing.

"I'm sure it'll be fine," said Iris. Her tiny hand reached over and squeezed mine. "Ruth didn't kill Bernard. And if he died from ingesting her potion, it was an accident. The Gray Council will understand."

"What do you think they'll do?"

Iris thought about it a moment. "They'll dismiss the charges if Ruth wasn't even involved. And if she gave Bernard something that he was deathly allergic to, she'll most probably never be able to work potions for anyone ever again."

"Right. Well, that's not so bad." I thought about how Ruth would be upset, but if she did accidentally kill Bernard, that would be the best outcome. I looked at Iris again. "And if they charge her?"

From her cloth bag at her feet, Iris pulled out a small photo album and opened it on her lap, her hands moving over the clear plastic overlay sheets. "We use these."

I leaned over for a better look. "We're going to use your family portraits to smother the Gray Council to death?"

"Portraits?" Ronin got to his feet and moved around me to sit next to Iris's other side.

Iris moved her hands away and I gasped.

"Not family pictures," I said, my eyes moving from one side of the album to the other.

What I first thought was an album with pictures of Iris's family was something else entirely.

I stared openmouthed at strands of hair and cut-out pieces of cloth that looked like they once belonged to a shirt. Some were small pieces of denim, teeth, strands of eyelashes, drops of dark maroon stains that looked a lot like dried blood, and various other small items I couldn't decipher. They were all placed in neat rows, all with labels neatly printed below each item on strips of white paper. Each was cataloged with names and dates.

"Iris," I said, my eyes still pinned on the eerie human toenail I'd spotted. "What is all this?"

Iris met my eyes and beamed. "This… is Dana," she said lovingly, as though the book was an actual person. "My little black book of curses. I've been collecting material from different half-breeds and humans over the years. I've done some of my best work with Dana. Biggest, baddest curses."

Ronin whistled. "Is it wrong that I'm so turned on right now?"

I wasn't sure what was more disturbing, Ronin getting excited at the toenails and teeth on display in Iris's book or the fact that she'd collected them.

I stared at what looked like a small piece of dried flesh. "Huh. And why do we need this?"

"Dana," Iris corrected.

Okay. "Why do we need *Dana*?"

Iris flipped the pages to somewhere near the middle. She pointed at a piece of gray cloth. "This is a piece of Hubert's gray robe. He's on the Gray Council. I recognized him earlier before he went in with the others."

"And we would use that to… what exactly?"

"To curse him." Iris's eyes were round with excitement. "Heart attack. Stroke. Brain aneurism. Explosive diarrhea. Projectile vomit. You name it. It can be done."

I was both impressed and a little scared. "Wow. Well… that's… great… uh… it's just…"

The door to the conference room opened.

I jumped to my feet, my heart bouncing inside my ribcage like a Ping-Pong ball as five gray-robed individuals stalked out the conference room, looking as out of place as Jedi knights at a tea party. They moved with a swiftness that belied their years. All had seen past their ninetieth birthdays, and they all carried themselves in a way that only really important people did.

"It's now or never," said Iris, suddenly next to me and shoving that creepy album on me. "Dana hasn't let me down yet. But you have to give her a little heads-up."

I shook my head, my eyes on the conference room. "I'm sure we won't need it—her." I wasn't sure at all, but I *was* sure cursing a member from the Gray Council was seriously illegal.

Next came Adira, followed quickly by her vamp cronies, the three males and the one female who were forgettable—and Marcus.

Our eyes met, and yes, I might have even stopped breathing, but before I could pull my eyes away, Marcus flicked his gaze at Adira and began a conversation with her, putting his back to me. I had a feeling he'd done that on purpose.

I felt a tearing in my chest that surprised me, like my heart was forming hairline cracks. I might have overreacted a tiny bit yesterday, but it was done. I had to accept it. Right now, I didn't have time to think about the consequences of my actions, or what it meant for us. If there had been an "us," there wasn't anymore.

Dolores came through the door next, and then Beverly with Ruth on her arm. Every muscle on my body went tense. No one was crying, thank the cauldron. I took that as a good sign.

With a sigh of relief, I rushed over, putting myself in front of Beverly and Ruth. "And? How did it go? What did they say? Ruth? What did the Gray Council say?"

Ruth met my eyes, and I couldn't understand what I saw in her face. "It's finished. It's over. Finally over. I am happy about that. The waiting… the waiting is the worst. But now I know."

I looked at Beverly. "What is she talking about?"

"She means the Gray Council ruled," said Dolores as she stepped in, staring at me, unblinking, her irises so dark I couldn't tell where her pupils were.

My heart was pounding, and my knees felt like they were about to give out as I searched Dolores's face. "What did they rule?"

Dolores's lips trembled, and she swallowed hard as though trying to reel in her emotions and having a hell of a time. "Ruth's been found guilty—"

"What?" I shouted, seeing Iris and Ronin pop into my peripheral vision to my left.

"The coroner's report stated that black belladonna was in her mix," instructed Beverly, her arm still hooked around Ruth's, and I couldn't tell which witch needed the support most. "It's what killed Bernard."

From my intense studying, I knew belladonna was used as a sedative, and sometimes it helped with asthma and severe coughs, even hay fever. Black belladonna? That was used as a pain killer and for paralysis. And if used too much, it would definitely lead to death.

"But Ruth would *never* put that in the gingerweed," I countered. "She knows better. And it's not like she hasn't done this a thousand times before. This is a mistake. They've got it wrong."

"The evidence is clear," continued Dolores, her voice drawn and tired.

I shook my head, staring at Ruth. "Ruth? Talk to me."

Slowly, Ruth lifted her eyes to me. "I… I don't remember if I put in the black belladonna or not. My mind's not as clear as it once was. I… I could have accidentally put it in."

"No." I shook my head. "I refuse to believe it."

"Well, it doesn't matter what you believe," announced Dolores. "The Gray Council found her guilty of negligent homicide. Of killing Bernard."

I gritted my teeth so I wouldn't gasp as I started to shake. "What does that mean?" Panic jerked through me. Part of me knew this might could happen, but I never thought it would.

Tears fell from Beverly's eyes as her lips trembled. She opened her mouth, but only a whimper came out.

"It means," said Dolores, her voice higher than usual. "That at the end of this month… on December twenty-third… Ruth will begin her five-year sentence in Grimway Citadel."

The witch prison. This time I gasped. A wave of nausea hit me, and I couldn't breathe. My eyes flicked back to Marcus and I found him staring at me, his eyes sad and filled with regret. I looked away before I started bawling.

"This can't be happening," I managed to say. "They can't do this. Ruth is innocent."

"They can and they did. Ruth confessed. She's agreed to do her time." Dolores clamped her mouth shut, and I knew it was her way of saying she didn't want to say more.

"How can she confess to something she didn't do?" The band around my chest tightened and I took a gasping breath that sounded like a sob.

"Ruth, no," I told her, tears finally escaping my eyes, in thick, heavy drops.

"Yes." Ruth smiled at me, but there was a bit of a grimace in it. "I killed him. I poisoned Bernard, left his wife a widow, and now I'm going to pay the price for my foolishness."

I stood there with my heart breaking as Dolores, Beverly, and Ruth made their way down the hall and out the front door.

How could things go so wrong so quickly? But it's like they say, it could always get worse. And they were right.

Tomorrow was my second witch trial.

CHAPTER

17

I felt like I'd been run over by a bus, which backed up and then ran me over again, just to make sure it had gotten all my bones, including the little ones.

The mental pain had elevated and morphed into the physical. The only time I'd ever experienced something like that was when my ex—John—had told me he didn't love me anymore. And yet, I had recovered surprisingly fast from that. Perhaps, deep down, I'd always known that relationship wouldn't last.

But this was different. This was Ruth. My beloved, gentle, kind, Ruth. The Ruth that saved house spiders and roaches and spoke to bees like they were tiny yellow and black kittens.

The aches and pains and the giant, constant throbbing was a result of lack of sleep from the previous days, if you could even call it a lack—more like nonexistent sleep.

I couldn't sleep. My aunts were hysterical, crying, sobbing. The news was just so damn devastating, and I was in shock or denial, probably both. Their world had been turned upside-down. And now, they were going to lose Ruth.

To make matters worse, Ruth had popped into my room last night to wish me luck.

"Good luck tomorrow," she'd said, her smile warm and reassuring. "But I'm sure you won't need it. You'll do just fine. Just fine."

I'd just stood there, my lips unable to form words. While her world was crumbling, she'd remembered about me and had taken a moment to wish me luck.

It took a great amount of restraint *not* to start bawling my eyes out.

Now, I needed to pass these damn Merlin trials more than ever. At least, I'd do it for my Aunt Ruth.

Ruth wasn't going to Grimway Citadel. Nope. Not going to happen. We still had sixteen days before she had to leave. Plenty of time to appeal the Gray Council's decision—or find out who put the black belladonna in her tonic. Ruth would never make a mistake like that, and I wouldn't rest until I found out who did.

Forgetting about getting any shuteye before the morning and not wanting Marina to sabotage my second trial (though no emails had been sent) I'd jumped out of bed, brushed my teeth, grabbed a few protein bars with a water bottle, and jumped the ley line at 4 a.m.

I'd been in such a rush to jump I'd forgotten how cold it could get in December that early in the morning without the sun to warm up the weather a little. Though I had on my winter coat, it wasn't warm enough to wait outside in freezing weather for another three to four hours until someone unlocked Montevalley Castle doors.

Imagine my surprise when I'd stepped up to the large front doors, looking for a spot to sit that wouldn't give me numbbutt, and they swung open and let me in.

Now, three hours and two protein bars later, I stood with the rest of the witches in training in a cold, cavernous space below Montevalley Castle.

We were in the castle's underbelly, its dungeon, the bowels of the log castle. Yup, and it stank too, like the cleaning crew had forgotten to clean out the toilets for a few years. The air was moist and hot, and though I was happy to have left my big winter coat in the common room, the air clung to my skin in a disgusting layer. Torchlights hung on the walls, the only source of light. I felt like I was standing in a medieval dungeon. Guess that's the vibe they were going for.

The ceiling height I estimated was about fifteen feet and supported here and there by pillars and beams that looked like they'd been added centuries ago by the amount of decay and rot. The cave walls were made of a mix of living rock and stone. The ground was compact earth and dirt. It was enormous, just as large as the castle's first floor with just as many rooms and passageways. Add the darkness and shadowed corners, and anyone could get lost here if they didn't know the way. It was a damn underground maze.

A witch servant or assistant had gathered us all in the common room a few minutes before 7 a.m. and instructed us to follow her down to the basement. She'd led us through twisting corridors and down more stone stairs, finally through an entryway to a chamber the size of the common room with a single door at the opposite end.

"Wait here," she'd commanded, and then she'd disappeared back down the same corridor.

I looked around nervously. I had no idea what to expect, but at least I'd gotten here on time for this one. A few mumbles carried around the chamber as witches conversed with one another, but most of the witches were silent.

The sound of feet approaching reached me and I turned to see a short, male witch with brown mousy-colored hair and glasses that seemed too big for him appear at my side.

"Hi," said Willis. The front of his shirt had a big toothpaste stain on it, and he was shaking like a leaf. "Tessa, right?"

"Right. Hi, Willis." I hadn't introduced myself to him, but Greta had done that for me, in front of everyone in the theater the day of the orientation.

Willis pushed his glasses up the bridge of his nose with a trembling finger. "Nervous? I am. I didn't pass the first trial. Can you believe it? Thirteenth time and I still couldn't do it. You'd think I'd be an expert by now." He gave a nervous laugh. "I'm probably the only one who didn't pass. If I fail the second one…" Willis glanced down at his shoes, unable to finish what he wanted to say.

My heart ached at the misery and defeat I saw on his face. Hell, he felt the same way I did.

"I didn't pass either," I told him, realizing we were probably the only ones. "Guess that makes two of us."

Willis's eyes were round behind his glasses. "Really? That's great—uh, no, I don't mean to say that it's great you failed, but at least I'm not the only one." He frowned. "It's not coming out the way I want it to."

I laughed. "Don't sweat it. I know what you mean."

I caught a few witches sneering at us. They were in their mid-twenties, three males and five females all dressed in the latest, expensive-looking fashions.

They were looking at us like failures, like losers. A couple of them laughed, their eyes on Willis. When his face went a shade of red I didn't think was possible, I knew he'd seen them.

But I was older. Wiser. And my lady balls were now huge.

So, I flashed them my best smile and gave them a finger wave. They all glared at me, but they did stop staring at us. I took that as a win.

And that's when my fun ended.

From the shadows of the basement, came a tall, thin man wearing only a pair of black pants, boots, and an evil grin. His dark hair was pulled back in a ponytail, making his goatee stand out. His bare chest was completely covered in tattoos. The runes and sigils covered his arms and shoulders, up his neck. The dude loved tats. He wasn't big like a bodybuilder, more like a CrossFit athlete, toned and wired.

Silas, the second arbitrator.

He folded his arms over his chest, displaying his runes and sigils. "Ninety-six of you entered the first trial, and fifty-two of you failed," he said, his voice harsh with the lilt of an accent I couldn't place.

Fifty-two?

Though I'd said it in my head. Willis turned up to look at me, his surprise mirroring my own. Guess we weren't the only losers here, but it didn't make me feel any better.

"Behind me, through that door, is your second trial." His voice was contemptuous, confident, and seething with absolute conviction. "The Merlin labyrinth."

I cursed. "I hate being right," I muttered to myself.

"And just like any labyrinth, you need to reach the center."

Someone laughed and Silas's attention snapped to the left. "You think this is easy? Do you?" His face twisted grotesquely. "Let me be clear. Since most of you morons already failed the first trial, which was the *easiest* one, by the way. It means there's not much hope for you losers."

"What a sweet talker," I said to no one in particular.

His head jerked in my direction. "What was that?"

"Nothing. Just looking forward to starting." I smiled. He didn't smile back.

Silas glared at me for a moment. "It's simple. Get to the center of the labyrinth, and you pass the trial." His scowl faded away, replaced by a careful, expressionless mask. "You'll be divided into two groups," he continued, a sneer to his voice. "The winners and the losers."

"Nice." What a bastard.

Silas's gaze traveled over the group of witches. "All those who passed the first trial, please step forward."

Together, all the witches who had passed the test—which to my utter disappointment included those who'd sneered at us—moved forward, leaving the fifty-two of us who'd failed behind. If his tactic was meant to embarrass us, it was working.

A tattooed rune on Silas's right arm glowed red. He snapped his fingers, and a giant digital clock appeared on the wall, left of the door. Glowing red numbers flashed 59:99.

My gaze moved back to the rune on his arm, and I watched as it faded from red to a dull black. I realized the guy drew his power from the runes and sigils tattooed on his skin. His ink was his magic. He didn't need to draw a circle, utter a spell, or recite an incantation. The dude was a walking spellbook.

I would have thought it cool if I didn't already hate the tat bastard.

"You've got sixty minutes to reach the center of the labyrinth," informed Silas. "If you can't do that, you don't deserve to be a Merlin." His gaze traveled over us. "Anyone who hasn't reached the center of the labyrinth when this clock hits zero—fails."

My group, the loser group, shifted nervously, the tension in the chamber growing as they kept flicking their eyes to the clock. I gathered sixty minutes wasn't a lot of time to face whatever we were facing.

"Losers," called Silas. "You'll have a fifteen-minute penalty."

"What?" I cried, unable to help myself.

Silas's dark eyes met mine and he raised a brow in challenge. "Losers will only be allowed through *that* door when the clock reads forty-five."

Willis gave a little squeak. The witch did sound like a mouse.

Okay, so they didn't play fair. Neither did I. Bring it on, Tommy Lee.

When my gaze flicked back to Silas, another rune, one on his right bicep glowed a deep red, and the door behind him opened. He moved to the side and I tried to peek through, but all I could see were more walls of stone that ended in shadows.

"Winners," Silas called. "You're up."

Like a pack of wild hyenas, the witches who were considered "winners" all burst into motion, pushing and shoving each other as they ran through the open door as though they were being sucked in by a giant funnel.

They looked like idiots, but I totally understood their haste. I would do the same when it came to my turn. I would for Ruth.

Just as the last witch was through, the door closed again.

Silas moved to stand in front of it like a bouncer at a club, and once again his arms crossed over his chest.

And he stood like that, without moving, like some creepy wax figure or movie prop for another fifteen minutes, while the rest of us found a spot to sit.

55:00

Willis didn't utter a single word to me as we sat next to each other, each of us lost in our own version of hell. It was clear. Us losers didn't expect to pass this trial, not with a fifteen-minute penalty off the clock.

50:00

It was the worst fifteen minutes of my life. Time was moving faster than normal, either that or staring at the glowing numbers decreasing was making it so.

47:00

I pulled out my cell phone from my bag and tapped on my clock app, setting a clock countdown to match the one on the wall.

Before turning it on, I glanced at the giant clock on the wall, waiting for it to change…

45:59

I tapped the countdown app on.

I stood up, and everyone followed my example, my body shaking with adrenaline as it pounded through my veins making my blood sing. Counting in my head, I took my position right in front of Silas. He didn't budge. I didn't care. As soon as the door opened, I would plow through him if he didn't get out of my way.

45:20

Fifty-two of us would go through that door in less than twenty seconds. It was an itty-bitty door, and a hell of a lot of witches.

May the best witch win.

45:00

I blinked. Silas moved to the side, just as the door swung open.

And I rushed through it.

CHAPTER

18

I ran along the dimly lit stone walls, feeling like a lab rat in some research facility, hunting for cheese.

Part of me felt like an idiot. The other part, the winning part, knew I wasn't just running for me. I was running for Ruth.

We, fifty-two losers, all ran blindly because, let's face it, we had no idea what to expect. Behind me, voices rose in the air with spells and incantations and labored breathing. The musty, wet, mineral smell of the maze filled my lungs.

With a power word on my lips, the tunnel opened up into a dozen other tunnels and openings. The labyrinth. I had no idea which of these led to the center. Maybe they all did. With that in mind, I picked a middle tunnel and ran—

Something hit me on the side, and I pitched forward like a stunt woman in an action movie. Unlike an experienced stunt woman, I had zero training on my landings. And with my already quick forward momentum, I knew I was going to hit that ground *hard*.

I did.

My breath escaped my lungs as I smashed into the hard dirt. Pain exploded on my left hip and elbow, and I might have swallowed some dirt.

I spat on the ground. "Ow."

I tried hard not to think about what I'd just had in my mouth as I pushed to my feet, wondering who had hit me and why.

A fist connected with my jaw.

Stars danced in my vision as I hit the ground again. My scream echoed around the tunnel as someone kicked me in the stomach—twice—before moving on. When I looked up, all I saw was a big witch male with red hair sprinting through the middle tunnel.

The bastard took me by surprise. It wouldn't happen again.

I was still unsure why he'd done this. Only when I looked behind me did I understand.

Our entire loser group was fighting each other. And when I say fight, I don't mean a few slaps and some hair pulling. I'm talking *serious* beatings in a mix of physical and magical hits.

I stared, opened mouthed at the most savage, brutal, magical brawl I'd ever seen.

Ten witches doubled back to the entrance of the labyrinth in obvious panic, their flight erratic and swift, dropping their bags, even phones, as they fled. High-pitched screams reverberated in the tunnel. A man's voice let out a ringing, defiant shout.

With a roar of light and sound, a flash of blinding red and purple sparks illuminated the tunnel like fireworks as witches flung their magic at each other like automatic weapons.

The ground and walls shook under the magical fire. Latin words soared above the screaming as witches frantically defended themselves. Through the shouts rose the dull, heavy, and familiar sounds of a closed fist hitting flesh, over and over. More screaming was followed by a pause and then the gurgling sound of someone choking before it died away.

I could make out at least a dozen dead or unconscious witches lying in awkward positions on the ground.

This was madness.

I clenched my teeth, rage filling me. "What the hell is wrong with you people!" I shouted. I looked for Willis, but I couldn't see anything past the flashes of multicolored magic and the blurs of arms and legs as the witches kept fighting.

The shouts and screams rose rapidly, growing louder and louder until it was a cry of madness. There was no dignity in the sound. No self-control. They'd all lost their minds.

There you have it. Put a group of people together, add fear and desperation, and you get Fight Club—but witch magic and no rules.

I had a feeling Silas knew this would happen. He wanted it to happen. He had added fuel to the fire by calling us losers and docking off fifteen minutes.

And time was ticking fast.

If I stayed, I might get killed by a flash of rogue magic. Not going to happen.

Making up my mind, I shot through the middle tunnel after the redhead. I owed him a few kicks in his manhood.

I darted through the passageway, my anger and frustration propelling me faster as I left the screaming behind me. I ran hard until I could barely hear the fighting anymore, until I all heard were my boots hitting the compact ground and my heavy breathing.

I moved with my senses on high alert, keeping my wits about me since I knew the redhead might be lurking in the shadows, waiting to jump me. Not this time. I had the perfect power word to use on that son of a bitch. And I couldn't wait to use it on him.

I slowed to a walk, listening with my heart pounding on my chest like it wanted out. It was tired of the constant abuse, and I didn't blame it.

I checked my phone. The countdown app read: 40:00. Still lots of time. Right? Probably not. But I didn't have a choice.

"You can do this," I whispered to myself. "Because... you have to."

I walked into a place that had never seen the face of the sun, never heard the whisper of wind. The tunnel was dark, close, cold, and intensely creepy. Who knew what kind of creepy crawlers lived here? Big, giant, slobbering, swallow-you-whole crawlers.

More stone walls moved past me with identical wall torches. The tunnels were narrow, forcing visitors to stay on certain paths. I peeked in a few openings, turns that took you nowhere, and claustrophobia began to take hold.

I wasn't an idiot. It would never be as simple as just wandering to the center because what would be the point? This was a trial. Trials required some level of struggle, a test of performance. Something or someone would be there to stop me. I just didn't know when they'd make their appearance.

After a few minutes of walking, a thread of panic slid through me. Maybe I'd been going around in circles this whole time? Was I lost?

I was so busy in my own head that by the time I saw the toad, it was nearly too late.

"Ah!" I screamed.

"Purrrreeeek!" called the toad.

Screaming like a banshee, I threw myself back and hit a side wall, my hands in the air in front of me with the power word still stuck between my tongue and my throat.

The toad was massive, the size of a bear, and nearly as tall as me. Its hide was rough, earth brown, and covered in large bumps. Two red eyes with a black horizontal line stared at me intelligently, magically. Strings of yellow spit drooled from the corners of its mouth, all the way to the ground. Nice.

And the giant amphibian was blocking my way. That was its purpose, which told me I was going the right way. But it also meant I needed to get past the damned creature.

So much for the trial being simple. "Hey, buddy. Think you can let me pass?" I was a witch and toads didn't scare me. Hell, most of us either had them as our familiars or dunked them in our cauldrons. I wasn't a fan of that last part.

But I wasn't accustomed to toads the size of grizzly bears. And the longer I stood here debating, the more minutes and seconds I was wasting. I was running out of time.

That's right, this sucker was big, uber big with an uber big belly and uber big hands and feet, with an even larger mouth.

Heart thrashing, I pushed off the wall and took a careful step forward, the toad's eyes never leaving me.

I grimaced at the smell. "Damn. You stink big. Big stink for a big boy." I laughed, thinking I was hilarious.

The toad's jaws parted in a silent hiss, and its throat constricted weirdly until it swelled like a balloon.

I'd watched enough of the nature channels to know what that meant.

I tapped into the elements around me, focused my will, flung up my hands, and shouted, "Accen—"

A giant bogie the size of a beachball came at me with frightening speed.

With the rest of my power word forgotten, I ducked, threw myself to the ground, and landed with an *oomph* of hard ground hitting my ribs just as the toad's snot hit the wall where my head would have been with a sickening thud.

And then something horrible happened.

The yellow snot sizzled and popped as rolls of steam rose. The hissing sound returned, and a round section of the stone wall just dissolved in a cloud of yellow mist and foul stench. Droplets of yellow liquid fell to the ground, and where they touched little holes appeared in the space of three seconds.

A hysterical laugh escaped me. "You've got acid snot? Of course, you would. How stupid of me," I said, pushing to my feet, and I gagged at the foul smell. I knew toads had toxic secretions. I'd just witnessed this beast's toxic secretion of gigantic proportions.

Fear licked up my spine until it was like I had an icicle instead of bones.

If that snot touched me… my skin, my bones, everything would melt away. Were these trials that sadistic? Were they willing to kill the witches in training?

Anger replaced my fear in an instant. I would not be beaten by giant bogies. Because, well, that would be humiliating.

I planted my feet. The giant toad barely moved, probably because it was just too damn big. I was going to barbecue this sonofabitch.

I turned toward the toad, fingers spread and palms out toward it. The toad's mouth opened again, and it made a slick, hissing sound.

"Accendo!" I shouted, willing my fear—not of the toad but of failing—to a tangible shape, and directed it at the massive amphibian. My terror and adrenaline roared out of my fingertips in the form of a fireball.

Another globule of acid mucus sped toward me.

The fireball caught the blob in midair — and it burst into a cloud of ash and embers.

"Hah!" I cried and did a little victory dance. A wave of nausea hit as the magic took its payment. But I was so high on adrenaline, I barely felt it.

The toad burped, pulling my attention to it again as it opened its mouth.

"Like why? Why can't I ever catch a break?" I readied myself, tapping into my will. "Accendo!" I cried, flinging another fireball at it.

The fireball hit the toad, and my confidence soared.

Then the unexpected happened.

The toad did not burn or explode into ash. Instead, the thing's body welled and shifted. Joints popped and flesh rippled and stretched to gigantic proportions. Its legs and arms thickened and lengthened. The toad grew and swelled until its body was so big, it filled out the entire tunnel space.

"This trial sucks," I grumbled, hating that flicker of defeat I felt.

The toad flicked its head at me. A grayish-brown tongue whipped out of its mouth.

I jumped to the left, only remembering too late that I was in a tunnel without much space, and hit the stone wall with a horrible thud.

That's going to hurt tomorrow.

The tongue wrapped around my lower left leg and yanked me forward. My feet left solid ground, and I was hauled across the tunnel and smashed into the opposite wall. I slid to the ground as I felt the tightness of the tongue release.

I gritted my teeth as agony sang through my body. My nerves pulsed into a burn, and a primal sound of pain and determination escaped me.

Think, Tessa. Think!

It was clear. If I tried another fireball, the toad would grow again. But then, how was I supposed to get past it?

I could try to climb over it, but if that didn't work, it would squish me to death.

There was just one way I was getting through to the other side of that tunnel.

"Screw this." I let out a breath. "Okay, stinker. If I can't go over you… and I can't defeat you… I'm going *through* you."

I'd made up my mind. I was going in through its mouth. Once inside I could either burn my way out or explode an opening large enough for an exit.

Yup. I was mad. The thing had acid snot. But everyone knew you needed to be just a little mad to be a witch.

I had to believe the impossible was possible.

"Bottoms up."

I moved to face the giant toad, crouched into a running position, and waited. I'd only have one shot at this. I prayed to the cauldron I was right. If I wasn't, the acid would kill me.

The toad's eyes flicked to mine.

My pulse thrashed as I lowered myself further. "This is going to suck."

The creature opened its mouth.

I burst into motion, making a beeline for its large, disgusting, sewer-smelling mouth—and leaped in.

I held my breath, my boots hitting something soft, like walking on a giant sponge. I blinked into darkness. I couldn't see. And for a horrible moment, panic hit. Maybe this wasn't such a good idea.

I felt a tug on my will and then my boots hit solid ground again and I blinked into the dimly lit tunnel.

The toad was gone. It had disappeared. I turned on the spot, looking for any evidence of the toad, but there was nothing. It was as though it never existed.

Silas had a strange sense of humor.

A trickle of excitement pulled my breath tight. But my happy mood evaporated as I checked my countdown app from my phone. The numbers 25:00 flashed back at me.

I had no idea how close I was to the center of the labyrinth or how many other toads or creatures I was going to have to face before I got there. Because I knew more were coming.

And with my luck, they were probably worse, much worse.

CHAPTER
19

My footsteps echoed hollowly back from the stone walls, unaccompanied by any other sound. I felt truly alone, like I was the only one in this underground maze, though I knew I wasn't. I had no idea if I was going the right way. I just kept on moving, hoping I was. The labyrinth of tunnels was enormous.

I never met anyone else. Never met that redhead who owed me a few kicks to his manhood. Maybe he was lost. Maybe his toad squished him. Or maybe he was already finished.

The thought that he'd attacked me infuriated me, but it also fueled my legs to pump faster.

I had now roughly less than twenty-five minutes to reach the center. It might sound like a lot of time, but having faced the giant toad, I knew whatever else Silas was going to throw at me would be more challenging. My brain also told me I'd have to do better and faster.

Yeah. No pressure.

And while in my brain, because there wasn't much else to do while wandering down dark, gloomy tunnels, I realized this trial wasn't just about testing our physical or magical strengths. The tests were measuring how well I could perform under stress and how well my mind worked under extreme pressure. They were seeing how my emotional and mental self coped with a tight deadline. I could do that.

I came to an intersection where the maze of passages and crumbling tunnels were seemingly ready to come thundering down at any moment, and they all looked the same.

With that in mind, I decided to take right turns from now on. And if that didn't work, I'd start to take left turns.

I continued like this for a long while, too long.

And when I made a right turn and faced a dead-end wall with nowhere to go but back the way I came, I kicked it hard, spun, and ran back.

Left turns it is.

Wiping the sweat off my brow, I took a moment to check the countdown.

15:52

My heart jumped to my throat. I'd been going around in circles for nine minutes.

My pulse rose, and I could feel the beginnings of a panic attack. Panicking would surely make me fail. I couldn't fail. Not now.

Somehow I'd taken the wrong tunnel. I was lost.

Voices rose. Loud shouts, but with so many of them, I couldn't decipher what they were shouting about. They were coming from inside the maze of tunnels, really close to me.

Sweat broke on my forehead. I crept forward, keeping to the shadows as my gaze swept the tunnel. Twenty or more witches were gathered in a space or chamber the size of three tunnels combined. And on the opposite wall, above a stone door, in glowing red letters was the inscription: WITH A BLOOD SACRIFICE, THE DOOR WILL OPEN.

Interesting. My first thought was, if I kill something and offer it to this wall, the door will open. But it wasn't that simple.

This was a test. And following that reasoning, this test was indeed more complex than the first one. I had the feeling Silas made sure we'd all amass here. I also had the nasty feeling he was watching.

And the witches, well, the witches were freaking out—again.

With deafening clangs, the stone walls shook as blasts of magic bounced off, hitting the ground, ceiling, and everything, as the witches attacked each other. A shudder ran through the tunnel like an earthquake. These morons were going to collapse the labyrinth on top of us if they didn't stop.

The blasts stopped for a few seconds, enough for me to hear a voice yelling.

"Get her!" shouted the same redhaired bastard who had kicked me when I was down, pointing at a small witch with round, terrified eyes, who reminded me of Iris. "She's the weakest link. If we kill her as a sacrifice, the door opens."

Mother f—

"Don't you touch her!" I yelled, stepping out of the shadows, relishing at the thought of kicking that witch's ass. Yup, I was going to enjoy myself.

But it was as though I'd yelled underwater. No one heard me.

The small witch screamed as she thrust her hands out. Green lightning shot out and hit the redhead's chest, sending him crashing into the wall.

I clapped. It *had* been an incredible hit. I wished it had been me.

And then all hell broke loose.

The attack came, sudden and vicious and horrifying. Cries rose in tempo as the witches collided with their bodies and magic. The screams of the witches and groans of the dying and injured melded together into an unbearable cacophony.

They've all lost their witching minds.

The witches all danced around each other in a dance of death and magic. Bodies flew, and the scent of scared flesh rose, making me gag. A male witch the size of Marcus was on the ground with his hands around the neck of another male witch while a female witch was playing spin the bottle with another witch twirling in the air above her.

Horrified I realized they were going to off each other. Pressure clasped me. My chest constricted. Around me, witches fell screaming in pain.

I stood there watching as the chaos that had been before skyrocketed. I wasn't an idiot. If I stepped in, I was witch toast. I planned on finishing this trial.

My gaze flicked back to the inscription. This was a riddle. And these morons had no clue. It was obvious they thought the last one standing would go through the door. Such idiots.

And I was going to let them be idiots.

Suddenly, there was a clap like thunder and an invisible force slammed into me, knocking me off my feet. I hit the wall with my back and slumped to the ground. Dizzy, I blinked through my blurred vision. And when I could see clearly again, the chamber was empty except for me.

"Huh. Will you look at that?" I stood up, rubbing my behind and feeling the giant bruise that would make its appearance later.

I knew they weren't dead. Silas had probably magicked their stupid asses back, which meant they failed—failed to understand the riddle.

Twisting my bag to my front, I pulled out the small pocketknife I carried to cut herbs, wiped it on my jeans, and sliced my palm. Dark red blood oozed from the thin cut.

I winced at the sharp pain, but it only lasted a second. "Okay. Now what?"

Not sure what to expect, I moved to the door and placed my bloodied palm on it. "Open sesame." I laughed and smeared my blood on it.

The effect was instantaneous.

Brilliant silvery light rippled through the frame of the door. The glow flared and streamed in a torrent of pure white. The magic aftershock pulsed through the tunnel and caught me in a dizzying whirlpool.

I felt it reach into my will, my core.

And then with a loud screech, the door swung open.

CHAPTER

20

Through the doorway, the tunnel was straight. It didn't branch off, nor did it look like it was going to end anytime soon. I felt like I was stuck in a dream where I kept on running forever.

I needed to wake the hell up.

Okay, so the blood thing hadn't been *that* hard, but it still cost me in terms of time.

Glancing at my phone's countdown the screen read: 04:06.

My chest constricted. I had just about four minutes to face whatever else Silas was going to throw at me and make it to the center. Easy peasy. Right? Not really.

Panting, I pinched the cramp at my side and took a few seconds to hydrate. Thank the cauldron I'd packed a water bottle. Without it, I would have fainted by now. With a last gulp, I shoved it back in my bag and sprinted down the tunnel.

My thighs burned as I pushed them faster and harder because I knew my time was nearly over. Would there be a fork in the path? A door? Something to tell me I hadn't taken a wrong turn? Would this path lead to the center of the labyrinth?

Being underground in the dark for what seemed like forever—with dirt crumbling onto my head, walls rubbing my shoulders, and a demon possibly waiting at the end of the tunnel—ranked right up there with this being my worst day ever.

Just when my lungs felt like I'd swallowed shards of glass, I saw a light at the end of the tunnel. Yeah, I knew how that sounded.

I staggered into a huge space. Looking around, it was oddly shaped, like a hexagon, with different tunnels leading to it, just as mine did.

Smoking braziers rested around the chamber, the only source of light. Warm air with the sharp scent of incense and some other, more acrid spice, filled my nose. Across from me, right in the center of the chamber and raised on a platform of stone was a gleaming, six-foot, silver star.

That was the center. I needed to get to that star.

I took a shaky breath and stepped forward—

A moan caught my attention to the right.

"Willis?"

The little witch was on his knees, blood trickling down his nose. "Tessa? Is that you? I can't find my glasses. They fell… and I can't see anything without them."

I was so shocked at seeing him that I just stared at him stupidly. He'd made it this far. That was something.

My heart clenched at the panic that flickered across his face. "Yes. It's me. I'll help you find your glasses." I made to move, but something else shifted in my peripheral vision.

Silas rose from the shadows of the chamber and faced me.

"Neat trick," I told him, wondering what the hell he was doing here. "Would love to know how you did that. But I'm kind of busy right now."

"Leave him," ordered Silas. "He'll never get past me." He shrugged. "Well, neither will you." He laughed and flashed me a smile that I wanted to kick off of him—if I could reach that high.

The runes and sigils tattooed to his chest, arms, and neck all began to glow red.

Damn. I cocked a brow. "Aha. So, I have to fight you? Is that it?"

"It is," said Silas and he crossed his muscular arms over his chest, his tattoos fading to their normal black. "You need to get past me if you want to complete this trial. So far, only sixteen have made it. And those who did were from the winning group. There are no places for losers within the Merlins."

Arrogant prick. "Yeah… well… we'll see about that." Did I just call myself a loser?

"Found them!"

I looked over my shoulder and found Willis on his feet, adjusting his glasses. The left lens had several large cracks running across it. He wouldn't be able to see through it, but at least he had one good eye.

He staggered like he was drunk and fell to the ground on his knees. "I think I'll just sit here a while. Until the stars go away."

"Good idea."

Now that I looked closer, I could see blood in his left ear, and a wet spot at the back of his head. Willis had taken a serious beating. If the rest of the witches had played fair, Willis would have had a real shot at this. But someone made sure he didn't. And that someone was long gone by now.

I didn't like these trials. In fact, I hated them. I honed my hate towards the tattooed freak. Behind him was my ticket out of this hell.

215

My eyes flicked to Silas. "Inflitus!" I cried, flinging up my hands as I pulled on the energy from the elements around me.

A saw a split second of red flashing from Silas's chest, and I went sprawling back in the air like I'd been hit by a giant fly swatter.

I hit the ground and rolled, my cheek smacking on something solid following a crack, which I knew was bad. But I didn't have time to worry about bruises.

Brushing the hair from my eyes and spitting the dirt from my mouth, I got to my feet with a groan, my lower back throbbing. How much time did I have left?

Silas hadn't moved. The cocky bastard was still standing in the exact same position.

"You're going to have to do a lot better than that, loser," said Silas. "Look at you. You're broken. If you want to give up now, I'll understand. It's what losers do."

"Shut up. I'm not giving up."

Without a single hesitation, I slammed down on my will and snarled, "Fulgur!"

A bolt of white-purple lightning blasted from my outstretched hand. It flew straight and true, right at Silas's dumbass head.

The bastard's runes flashed red, he snapped his fingers, and my beautiful bolt of lightning turned to water. It fell to the ground in a puddle next to his feet.

Silas laughed. "You're pathetic. What was that? And you call yourself a Davenport witch? Tick-tock, loser." His smile faltered, and something dark moved behind his eyes.

Call it my witchy instincts, but I tapped into the elements just as a rune on his neck glowed red.

"Protego!" I howled. A sphere-shaped shield rose above my head just as a red blast of magic hit it.

Both my shield and I flew back by the sheer force of the blow. Without the shield, I would have been witch toast. The force of Silas's magic reverberated inside my shield, and I felt it in the ground beneath my feet. The tattooed creep was strong. How could anyone beat him?

"Tessa? Are you all right? Tessa?" came Willis's voice from somewhere off to my right.

"I'm fine," I called back, peering through my shield as I found Silas's shape.

A volley of a hundred red, glowing darts sprouted from Silas's chest, flying straight for me.

"Okay, not fine."

I ducked, just as I felt a release on the hold on my magic. There was a pop of displaced air, and my shield fell.

"Crap."

"Oops, my bad. Guess I burst your little bubble," said Silas. I raised my head to find him grinning. "Just accept it. You're not strong enough to beat me." He pointed at himself. "Winner," he said and then pointed at me and added, "Loser."

"Very mature." I pushed to my feet and staggered. The power words were stealing all the energy I had left. I shook from just the strain of standing. I couldn't keep this up much longer.

"Don't listen to him," encouraged Willis, still on his knees. The blood that kept dripping from his ear worried me. "You're not a loser, Tessa. You wouldn't have made it this far if you were. He's a liar and a bully."

A well of gratitude filled my chest. I really started to like this little witch. "I hate bullies," I told him with a smile.

"Me too."

My heart pounded as I strained my body from shaking. Yes, I was tired and yes there was pain. But I still had a hell of a lot of fight in me. I lowered my body and spread my hands in a fighting stance.

He's a liar. This wasn't about beating him. It was about getting *past* this a-hole and reaching the platform.

I just didn't know how to do that.

A smile of satisfaction blossomed over the tattooed witch's face at what he saw on mine. "Loser," he crooned. "Can I call you loser? Okay then. This is pointless, loser. You look like hell, loser."

"I look better than you," I said, making Willis laugh. Yeah, he's a keeper.

Silas gave a mock laugh. "You're out of time," he warned. "Face it. You were never going to be a Merlin. Your aunts were idiots to think they could make you one. Hell, they're so old, they're not even real Merlins anymore, more like Merlin shadows."

"You shouldn't have said that," I growled, feeling feral. I was going to peel off those tattoos.

Silas flashed his teeth. "Why's that?"

"Because I'm going to kick your ass."

Willis laughed and clapped his hands, reminding me of Iris.

Silas spread his arms, and his biceps bounced, the tats glowing red. "Losers don't make Merlins. You're a loser," he said and dipped his head toward Willis. "And he's a loser. You're both finished. It's over."

I didn't like the way he'd said that, with so much finality in his voice.

"Oh no!" cried Willis.

I pulled my head back to Willis, who had a watch practically stuck to his right eyeball. "He's right," said Willis as he dropped his watch looking defeated. "I'm sorry, Tessa. I was rooting for you. You'll have a chance next year. Me…" he didn't finish.

I frowned. "What are you talking about? There's still time."

Willis looked at me and shook his head. "Can you get to the platform in twenty-five seconds?"

"What!" Panicked, I yanked my phone out of my bag and gasped.

00:24

No, I thought in horror, seeing that everything I'd accomplished so far had all been for nothing.

Silas laughed, a deep, horrible, self-satisfying, mocking laugh that made me sick to my stomach.

No. No. *No!*

I hadn't come all this way for nothing. My panic rose anew, and I shifted from foot to foot, trying to jumpstart my brain again.

I needed to get past Silas. But how? If only I could slip past him and reach the platform without him being able to stop me.

A thought occurred to me. The only way I could do that was with a ley line. But the nearest ley line was miles away from the castle.

If only I could *bring* it here…

A spark of energy blossomed in my chest.

Hello.

It grew, and stretched, and squeezed. I recognized the source. This was the ley line…

But how? It was as though the ley lines were answering my desperate call.

And then it hit me. Could I move the lines? Could I *bend* them?

220

As if in answer, another spark of energy welled in my core, only faster this time, stronger. The ley line was answering me. It *wanted* me to do this.

With my heart thrashing with exhilaration, I drew in my will and reached out to tap the ley line. A burst of sudden energy hit me as it answered, like a rushing river, ready to sweep me away. I felt it in my body, my bones, vibrating with its power. With the ley line's power.

I'd never done this before, and yet, somehow I knew what to do. As though I was born to do this.

I glanced at my phone and gasped.

00:15

"Time's up," said Silas. "You've failed. But it's like I said, losers don't make Merlins."

A powerful wind rose. Silas lost his smile.

"What's happening?" cried Willis.

I leaned my energy, focused on the ley line—and pulled.

With only my will, I yanked the ley line closer and closer to me, like pulling a rope. I could see it clearly in my mind, like a translucent river. And like an elastic band, I manipulated it. I bent it until I could feel its trembling energy beneath my feet, until I could see it race across the chamber to the center of the labyrinth, to the star on the platform.

00:09

Silas's roar of outrage echoed around me.
00:08
It was now or never.

I rushed over, hooked Willis's arm through mine, pulled him to his feet—and jumped the line.

I'd never brought anyone else with me, so I was purely running on instincts. *Please don't fail me now.*

Willis screamed like a girl as we both landed together, speeding forward in a howl of wind and colors. Energy rushed through my head, my body, everywhere. The stone walls of the labyrinth blurred as our bodies shot forward. Silas's angry face blurred past us like we were on a speeding train.

And of course, I *had* to flip him off.

Then, I felt a sudden release as the images around me slowed until they weren't blurred anymore, until I could make them out—as though time itself had slowed, just for me.

All the while Willis kept screaming, but I never let go of him.

I focused solely on the platform, on the star, on where I needed to go, knowing I was about to jump.

A dark shape appeared in the ley line with us that wasn't there before. It resembled the outline of a man, tall and fit. At first, I thought it was Silas. But it wasn't him. I couldn't see his face clearly, but his eyes, silver and gold reflected the dim light of the labyrinth, luminous and eerie.

And just as I tried to see him more clearly, he was gone.

I'd hit my head, but he was not a figment of my imagination. He'd been there for only half a second, but long enough for me to see him. I couldn't think about that right now because if we didn't jump at the right moment, we'd end up in Canada.

With the last of my strength, I leaped, pulling Willis with me, and we landed on the platform.

I let go of Willis, just as he bent over and began puking his guts out. Totally understandable. Adrenaline pumping, I checked my phone.

00:02

We made it. Two seconds left. We made it!

"We made it." I turned and looked down at Willis who was wiping his mouth with his hand "We did it," I told him. "Two seconds left!" I did a little happy dance, which was a twirl and an awkward side kick. Don't ask.

Willis blinked up at me, his face twisted in wonder. "How did you do that?" He looked past me at what I figured was our point of departure.

223

I looked back over my shoulder. "I have no idea." Which was partially true. I had no idea how I'd bent the ley line, but I did.

But the real winner was the shock on Silas's face.

Yeah, there's the ticket.

CHAPTER
21

"**W**hat do you mean you *moved* the ley line?" exclaimed Dolores as she paced around the kitchen. "That's preposterous. It makes no logical sense."

"And ley lines are logical?" I countered.

Dolores gave me a hard stare. "Don't patronize me. Everyone knows you respect those *taller* than you."

I laughed. "Yes, ma'am."

Beverly popped an olive in her mouth. "She does have a point. I never did understand how those ley lines work. All those courses of lines and stops, ups and downs, and side to side. It's exhausting." She fanned herself with her hand. "I'm breaking a sweat just thinking about it."

Dolores patrolled the kitchen, stopped, and gestured with her right hand while her left was on her hip. "Just… start from the beginning. I need to hear it again."

"It's like I said. I reached out to the nearest ley line and I pulled it to me. I bent it," I said again, seeing my Aunt Dolores's eyes widening more each time.

The moment I got back, I'd hurried inside Davenport House in search of Ruth to give her the good news. I'd finally found her upstairs in her bedroom, standing next to her window and staring absently outside.

"I did it, Ruth," I'd told her as I came to stand next to her. "I passed. I passed the second trial." When she didn't answer, I tried again. "Ruth? Did you hear me? I passed the second trial."

When my aunt had finally turned around and acknowledged my presence, I'd stifled a gasp.

Her face. Her face had aged twenty years. Heavy layers of skin drooped down around her eyes and mouth, pale and dry. Her hair was a mess like she hadn't brushed it in years.

"That's wonderful," she'd said to me, her eyes distant and not really seeing me. Then, she'd looked away, back at whatever had gotten her attention outside.

My throat and eyes had burned as I'd bitten back a sob. I didn't want to break down in front of her. Not when she needed me to be strong.

I'd left her room feeling devastated that I hadn't helped her in some way.

There was still time to prove her innocence. I didn't know how I was going to do it, but I just knew I *had* to do something.

"Let me get this straight," Dolores was saying, and my attention snapped back to her. She stopped pacing and spun to face me. "You're saying that you pulled the ley line that was miles away into this labyrinth... pulled it right next to you... and then you used it—"

"She *bent* it," interjected Beverly who flashed me one of her smiles and popped another olive into her mouth. "She's flexible." Her green eyes met mine and she raised a perfectly manicured brow. "Speaking of flexible," she said, her voice low and sultry. "Oliver said he's never been with someone so flexible." I had no idea who this Oliver was, probably her man of the week.

"He said he could just bend me like he wanted. Like a doll."

"Yes, an inflatable one," snapped Dolores.

Beverly glared at her sister. "You're just envious because you haven't had a date in months," she replied, casually tossing her hair back and casting a glittering smile my way. "It's not my fault you don't put yourself out there. You might get lucky and find a man who doesn't mind dating a big ol' sasquatch."

"As opposed to dating what? A walking mattress?" Dolores shot back. "I'll take those odds anytime."

I cleared my throat at Dolores's hard stare. "Umm... we're getting sidetracked. We were discussing the ley lines?" I didn't want them to start a fight again. The tension between my aunts was getting worse. The closer we got to December 23, the higher the tension. We were all under a lot of stress. The last thing we all needed was a wedge between the sisters.

Dolores nodded and made a sound in her throat. "You said you bent the ley line and used it to finish the trial?"

"Yes. That's exactly what I'm saying." I leaned forward in my chair, grabbed a piece of cheese from the large platter piled with an assortment of cheeses from different countries, and stuffed it in my mouth. I was ravenous. The trial had used up all my energy. High-fat dairy was my healing food. The creamier the better.

"So?" I asked, swallowing. "How come Ruth never told me I could *bend* the ley lines? I mean... I've been over and over the ley line book she gave me. But I couldn't find anything on that."

My chewing was loud in the sudden silence. I swallowed and grabbed another slice of

Italian cheese with chunks of cranberry in it. Yum.

Dolores pulled a chair from the kitchen table opposite me and sat. "That's because it's never happened before."

I choked on my cheese. "Excuse me?" I coughed, my stomach tightening. "What do you mean… it's *never happened before*?" My heart slammed against my chest at their silence, my eyes darting to each aunt. "Are you telling me… there's never been a witch who's done this before?"

Dolores watched me for a long moment. "That's exactly what I'm telling you."

"Bullshit."

Dolores raised a brow. "Language."

I leaned back in my chair. "Clearly it has something to do with me being a Shadow witch. Right?" It was the only thing that made any logical sense. From what I knew, it was a rare gift. Only a handful of witches were considered Shadow witches. I knew being able to weave both Dark *and* Light magic had its perks. This was just another badass magic bonus. The image of Silas's utter shock brought a smile to my lips. It had been so worth it.

Beverly drummed her red manicured fingers on the table. "I've never heard of a Shadow witch or any witch with the power of drawing ley lines to them and *bending* them. We all know ley lines run straight. Like a grid that wraps around the earth. I don't think any witch or magic practitioner can."

"Maybe you just haven't heard of it," I told them, my pulse rising with excitement. "Because," I continued as I reached for another piece of that fabulous Italian cheese, "it's so rare that the witches who can bend the ley lines have kept it a secret. I mean, it's possible they were afraid to tell anyone. You know how witches get when they hear of something that could potentially make them a crapload more powerful. Take Adan and the Elder ring. He kind of lost his mind."

Beverly let out a puff of air. "He was already a jerk, darling. I doubt the ring had any part in that. That was all him."

"Even so," I said, chewing. "Hmmm. Good cheese. Um… I think it's really unlikely that I'm the only one."

"I don't think you're hearing us, Tessa," said Dolores. The tension in her voice pulled my eyes to her. "Moving, bending, manipulating ley lines the way you've described to us… it's never been done. By anyone."

"I'm pretty sure I remember seeing the sorceress Samara doing just that in the woods." I had a good visual of the psychotic sorceress pulling the ley lines to her.

"That wasn't the same." Dolores shook her head. "Samara pulled the town's ley lines' energy into that fortress. Not the ley lines themselves. She was drawing on their power. She never physically moved them like you did. She never bent them."

I should have been feeling excited at the prospect of being able to do something that apparently no other witch could. But the grim faces my aunts wore made me feel like puking. I really wasn't getting why they didn't see this as an opportunity.

If I could bend ley lines... what else could I do with them?

So, so much.

I took a sip of water from my tall glass to wash down the cheese, not liking where this conversation was going. "But this is good. Right? Being able to bend ley lines is good," I blurted out, remembering how badly things had declined for me when I told them I was seeing a goat, who turned out to be a cursed Iris.

"I'm not entirely sure," answered Dolores as she glanced at Beverly. The two sisters did that thing again, that unspoken conversation between them that only close siblings could share.

My jaw tightened. "What?" The look didn't settle well with me. The cheese I'd just gobbled down threatened to come back up. "Why are you both looking at me like I'm crazy. I'm not seeing dead people or demons or ghosts that no one else can see. This is entirely different."

231

Dolores folded her hands on the kitchen table. "Not necessarily."

I leaned back and wrapped my arms around my middle. "Okay. Can you tell me why?" My voice sounded harsh, but I was getting a little ticked off at how ominous this whole situation was getting.

I was kind of glad I hadn't mentioned the man I'd seen in the ley line earlier. If they were freaked out about me bending ley lines, imagine what they would do if I told them a dude was in there with me.

Yeah, I wasn't going to tell them about that just yet.

Thinking of said man reminded me of Marvelous Myrtle's warning to me months ago before she died. *"A dark presence is following you. It's… around you… around your aura."* Had he been this dark presence? The man in the ley line?

Dolores pressed her lips together in thought. "As you know, not many witches are capable of drawing power from ley lines. To most, ley lines are still an unknown territory in terms of magic. And most witches are afraid to even use a ley line. They're unpredictable. If you're not in tune with them, you might lose a limb."

"Or your life," added Beverly and then took a sip of her red wine.

"Yes, but some witches do," I countered, staring at my glass of red wine, which was still full. "Even Ruth told me she used to ride the ley lines."

Dolores sighed through her nose, and I could see the pain that just mentioning Ruth did to her. "Riding ley lines is like riding a race car," she said.

"Good analogy," agreed Beverly, lifting her glass in a salute.

"Thank you." Dolores shifted in her chair. "Race cars are dangerous. Deadly. And only a few people are crazy enough to ride them."

"You mean someone like me," I said.

"And a handful of others, yes. The thing is, ley lines are still in the gray area of magic. Because of their nature, we don't know much about them. It's not like elemental magic, or even borrowing magic from demons like the Dark witches do. It's been practiced for thousands of years by millions of witches all over the earth. All magic is risky. But ley lines… the energy drawn from ley lines is a magic that's still raw, unsure, and unused. We just don't know that much about it. But I am a hundred percent certain that bending or moving lines has never been done before."

"To your knowledge," I said, ignoring her frown. "I did it. I'm not lying."

"We believe you," added Beverly quickly.

"That's the problem." Dolores sighed. Fear simmered in the back of her thoughts, showing on her face. "Tessa. If I'm right, and I have a

233

feeling that I am, you are the *only* person on this earth who can." She hesitated, searching my face. "Do you now understand what I'm trying to say?"

"Maybe if you stopped talking like Obi-Wan Kenobi, I might have a chance." My heart did a little flip-flop of dread. "What kind of freak am I?"

Of course, if there had to be a freak in the world, it would be me. And if I was the only one who could bend the ley lines with my will, what did that make me?

"Sorry, darling." Beverly reached over the table and tapped my hand. "It's better to be a witch freak than a human freak."

"That's not exactly helping," shot Dolores.

Beverly leaned back in her chair. "Of course, it is." She tipped her glass to her lips and finished her wine. "She's here with us," she said as she reached for the bottle and poured herself another glass. "In this town, she can be as freakish as she wants. This is Hollow Cove, for cauldron's sake. We're all freaks. Nothing new here."

A dark cast came over Dolores, and I could see that she was really worried. "Tessa. Did the arbitrator—this Silas—see you when you bent the ley line?"

I stiffened in my chair. "Yes. So what? It's not illegal to use the ley lines. I used what I could to finish the trial. What? You think I shouldn't have?"

Dolores bit her bottom lip. "I'm just trying to understand. If he saw you, then Greta knows."

"And you don't want her to know?"

"I would rather less people know until I know more about this. It's all very new and unexplored." Dolores was quiet for a long time. The only sound was Beverly drinking her wine.

This was not the reaction I'd expected from my aunts. I thought they'd be excited at the prospect of my being able to do something extraordinary. I had let it go to my head. And now, well, now it seemed like bending the ley lines was a bad idea.

"So, what now?" I asked. "You think Greta is going to use that against me?" A new dread rushed through me at the thought. "You think they'll take away my win?" If they did, I thought I would murder that old witch.

"Settle down, Tessa." Dolores gave me a weak smile. "They can't fail you for using a ley line. But, knowing Greta, she's probably already looking into it."

"And?"

"And," said Dolores, her features twisting in bitterness. "I would hate it if she knew something I didn't." Dolores pushed back her chair, a dark gleam in her eye. "I have some work do to."

"What about Ruth?" I called out as Dolores walked out of the kitchen and into the hallway.

Halfway down the hallway she turned around, opened her mouth to say something, but then shut it and walked away.

"I'm afraid we've failed Ruth." Beverly's voice was small, and when I looked back, her green eyes welled with tears. She put her glass to her lips and downed the entirety of her wine in one gulp. "It's over."

I clenched my jaw. "It's not over. She's still here. And she's innocent. She didn't put that black belladonna in her potion."

"I know, darling." Beverly grabbed the wine bottle. Her hands shook as she poured herself another large glass. The wine spilled from the rim of the glass and onto the table. "She didn't even have any left."

Alarmed, I froze. "What did you say?"

Beverly wiped a tear from her red cheek. "She'd run out. Months ago. It's not an herb she likes to use, so she hadn't bought any for a while. It couldn't have been her. We didn't even have it in the house when she made that gingerweed for Bernard."

"Oh, my god."

"It wasn't Ruth." Beverly bent her head over her glass, slurped the excess wine, and giggled. She picked up her glass, spilling the wine over the table and her wrist as she took another sip.

I leaned over the table and grabbed Beverly's wrist. "Did you tell them that? The Gray Council?"

"We did. They didn't care. They said it didn't prove that she didn't put it in there. They said she could have gotten it somewhere else."

"Idiots." And then it hit me. "Where did Ruth get her orders of black belladonna from?"

Beverly laughed, but tears fell from her eyes just as more wine spilled down her hand. "From Gilbert's store. He has an aisle reserved for exotic herbs. It's seriously overpriced too. The little worm of a man."

My pulse thrashed with excitement. This was it. This was what I'd been waiting for. It was right in front of me, so simple. I knew exactly what to do.

"Where's Iris?" For my plan to work, I was going to need her help. Possibly Ronin's too.

"She's probably banging that vampire," said Beverly, her green eyes unfocused. "Good for her. Good for her for getting some. Orgasms are the best stress releasers." Not this again. She started to laugh as she pointed a finger at what I expected she thought was me—but was the refrigerator. "Do you have a good vibrator?"

"Okay." I jumped to my feet. "Time for me to go."

"What?" Beverly kept laughing. "Martha's got a two for one special."

"Two for one vibrator special?" This was beyond weird.

"No," she dismissed me with a wave of her free hand. "You get a facial and a vibrator for the price of one."

That was my cue. "I'll see you later," I said, tense and excited all at the same time.

Grabbing my phone, I rushed down the hallway, my pulse racing with anticipation because I knew how to get Ruth's charges dropped.

CHAPTER

22

All my life, I always dreamed of becoming an artist and a witch, but never in a million years did I think I should have added thief to my résumé.

I was getting really good at it too. And by the rate of breaking and entering I was doing, I'd be an expert by the end of the year.

I'll admit there was a high about breaking and entering. Breaking into someone else's house to snoop and take something that didn't belong to you and not knowing if you were going to get away with it was incredibly exciting. I was definitely losing it.

The streetlights glowed with silver halos as the snow came down, leaving dark shadows where the light didn't reach. The cold air was speckled with occasional flakes of wet snow that wouldn't last as it hit the ground.

The sound of keys pulled my attention to Ronin as he stood in front of Gilbert's Grocer & Gifts' glass door. The streetlight cast dark shadows across his face as he flipped through his keys. Iris, dressed all in black and looking like a gothic doll with pigtails, black lipstick, and eyeshadow, stood facing the street, her fingers moving in a dark spell in case we were discovered.

I leaned closer. "You have Gilbert's keys?" I laughed. "Did you steal them? He's going to be pissed."

Ronin slipped a key into the keyhole and turned it. The deadbolt rattled dully. "Of course not. These are my keys."

"*Your* keys," I questioned. "I'm not following."

Ronin glanced over his shoulder at me. "I own the building. Gilbert's my tenant."

I stood there staring at my half-vampire friend like an idiot. I knew he'd wanted to buy Marcus's building because the apartment on the second floor had more square footage. I just never expected him to be Gilbert's landlord.

"I invest in real estate," continued the half-vampire. "It's how I make a living and how I can afford to stay in bed until noon." He looked over at Iris who flashed him a smile.

I didn't know the exact date when the two had become an item, but they had been inseparable for months.

"How many other buildings do you own?" I asked curiously.

"A couple more in Hollow Cove and some in Elizabeth Town," he answered, looking happy that I was interested.

I was impressed. "When you said you had a way in, I thought you meant like a side door or something. Never thought you meant the front door. So, technically, this isn't breaking and entering since this is your building."

"Oh, it is." Ronin pushed open the door. "I can't just bust in Gilbert's place of business in the middle of the night without giving him a twenty-four-hour notice. This is illegal."

Iris squealed and clapped her hands. "We're so totally doing this."

Ronin bowed from the waist as he held the door open. "Witches first."

Iris sneaked through the door. I glanced over my shoulder one last time, making sure no one was in the street watching this display, and followed Iris in. I heard the door shut behind me.

We stood in the darkness, and I waited a few seconds for my eyes to adjust. The streetlight from the outside cast enough soft light through the glass windows and doors to see shapes.

"Where do you think he keeps his records," asked Ronin as he appeared next to me. "That's if he keeps track of the stuff he sells."

"He does. I know he does." Now that I could see better, I looked past the aisles of food and produce to the back of the store. "In the back. It's where his office is. It'll be there." I didn't know Gilbert well, but from the little I knew, he was meticulous when it came to his store and the items he sold. I was certain he kept a list of his inventory—especially the exotic kind.

Quickly, I hurried across the store, pulled the office door open, and stepped through. I was met by a solid wall of darkness. There were no windows in this small office.

Yanking out my phone, I tapped on the flashlight icon and flicked it around the office.

"There," I said, pointing to a small desk sandwiched between boxes of bananas and oranges. I rushed over, angling my cell phone as I was hit by a feeling of déjà vu. "Just like old times," I said to a smiling Ronin.

Ronin lost his smile. "I hope we find something. For Ruth's sake."

My stomach churned. "We will. We have to."

"Found a laptop," informed Iris as I spun around and saw her eyes wide, holding her cellphone's light in one hand while she dangled a small laptop in the other.

"Open it and see if you can find his list of inventory." I turned back around and searched Gilbert's desk.

"The dude's a hoarder," said Ronin after a moment, standing next to a pile of magazines that were nearly as tall as him. "These *National Geographics* date back to the nineteen seventies."

I laughed. "Good. That means he has a record of the black belladonna somewhere. We need to find it. I don't care if it takes us all night, I'm not leaving until I have it."

"Me neither," said Iris as she sat on the floor and flipped the laptop open on her lap. "Don't worry. We're going to find something to help Ruth. I can feel it."

My throat contracted at the mention of my aunt. We didn't have much time left. If I was wrong, if there wasn't anything here, I had nothing left.

After ten minutes of searching, dread started to sneak into my head. Ronin was right. Gilbert was a hoarder, which also meant we had piles and piles of papers and magazines and bills to get through. And we were still not close to finding anything.

"Iris? Anything?" I looked down at her.

Iris shook her head. "Not yet. This is just pictures of—oh. Look here. Gilbert's on a dating app." She laughed. "Oh, my, god. What a liar. He says he's five-eight." She let out a sigh. "I don't think there's anything here, Tessa. This is mostly personal stuff."

"Keep looking." I spun around, pulled open the first drawer, and began looking through a stack of bills.

"Nice," said Ronin, and my heart skipped a beat.

"You found something?"

"Yeah." Ronin held a magazine open. "*Playboy* 1982. These gals had more meat on them. They were more natural. And a lot hairier down there too. Look. I'm digging the more native style."

Iris kicked him with her foot. "Don't be a douche."

I pushed the drawer back and yanked the next one underneath. A small red book blinked up at me. Fingers trembling, I flipped it open on the desk.

"Found it," I said, seeing a list of ingredients, names, and dates scribbled at the top of the first page in blue ink and cataloged into neat rows.

"You sure?" Ronin stepped in next to me.

"Yeah. Look. I've got names, dates, and the exotic herbs written in neat little rows. This is his exotic herb inventory."

Iris brushed up on my other side. "Look under B for belladonna."

I had to bite my tongue not to laugh. "Gotcha." I flipped through the book. "It's not

244

categorized alphabetically. It's by month." Knowing that all this mess started at the end of October, I flipped the pages back until I saw the month of January of this year written at the top. With my flashlight illuminating the page, I flipped through every month, searching for the herb that had landed my aunt in cuffs and the witch prison.

"There!" I said, my heart thrashing.

Ronin's shoulder bumped against mine as he leaned closer. "Two people bought the black belladonna."

"Estelle Watch and Michael Blackwood," read Iris before I could.

"Ruth's name isn't here," I voiced, every nerve in my body pulsing with our discovery. "She never bought any. No one did until these two in September. It proves she didn't put it in there." It didn't prove that she didn't drive to another paranormal community to buy black belladonna there, but I was going with what I had. Besides, Ruth hardly ever drove. She didn't like it, and the closest paranormal community was four hours away.

I looked at the two names. "One of these is the murderer. One of them killed Bernard and has been letting Ruth take the blame."

"Yeah, but which one?" asked Iris, her voice hopeful.

I glanced at Ronin. "Do you know them? Do the names sound familiar? I've never heard of either of these people."

Ronin shook his head. "No. Sorry."

I sighed. "It doesn't matter. We have them. We know who bought the black belladonna." I let the names settle in my head, knowing that one of these people was the murderer. One of them had let my aunt take the fall for Bernard's death. Just for that, I'd skin them alive and drop them in a boiling cauldron while I danced around it.

"This is it," I said, shaking like I was cold, but I was seething inside. "This is how we're going to prove that Ruth didn't do it."

"But how?" asked Iris. "It's like what Dolores said. It doesn't prove that Ruth didn't buy it from somewhere else. If it were me, that's what I would do if I was planning on killing someone in my town. I wouldn't buy the stuff here."

I picked up the book and looked at both of my friends. "We have names now. One of these people killed Bernard. One of them had it out for him. So much so that they were willing to kill him. With a little investigating, I'm going to find out which one."

"Which one, what?" said a female voice behind me, making me jump.

Iris screamed.

So did Ronin.

The red book slipped from my hands and landed on the floor at my feet with a thump.

I spun around as bright light exploded in my eyes. I blinked slowly, waiting for my eyes to adjust.

Once they adjusted to the light, I blinked into the faces of Adira, two men I recognized as her vampire deputies, Jeff, Cameron—Marcus's deputies—and the chief himself.

Oh, goodie.

CHAPTER
23

In my life, things most always get worse. And at this moment, it was the understatement of the year.

We'd been caught. Guess I could remove "expert thief" from my résumé now. I felt Ronin and Iris stiffen next to me. I could deal with going to the witch prison, but I wasn't ready to have my friends go down with me. Not when this was my idea in the first place.

With a snap of her fingers, Adira gestured to her two vampire dogs to stay put outside the office. Then she strolled in, her motions stiff and hurried, trying to make herself look important, but it just looked like she really had to pee. The light of the room shone on her red hair, making it look on fire. I could make that happen.

Her eyes flicked everywhere at once. Her face held the cold beauty of someone who was going to get the prize she'd been waiting for.

I'd never hated her more than I did at this exact moment.

Marcus walked in next. I hated that my pulse increased at the sight of him, at his thick luscious dark hair, his wide shoulders, and his incredibly tight behind. I hadn't spoken to him since I'd verbally thrown him out of Davenport house. Okay, it had been a little extreme, but I'd been out of my mind with fear and anger that he wouldn't help Ruth. I'd lost it.

Now that I'd had a few weeks to calm down, guilt gnawed at me. I'd lost control. And I'd taken it out on him. I wasn't sure he'd ever forgive me for that. He looked at the book on the floor at my feet for a moment. Then he pulled his head up and our eyes met. His face was blank of emotion, but such a coldness shone in his gray eyes, a finality, that gave me my answer. My heart squeezed itself into a hard fist.

Marcus wanted nothing to do with me. Not anymore.

I was crushed. My heart seemed to split in half, but I stood. I would not break down now because of a man… because of what I'd done. It was over. I had to move on.

Both Ronin and Iris felt the change in me, and they both squeezed in tighter around me, like a safety net.

Jeff and Cameron stayed outside the office too, though I was sure it was more to keep an eye on the vampires than anything else.

Both of Marcus's deputies had disappeared a few days before Adira had arrived. As the new chief, I had the distinct feeling Adira had removed them to bring in her people.

Burying my feelings into that part of me where I could take them out later, I stared at Adira.

"You following me?" I accused, hoping Adira didn't see the book on the floor. Damn. How was I going to sneak it out now without her or Marcus noticing? He'd already noticed the book. Now I had to wait and see what he was going to do about it.

A slow, lazy, carnivorous smile touched Adira's lips. "You triggered the silent alarm, silly witch."

I shot Ronin a look. The half-vampire shrugged. "What? I had no idea," he said.

I knew I should have been scared, but all I felt was rage.

"This is Ronin's building," I seethed, shaking with fury and calling her all kinds of obscenities with my eyes. "He's allowed to do whatever he wants with it."

"Really?" Adira's gaze shifted to Ronin.

"Solidarity, sister," said Ronin as he stepped forward and attempted to high-five her.

Adira's face twisted like she'd just stepped in dog poop. She eyed Ronin like he was foul, beneath her, as though being half-vampire made him lesser somehow.

Yup, I hated her even more after that.

"What the hell are you still doing here," I growled as Ronin dropped his hand and stepped back. His pale face reddened, and I knew he was angry and embarrassed. I'd stake her in the heart just for that. "Shouldn't you return to your coffin? Preferably in the bottom of the ocean?" I asked, matching her smile.

Iris leaned and whispered in my ear, "I can make that happen."

A nervous laugh bubbled up. The visual was awesome.

Adira traced her long fingers on one of Gilbert's shelves. "Believe me," she said, flicking her fingers with what might be dust or something more sinister. "I can't wait to get out of this crappy little town. But I'm stuck here. You see… since I made the arrest on your aunt, I'm the one who has to escort her to Grimway Citadel."

I cringed like she'd bitten me on the neck with her vamp teeth. "You mean when you made a false arrest."

Adira turned to face me. "I made the proper call." She pulled a pair of iron handcuffs from inside her short, leather jacket. They looked just like the ones she'd put on me before. "Looks like I'm about to make another."

Magic pulsed, fed by my anger. I trembled with it. I didn't even have to pull on the elements. My emotions channeled them on their own, charging them to full. My hair shifted in a breeze that touched only me, and a crapload of power filled my chi. If she took a step toward me, I was going to blast her into vampire pieces.

"Come on then," I challenged, my voice so hard I barely recognized it. "Come and get me. I dare you, fang bitch."

Ronin smacked his thigh and laughed. "Good one."

The tension in the room escalated.

Adira had gone deathly still, gathering intent and power about her as she readied herself to come at me. Her beautiful face was as savage and pale as it was hollow, hard, and unyielding.

If I killed her, that would make me a murderer. Yeah, not that smart. How could I help Ruth if we were roomies at Grimway Citadel?

Ley lines.

It was so simple I almost burst out laughing. Almost.

Apart from my aunts, no one knew how I could bend the ley lines with my will. Right now, all I had to do was reach out and grab one to pull myself, the book, and my friends away from here. No doubt it would make us guilty if we ran, but I'd figure out the logistics later.

There was no way in hell she was going to put those on me.

"Tessa is right," announced Marcus, and I turned my eyes on him surprised, but he was looking at Ronin. "Ronin is the owner of the building. Here in Hollow Cove, that's a free pass. As far as I'm concerned, he's not breaking any laws."

"They were sneaking into a place of business in the middle of the night in the dark," said Adira. "Where I'm from, that's what we call criminals."

A hard expression flickered across Marcus's face. "You're not from here." His shoulders tensed. "And I'm the chief. If Ronin feels like showing his lady friends a good time in *his* building after working hours, that's his call. No harm done."

Lady friends?

A cruel smile curved the corners of her mouth. "If that's true, why did he set off the silent alarm? I'll tell you. It's because he didn't know there was one. For all we know, he was trying to steal something in Gilbert's safe."

Ronin howled in laughter, a tad over the top. "There's nothing in that safe worth

253

stealing," he snorted. "Trust me. The only thing that's worth some money in here is his collection of vintage *Playboys*."

"Shut up, Ronin," I hissed. "Not helping."

Ronin lost his smile. "Right. My bad."

Marcus's expression went hard as he eyed the vampires. "This is my town," said the chief, an underlying threat in his voice. "You're not acting chief anymore. And honestly," he added, "I don't care what you say. You don't belong here."

"Tessa Davenport has a penchant for breaking the law," expressed Adira, her focus on me again. "I've asked around. It's a well-known fact."

"Oh, please. Pack of lies," I voiced, knowing full well it was the truth. *Oops.*

Marcus stepped up to Adira until they were face to face. "I'm the law here, and I say they didn't break any."

Adira leaned forward, her green eyes now black. Damn. She'd vamped out.

"Is that so?" she hissed. She made to step toward me, but Marcus blocked her way.

Marcus watched her for a long moment. "Tessa. Ronin. Iris. Please leave the building. You're not under any charges. You're all free to go."

I stared at my friends' open mouths. Marcus was letting us go? We all knew we were breaking all kinds of laws, but he was letting us go. Why?

Emotions welled in me, and the winning one was guilt. But it was obvious Marcus wanted nothing to do with me. Yes, he was letting us go, but I was willing to bet it had more to do with Adira than me—his way of showing her who was boss.

My eyes flicked to the book at my feet.

"Get out," said Marcus, his voice dangerously low.

"Aye, aye, captain," said Ronin, and he gave Marcus an army salute. "You heard the man. Let's go, my beautiful *lady friends*."

Ronin hooked his arms through mine and Iris's. Before I could attempt snatching the book without anyone seeing, he steered us away from the two chiefs and ushered us out of the office, past the two vamps who were getting an eyeful from Cameron and Jeff, and out the front doors of Gilbert's store.

Ronin let us go when we reached the sidewalk. "Man, I don't know about you guys, but I need a drink."

"I really hate Adira," said Iris, looking angrier than I'd ever seen her. "I was just about to give her chlamydia."

I burst out laughing loudly from the pent-up stress. It felt amazing.

"God, I love you." Ronin pulled Iris against his chest and kissed her. "Love it when you talk STDs." Iris giggled and kissed him back fiercely.

My relief was short-lived. I'd lost the only proof that could get Ruth off the hook for murder.

The sound of a door shutting had my gaze flicker to the front of Gilbert's store. I clenched my jaw as I watched Adira and her cronies walking away. She never once looked in our direction as she and her vamp posse team disappeared down Shifter Lane with Marcus watching them leave.

I tried to shake off my discomfort as I stared at the wereape who'd probably broken some chief's code by letting us go.

As though he'd heard me, he turned, and our eyes met. His gray gaze seemed to pierce a hole through my soul. I felt like I'd been hit on the head with a shovel.

And when he started my way, I felt like I'd been hit in the head by *two* shovels.

Vertigo hit me. Had I been wrong? Had he lied to Adira just to spite her and was indeed going to arrest us?

He stopped silently when he was facing me. My head was going a million miles an hour. I tried to read him, but his face was a careful, an expressionless mask.

Marcus reached inside his coat and pulled out a familiar red book. "Here. You forgot this."

Ronin cursed and I caught a glimpse of Iris pinching his butt. Weird.

I took Gilbert's book in my hand, though my lips were unable to form any words as so many questions flooded my brain at the same time.

"Thanks," I said, looking up into those beautiful gray eyes.

"Don't mention it." Marcus watched me for another moment, and then he turned and walked away.

I watched him slip into the shadows between the nearest building and vanish from sight, leaving me confused and feeling like the biggest ass on the planet.

CHAPTER
24

Estelle Watch and Michael Blackwood.

I had two names, which meant I was two names closer to finding out who the real murderer was. And I was certain one of these people had poisoned and killed Bernard the baker. Hell, I'd bet my life on it.

Too bad I was stuck doing my third witch trial.

Today was December 22, and I was back in Montevalley Castle, in the theater where I'd sat on my very first day of the Merlin trials. I took a seat in the back, perhaps even the same seat, and as far away as possible from the stage at the end of the room.

Though this was the same theater, glancing around now, it was a far cry from the ninety-six witches who'd sat in those seats on October 31.

Now, we were only eighteen, including me and Willis.

My eyes moved to the mess of brown hair and round eyes behind a pair of glasses that were way too big for him and might have been in style back in the eighties. A strange, mothball smell was rolling off of him. Yes, Willis was an oddball, but I liked him.

Only four minutes ago, when my butt had barely made contact with my seat, Willis had called out my name and hurried to grab the one next to me, as though it were the only available seat left in the theater. Looking around, Willis and I were the only ones sitting next to one another. In fact, all sixteen other witches were sitting as far away from one another as possible. They were avoiding each other like the plague. Yet, they kept throwing covert glances filled with disdain and hate our way.

I let out a breath. That was way too much emotion for me. At least Willis and I were on the same page. Trial besties. They could go on hating each other for all I cared. What did it matter anyway? We'd all made it this far. We all deserved to be here. What was their problem?

I had no idea what the third trial would entail. All I knew was that: one, it was the last trial; and two, it was the hardest trial yet.

Excellent.

My eyes scanned the stage. Greta wasn't here yet. No one was, except for the two witches standing at the roped-off section at the far right of the stage, who I'd presumed worked at the castle. They'd ushered us inside the theater when we'd first arrived and now stood in the shadows, where they could overlook the crowd.

The longer we waited, the worse I felt. Glancing at the heads of the other witches, we were all literally squirming in our seats, awaiting our fate.

I had a feeling Greta was doing that on purpose. She was probably hiding behind a curtain or a door, enjoying the show and sneering at us.

"What do you think the third trial's gonna be?" asked Willis, his voice low and shaking so much I barely understood him.

"No idea," I answered, my gaze on the stage. "Harder than the other two. Worse. A lot worse."

Willis nodded. "Okay. Okay." He rubbed his hands along his thighs. "You can do this, Willis," he told himself, and I felt a tiny pang in my heart. "You've got this. You've made it this far… I have faith in you. You're the man. *You* are awesome."

"*You* are weird," I snorted.

The middle-aged witch beamed. "Better to be weird and unique, than to try being something you're not."

"Amen."

"I don't know how you did it," said Willis. "How you pulled me into that ley line? But thank you, all the same. I wouldn't have been able to do it without you." He hesitated. "How *did* you do it?"

"You mean, pulling you in there with me? I'm not exactly sure," I told him. "And that's the honest truth." I hadn't had the time to think about it much. I'd been too busy trying to figure out who those two people were who'd bought the black belladonna.

"Willis." I waited for the witch to look at me. "You would have been fine without me. If those witches had played fair, you wouldn't have needed my help," I said, remembering the blood in his ears and nose with the bloody gash at the back of his head. Willis would have had a real shot at defeating Silas if he hadn't been suffering from what I suspected was a severe head trauma. I cast my gaze around the witches, wondering which one of these bastards had done that to Willis.

"They hit me too," I told him.

"But you got up. I was down, Tessa. I was the one beaten."

"But you weren't beaten," I said. "After what they pulled? They don't even deserve to be here. But you and me? We do. We're the underdogs. And they're jealous that we have a shot at winning this."

Willis looked down. "Well. We'll see. My Wilma doesn't want me to give up."

"Wilma?" *No way. Willis and Wilma?*

Willis looked back at me and smiled. "My wife. I'm doing this for her, you know." He moved his eyes back to the front stage. "She believes in me. I don't know why, but she does. I've already failed the Merlin witch trials twelve times. I've never been this close to winning before. Never even got past the second trial. I want this, Tessa. I want to win this for Wilma. She's my everything. You know?"

Not really. I patted his shoulder. "You will." My heart clenched at how he spoke of his wife. There was so much love there, and it made me jealous. I wanted a Wilma too—well, a Marcus.

Marcus…

My heart shattered into tiny pieces just as my phone *beeped*. I glanced down at it in my hand. It was a text from Ronin.

Ronin: *I said I'd give you an update. Here it is. Nothing. We're stalking Facebook but still can't find anyone by the names of Estelle Watch or*

Michael Blackwood. Do you want me to ask Gilbert?

Damn. The last thing I needed right now was for that little shifter owl to start a fuss about us having those names. He'd figure out we broke into his store, and then he'd have a fit. Next, he'd figure out his precious book of exotic herbs was missing—another fit—and then he'd blab. Estelle and Michael would hear about it, and they would take off. And that would be the end of that.

We had proof that they bought the black belladonna. Next, we needed a motive, the drive that propelled them to commit murder and poison Bernard the baker.

Me: *No. DO NOT TELL GILBERT!!! Sorry about the caps. Please keep looking.*

Ronin: *Yes, ma'am.*

Ronin: *Iris here. U doing ok?*

Me: *Yes. Tell you all about it when I get home.*

Ronin: *K*

"It's starting," whispered Willis and I switched my phone to vibrate mode and shoved it in the bag on my lap.

From the right, roped-off section, Greta strutted her way to the middle of the stage across from us, followed by Marina and Silas who stopped and stood a few paces behind her. Each had a stack of white envelopes hanging in their hands.

Greta walked like a disciplined businesswoman. She wore a white robe trimmed with gold cloth. The light from above shone down on her nearly bald head. Her eyes were no less calculating, but there was an edge of something there that I recognized—cruelty. The love of power, to the exclusion of the well-being of one's fellow beings.

Willis shifted next to me. There was a general murmur of restlessness from the witches in the room. My own nerves were shot. My entire body shook with them. I felt like I was about to shoot off from my chair to the ceiling like a cartoon character.

"Welcome," she said finally, "to the final Merlin witch trial." Her voice resonated around the theater. "Ninety-six of you began this journey," she continued. "And only eighteen of you are left. I expect only half of this group will graduate with their Merlin license. Perhaps less." She delivered that last while giving me a pointed look, making sure anyone in the room who hadn't noticed me would now.

I felt my face heat up.

Fan-freaking-tastic.

Gasps and low murmurs did another run around the theater. The witches in attendance all muttered and grumbled their disapproval. Obviously, like me, none of them intended to fail. We were here to pass. To get our licenses.

264

And if the last two trials weren't evidence enough of what they were willing to do to each other, this third trial was going to be hell.

Greta stared at me for another long moment with animosity and I swear a flicker of curiosity behind her eyes. A-ha. Silas had told her about my using the ley lines in the second trial. Either she was curious about them, or she was wondering if I should be disqualified. I was here. Wasn't I? Which meant the old witch was curious about my ability. My aunts had said it was unique. Maybe they'd been right. Maybe no other witch could bend the ley lines. *Yay me.*

"Why is she looking at me?" whispered Willis, his eyes wide with panic as he slipped slowly down in his seat until he was practically on the floor. "She thinks I'm going to fail!"

"Shhh," I told him, pulling him back up by his shirt. "She's looking at me. Not you. Our hatred goes wa-a-a-y back." Like a few generations back.

So, she thought I was going to fail. If she thought I would shrink away like Willis, she was wrong. It just made me that much more willing to succeed.

Greta let silence fall afterward and I looked to Silas and Marina whose heads were bent together, deep in conversation. And by the smiles on their faces, I had to infer they were probably placing bets on which one of us was going to make it.

Greta regarded us with passionless, distant features. "You've passed the first two trials and now you are here. You think you're something special. Don't you? Well, you're not."

"Always liked her," I murmured, seeing Willis slip down again from the corner of my eye. "Does wonders for our egos."

"Don't be fooled," continued Greta, her eyes scanning the rows of seats. "Being a Merlin not only means you need to be able to use your magic abilities, but you need to use your brain. Your investigative skills need to shine. You can excel in your magic, but it means nothing if you can't use your brain." She raised her brows and enunciated loudly, "Magical Enforcement Response League *Intelligence* Network. That's what a Merlin is. You need to become analysts. Intelligence analysts. You need to prove to me that you're capable of solving a case."

A rush of whispers shot through the auditorium.

Willis jerked up in his seat. "Did she just say case?" He pushed his glasses up the bridge of his nose with his finger, looking excited for the first time since he sat down.

"She did," I answered, tense, edgy, and eager all at the same time. I leaned forward in my seat.

Pulse racing, I stared at Greta as the old witch moved her gaze along the witches. Excitement rushed through me in waves. I could do this. I could solve a case. Right?

Greta cleared her throat. "There are eighteen cases, one for each of you," she instructed. "Each case is specifically designed for you and you alone. If you need assistance from friends or family, you may do so. Or you can choose to work alone. It's up to you. You need to collect data, make assessments, investigate your crime scene... your case. Once you have collected all your evidence," she said, her gaze on us again, "you will come here and present your case to me."

My lips parted. So, Greta was playing judge, jury, and executioner? Why was I not surprised?

"If you don't solve your case in the designated amount of time..." She paused. "You will fail." Again, her eyes pinned me, and I had to resist the urge not to flinch. "Listen up, witches. It's simple. Solve your case and you will become the next Merlins. Fail... well... better luck next time."

Willis gave a little whimper and I reached out and patted his head like I would a puppy.

"Now, when I call your name, please come up to the stage to get your assigned case," ordered the old witch. Greta turned and motioned for Silas and Marina to come forward. They gave her the stack of envelopes they were holding and stepped back.

The old witch glanced down at the first envelope and called, "Craig Allen."

A twenty-something witch with a shaved head and latte-colored skin stood up and jogged his way to the platform to get his envelope.

The pulsing of adrenaline hurt my head, and I barely heard the other names she called as, one by one, witches in the theater stood. Their movements were fast with barely controlled excitement as they milled together and walked up to the stage to get their envelope, their case.

"That's me!" exclaimed Willis as he tripped, pushed himself up, made it out of our row, and of course, tripped on the steps on his way up the stage. My eyes were glued to him as he took his envelope and moved away, clutching it as though his wife's life depended on it. He took three steps, ripped it open, read what it said, and gave me a thumbs up.

I released a shaky breath.

"Tessa Davenport."

Somewhere in my frazzled brain, I heard my name. I was last. Who knew why? Clearly, it wasn't alphabetical. Maybe it was by merit. Willis and I both were last to make the second trial.

Numb, I moved out of my row and walked down the aisle to the platform. I barely registered my legs moving, but they did.

I faced Greta. We stared at each other for a moment. Her face was empty of emotion, but her eyes were hard. I flicked my gaze down to the last white envelope in her gnarled fingers. Without uttering a single word, Greta handed me the envelope.

I snatched it up, fingers trembling, as I stared at the simple white envelope with the name TESSA DAVENPORT written in elegant black letters.

I moved down the platform to a space away from the others. I did not want anyone to see me while I opened my envelope, just in case it was bad. I would do badly alone, thank you very much.

With my heart jackhammering in my ears, I ripped open the envelope with shaking fingers and began to read. There was just one sentence, one tiny sentence on the entire piece of eight-by-eleven paper. Yet I had to read it over twice.

You have until midnight tonight to prove Ruth Davenport's innocence.

Holy hell. She'd given me Ruth's case.

CHAPTER
25

I had less than sixteen hours to solve my aunt's case and present it to Greta.

Yeah, no pressure.

My Aunt Ruth had already been found guilty by the Gray Council. She'd been tried, convicted, and was going to see the inside of the witch prison tomorrow morning.

Yet Greta had given me a slip of paper that suggested otherwise. At least, *if* by a miracle I could prove her innocence. I believed there was still a chance to dismiss the charges. The question was *why* did Greta?

Did she hate my family so much that her desire to fail me amounted to her giving me a case that couldn't be solved? Is that what she hoped? Was she that evil and devious? Or was there another reason?

My mind was flaring with questions as I jumped the ley line home. Right now, it didn't matter why she'd done it. I had planned on solving it on my own anyway—with the help of my family and friends, of course.

And I was going to need all the help I could get.

"*Estelle Watch and Michael Blackwood*," read Dolores, her finger on Gilbert's red book that rested in the middle of the kitchen table. She pursed her lips. "Never heard of them. Beverly?"

Beverly cocked her head, her coffee mug wrapped in her delicate fingers. "Never heard of Estelle Watch. And I'm afraid Michael Blackwood doesn't ring any bells either."

"You sure?" pressed Dolores. "I thought you knew all the males here in Hollow Cove. Married or single."

A smile curled over Beverly's lips. "Why, yes, Dolores. Forgive me, but my memory's not like it used to be. I'll have a look in my book."

"Does that include the names of those you've had sex with?" asked Ronin, his face transforming into a goofy grin.

Beverly flashed him a smile. "Maybe."

"Nice." The half-vampire moved next to Dolores and started snapping pictures with his phone as he turned the pages of Gilbert's book. He caught me staring and said, "Leverage."

I did not want to know.

Beverly pushed her chair back and stood. "I'll see if Ruth recognizes those names. She might." Beverly lost some of her smile at the mention of her sister.

"Good. That's a good idea." Dolores's face went blank as she stared at Ronin flipping through the pages and snapped more pictures.

Ruth had been the first person I'd gone to see as I walked through the door at Davenport House. I'd run upstairs to tell her the news that I'd be officially working on her case—sort of— but my aunt didn't even acknowledge my presence. She sat at the edge of her bed staring at the floor as though she didn't see me and couldn't hear me.

It had freaked me out. I didn't recognize her like this. Gone was her bubbly charming personality, replaced by a morbid, lost soul. I wanted my aunt back, and the only way I was going to get that was to solve this case—my way.

From my pocket, I yanked out the folded piece of paper and flattened it on the table. "Why do you think Greta would assign me this? She knows Ruth's already been tried by the Gray Council. I don't get it. What am I missing here?"

Dolores moved to stand next to me, her eyes on the piece of paper. "I don't know, Tessa. She's angry with us. Not with you."

"No, I'm pretty sure she hates my guts too."

"Well, she shouldn't. *We* made you a Merlin."

"And she took it away." Angrily, I grabbed the piece of paper, folded it again, and stuffed it back in my jeans pocket.

Dolores watched me for a few seconds without a word. "I'll have a word with Gilbert," she declared suddenly. She looked at me. "He'll tell me who these people are and where to find them."

"And if he doesn't?" asked Beverly, as she set her coffee mug in the kitchen sink. "You know how he can be. Useless little rat. I should show him to the basement."

The idea of Davenport House giving Gilbert a lobotomy didn't sound so bad.

"And you know how *I* can be," said the tall witch. "I'll pluck the feathers off that owl if I have to. I don't care. This is Ruth's life we're talking about. Not his overpriced bags of flour and table salt."

"His table salt tastes like vinegar," said Iris as she entered the kitchen with Dana tucked under her arm. "My theory is that he takes the leftovers from the restaurant across the street — Garden of Eden — repackages it and sells it."

273

She pulled out a chair from the kitchen table and sat, securing Dana on her lap.

I stared at Iris for a moment. "If you're right, makes me wonder what else he reuses and repackages."

Ronin shook his head. "If you say condoms, I'm going to hurl."

I pursed my lips. "I didn't say anything, you big baby," I told him, making Iris laugh.

Dolores moved to the wooden peg rack on the wall, put on her long gray wool coat, and wrapped a scarf around her neck. "I'll be back as soon as I can."

"Please don't murder anyone," I said, letting go of the breath I was holding. "I can't lose another aunt."

Dolores stared at me and then made for the back door. "Can't make any promises," she said, as the back door thumped shut behind her.

I frowned at the door. "Damn it."

"You think she'll hurt him?" asked Ronin.

"I'd hurt him," interjected Iris.

I shook my head. "I don't know. Maybe? She's under a lot of stress. The guy's a little anal."

Iris looked at me expectantly. "What do we do now?"

My eyes moved between my friends. "Well, I can't just sit here and wait for Dolores who might or might not have any information to give. This is my case." I stared down at Gilbert's book. "Who besides Gilbert has a list of all the people in this town?"

"The town clerk," said Ronin.

Hope blossomed in my chest. "Excellent. This is good. Why do you look like you just ate raw liver?"

"Because Gilbert's the town clerk," he answered.

My hope bubble burst and I hid my face with my hands. "Great. I'm so screwed. There *has* to be someone else. Someone who would keep tabs on—" My hands fell from my face. "Marcus would know," I said. My stomach clenched at the mention of his name. I remembered him telling me how he had a list of all the visiting paranormals when Hollow Cove had hosted the Night Festival. I was certain he had a list of everyone in this town. "We could ask him."

"No. *You* should ask him," said Iris. "If you tell him why, I'm sure he'll be willing to help."

"I'm with Iris, Tess," agreed Ronin as he slipped his phone in his pocket. "*You* need to do this."

"I don't think that's such a good idea," I told them, my stomach playing tug-of-war with my intestines at the thought of speaking to Marcus. "Not after what I did. I was a total jerk to him. I doubt he would want to speak to me.

Probably will slam the door in my face. That's what I would do if I were him." I totally deserved that.

"You're *not* him." Iris exhaled, looking at me like I was a five-year-old kid who didn't understand grown-up conversation. "He gave you this book. Didn't he?" she said, gesturing at Gilbert's red book. "He didn't have to, but he did. And he did it because he cares. He cares about Ruth, and he cares about you. We all lose our tempers. No one's perfect."

"Speak for yourself," said Ronin, hooking his thumbs at himself. "Ten out of ten right here, baby."

Iris did have a point. Marcus didn't have to give me the book, but he did. That had to mean something.

"You're right." I had grown some serious lady balls over the past weeks. I had to own up to my mistakes. I had to deal with what I'd done. I had to face it. There was no going back, only jumping forward.

Part of the problem was I didn't want to admit to myself that I'd probably ruined my chances with a wonderful man. Men that good, that honest, were practically an endangered species. And I'd screwed it up.

My love life was inconsequential at the moment. None of it would matter if I didn't help Ruth.

And to save Ruth, I knew what I had to do. I had to ask the man I'd been horrible to for help.

It was going to be awesome.

CHAPTER
26

I was running.

My boots slipped on the uneven sidewalk covered in a thin layer of wet snow as I ran down Stardust Drive. The searing pain in my thighs, the cramp in my side, and the reminder that time was running out were all nothing compared to the pain Ruth would suffer if I didn't do this.

This is not about me, I reminded myself. *This is about Ruth.*

The sun was right above me, peeking through clouds as it made the day a little warmer. I splashed through a puddle, too anxious to care if my ankles got wet.

Crossing Shifter Lane at a jog, I hit the sidewalk and rushed to the Hollow Cove Security Agency building.

The rattle of a glass door opening was my only warning, and I jerked back just as Marcus came rushing through, nearly smashing the door in my face.

"Tessa," he called out, looking great in his casual jeans and bomber-style winter jacket over a black T-shirt.

"Hey." I stepped back, slipped on some wet snow, and caught myself before I went sprawling on the wet sidewalk. Heat rushed to my face as I righted myself. "Hey… you…" I added awkwardly, feeling a sharp pain on the left side of my lower back, knowing I probably twisted something while I attempted to stop my fall. "I was just coming to see you."

Marcus raised his brows, looking genuinely surprised. "You were?"

"Yes." I nodded to myself like an idiot. God, why was this so hard? "Um… Hi," I said, giving him a wave. I *waved* at him? I was going mad.

"Hi," answered Marcus with a smile that was damn near hypnotizing.

"That should be illegal," I blurted, realizing too late that I'd spoken my thoughts out loud.

Marcus frowned. "What should?"

"Mmmm. Nothing." I was a stammering, blabbering idiot. "Uh—you look great. Really great. Thank you." *Thank you?*

Marcus laughed softly. "No, thank *you*." He laughed again. The chief thought I was hilarious.

Yup, the jumping of the ley lines was seriously affecting my conversation skills. They were taking a colossal hit.

We stood in an awkward silence for a while, my heart making music in my ears in the swirl of conflicting feelings while my entire body thrummed with heat that had nothing to do with my warm, down jacket.

"Did the book help?" asked Marcus, finally, his tone caring and soft, and I wanted to wrap myself in it.

"Yes," I said, feeling a little more relaxed that he didn't look or sound angry. I took that as a good sign. "It's why I'm here."

A frown rippled over Marcus's features. "Is it Gilbert? Does he know? Did he say something to you?"

"No, he doesn't know about the book. Well, I don't think he does. Not yet, at least. But I'm here about the names we found," I said speaking fast. "Estelle Watch and Michael Blackwood. These were the only two names who bought the black belladonna from Gilbert's store. Ruth's name's not even in the book. She didn't buy any. The Gray Council doesn't care. They think she could just have easily bought some at another store. But Ruth didn't. And I *know* one of these people killed Bernard. I just need the proof to solve my case."

"Your case?"

I met his gaze. "Long story. But it's my third witch trial," I added with a laugh. "It's absolutely insane. But I have until midnight tonight to solve Ruth's case."

Marcus watched me. "Got it."

I sighed. "So, do you have a list or do you recognize these names?"

"Just a sec." Marcus pulled out his phone and started scrolling through it. "I can remotely access my computer with my phone. I keep the same records as the town clerk in the system."

"Gotta love modern technology." I anxiously held my breath and watched Marcus's fingers tap his phone while I was tapping with my left foot. "And? Anything? You got something?"

"Well," said the chief, still staring at his phone. "I can't find Estelle Watch on the list, but it says here that Michael Blackwood is dead."

"Dead? When?"

Marcus tapped his finger once on the screen of his phone. "September sixteenth."

I fixed my eyes on his. "That was before Bernard was found dead." My blood pressure spiked. "It means Estelle Watch killed Bernard."

And she was going down…

"Maybe." Marcus slipped his phone back inside his jacket pocket. "But there's no record of her here." He narrowed his eyes in thought.

"What? What is it?"

He looked at me and shook his head. "It's weird. But that name—Estelle Watch—I know I've heard it before. I just can't remember where."

I let out a long sigh through my nose. "They say women killers use poison. Right?"

"Sometimes."

"Estelle came into his store, and when he wasn't looking, she dumped the black belladonna into the vial that contained Ruth's gingerweed," I said, seeing the scene unfold in my mind. "That way, it was hidden. He'd never smell it either, even if he tried, not with the strong ginger scent."

"It's a possibility," said the chief. "But why would she do that?"

Right. "No idea."

"Before we can make any kind of assumptions…"

"Theories."

"Theories," said Marcus with a smile. "We still need to find her. And according to my list, she doesn't live here in Hollow Cove."

"Could she be from a neighboring town? Black belladonna isn't your regular healing herb. It's dangerous. It isn't easy to come by. Maybe she drove from out of town?" It was a stretch, but I was desperate, and I was running out of time.

"I'll have Grace go through the list again. She's really good at finding people."

"Bet she'll love that." Especially if she knew it was coming from me. I looked over his shoulder at the shadows inside the building. "Speaking of people who despise me... where's Adira?" I searched for the sexy redheaded vamp, thinking of ways to give her chlamydia or a severe case of acne.

"Gone."

"Gone like gone for the day to get her back waxed? Or like *gone*, gone?"

"I made the arrangements to escort Ruth myself tomorrow." A shadow crossed Marcus's features. "I thought it would be better for her to be with someone she knows. Someone who cares about her." His eyes met mine, his jaw clenching. "I know you think I don't care about Ruth, but I do."

Ah, hell. I raised my hand. "No—I mean— yes, I know you care." I was a stammering idiot once again. "What I mean to say is, I *know* you care. And I'm sorry about what I said. I was rash, impulsive, a total jerk." There, giant lady balls for an apology. "I was an asshole. You didn't deserve that. I'm sorry."

Marcus smiled at me, a smile that was both caring and at the same time a little wicked. That kind of smile would have had me ripping off my clothes in the middle of winter on a sidewalk. It was *that* dang hot.

"Don't apologize," soothed Marcus. "I get it. What's happening to Ruth is unimaginable. Tempers are flaring. It's understandable." His voice was so dreamily and calming, it sent a shiver through me.

Crap. He was soooo nice and he genuinely cared about Ruth. He watched me, his eyes filled with a fervent, unashamed desire. And when they flicked to my lips, a pulse thundered to my core.

Don't do it, I told myself, straining not to look at his full, kissable lips —

Shit, I did it.

Pulling my eyes away from ground zero, I willed myself to take a step back, but my legs seemed to be cemented to the sidewalk. Oh dear. I could hear my heartbeat in the silence, as the chief kept watching me, unabashed, with a half-smile, clearly enjoying whatever display my face and body were doing at the moment.

He stood there, all hot and sexy as hell, looking at me with those damn pretty gray eyes, that damn sensual body, and those damn illegal lips. I didn't even realize what I was doing before it was too late, before I felt my feet leave solid ground—

I jumped him.

Not in the exact sense, but I did jump his lips.

Crushing my body against his, I reached out, grabbed the back of his head, and pulled him to me.

Yup, I had some serious lady balls today. Yay balls!

His lips were soft with a moist warmth despite the cold. My breath came and went in a pant and a soft sound of real bliss escaped me. He opened his mouth, and my tongue found the smoothness of his.

He let out a sound, part growl, part moan, adding to my fervor. He wrapped his strong hands around me, pulling me harder into him. I moved my tongue around his, stopping only to nibble at his lips.

Yup, his damn mouth and tongue catapulted me past my sensibilities and into a reckless crazy woman.

I pulled away, shocked at my own impulsiveness. "Oh, my god. I can't believe I just assaulted your mouth," I said, my lips still throbbing with the warmth of his lips.

Desire flashed in his gray eyes that made me tingle inside. "I'm not. You can assault my mouth anytime," he added smugly.

I met his eyes—his faultless gray eyes—studying them with the breathless understanding that I didn't know what was going to happen between us but praying something would.

But it would have to wait…

"Ruth…" I said, feeling a sudden crushing weight, as an image of my aunt's gaunt face flickered in my mind's eye.

Marcus gave a nod of his head. "I know."

I swallowed hard and took a step back. "I have to go."

"I know."

"I have phone calls to make, some social media stalking," I said and then realized I shouldn't be saying that to the chief. I also wanted to see if Dolores was back with a plucked owl. Maybe she had the scoop on Estelle Watch or maybe not. "Will you call me if you find out anything about Estelle Watch?"

Marcus's eyes were bright. "I will."

I turned around and walked back up Shifter Lane, acutely aware that Marcus was watching me walk away. He was most probably staring at my ass, which would have made me self-conscious on any other day, but today I had lady balls.

And a name. *Estelle Watch.*

Time to put on my Merlin cap. Time to work my investigative skills like never before.

Because my midnight deadline was coming up fast.

CHAPTER
27

What is that saying again? Time flies when you're having fun?

Nope.

Time also flies when you're under extreme duress and trying to find a ghost.

That's right. Estelle Watch was a ghost. Not in the literal sense, but more in the figurative can't-find-evidence-that-she-exists kind of way.

After spending hours on the phone, calling every paranormal town in a day's driving distance, and stalking social media until my fingers had cramped up, I hadn't found a single thing on Estelle Watch. Nothing. No employment records, no Facebook account, or any other social media presence.

It was as though she never existed, hence my term ghost.

The clock on my phone said 11:49 p.m. and we weren't any closer to finding out who Estelle Watch was.

Thinking that perhaps Gilbert had misheard her surname—he was coming along in years—I'd spent hours looking under different last names that started with the letter W like Estelle Watson, Estelle Ward, Estell Wallace, Estelle Wagner, and Estelle Walker. But that was a bust too.

Maybe I'd been looking at this wrong the entire time. Maybe I'd run out of options. Maybe I'd already failed, but I was too stubborn to admit it.

Davenport House's kitchen had become Research Central for my case. Books and boxes of books lined the walls and covered most of the kitchen floor. Binders, files, and folders covered every inch of counter space. A half-empty pizza box lay on the kitchen island above file folders and documents along with boxes of Chinese takeout.

The kitchen table, my workspace, looked as though someone had a food fight but with papers instead of actual food. Topped with so many books, files, notebooks, and slices of half-eaten pizza, it had gained an extra five inches in height.

Ronin and I sat across from each other at the kitchen table, fingers typing away on our laptops while Iris mumbled some dark magic incantations as she stood over her small boiling cauldron on the stove.

The smell coming from her cauldron made me gag. It was the musty, moldy smell of old dirty socks mixed with pond scum as well as a few traces of something spicier, maybe some kind of incense. My stomach rolled uncomfortably, and the rising sense of dark energy didn't help me keep it calm.

I didn't care what Dark magic Iris was brewing. If it could bring us Estelle Watch, she could do conjure up an army of the dead if she wanted, even throw a few demons in the mix if she thought that would help. Right now, I was desperate.

As I typed, I could hear the constant sobbing from upstairs. Dolores and Beverly had been crying for hours, a heart-wrenching, desperate melody that caused me physical pain.

Dolores, up until two hours ago, had been helping us search for Estelle since this afternoon.

"What a waste of my time," she'd shouted as she burst through the kitchen's back door about an hour after I had returned from my encounter with Marcus.

I'd looked up from my laptop. "Gilbert wouldn't talk?"

Dolores had flung off her coat, purse, and scarf as she came in. They floated to the wooden peg rack and all hung themselves neatly as though an invisible butler had caught them and hung them for her. "He talked," she'd said. "The little owl had lots to say, all right. But nothing on Estelle."

"Couldn't you spell him with a truth charm or something?"

Dolores had raised a brow. "Who do you think I am? Of course, I *spelled* him. But he simply *didn't* remember who those people were. Nothing. He drew a blank. So, I had him go to his computer and go over the list of all registered residents of Hollow Cove. I thought that might jog his memory. Unfortunately, Michael Blackwood—"

"Is dead," I had said and quickly told her about my run-in with the chief.

"I'm glad that horrid redhead vampire is gone," Dolores had said and seated herself at the table. "But it doesn't help Ruth. Well, if there's a record of Estelle Watch in the witch community—because I have a feeling she's a witch—they'll know of her." She stood up and said, "I have some phone calls to make."

She'd been at it for seven hours straight. And then two hours ago… she just… stopped.

Another sob came from upstairs, a heart-wrenching one that had my eyes burn. If a heart could literally break into pieces, mine just did. I could almost feel the pieces fall to the bottom of my stomach. A tear escaped from my eye, and I could feel it trace down the length of my cheek all the way to my chin.

"Tess," said Ronin suddenly, drawing my attention to him, his voice loud in the silent kitchen. "Maybe we should—"

"I'm not giving up," I growled, my voice high and filled with emotions. I brushed my tear from my chin. This wasn't the time to cry. I wasn't giving up.

Ronin let out a breath. "I was going to say… let's try something else. We've been through every possible lead to find this Estelle Watch. She doesn't exist. Not where we're looking. And not with the resources we have."

"She exists enough to sign her damn name in Gilbert's book," I shot back. "She's real." I felt Iris's eyes on me, but I kept my attention on Ronin even with the stab of guilt I felt at the look on his face. "Sorry. I'm just… I'm just frustrated is all."

"No worries," said the half-vampire. "You can abuse me all you want. That's what friends are for. But, Tess? You have to accept that maybe this Estelle is a dead end."

I met his gaze. "Can't. It's the only name I've got." I leaned back in my chair, my lower back throbbing as I suffered from numbbutt from sitting most of the day and night. "I've got nothing else to go on… I'm running out of ideas… and I'm running out of time."

The truth was, I didn't want to admit that Ronin might be right. Because if he was, it meant all of this, all this hard work, had been for nothing. If Estelle Watch was a dead end, who had poisoned Bernard?

"Estelle Watch," recited Iris, as though reading my mind, and I looked over to see her drop a small piece of paper with blue-pen lettering into her cauldron for the fifth time. She'd been at her Dark locator spell for hours. With only a name and nothing tangible—like the person's toothbrush, an article of clothing, even just something that was owned by a person, provided it had their DNA on it—the odds of it working were slim. They were practically nonexistent.

And there was still the artifact you needed to use like a compass of sorts to show the way. Or a map, like the way I'd found Marcus. Still, all that was useless if you didn't have a part of the person in question's aura. But I was betting on a miracle and Iris's skills as a Dark witch.

Iris leaned over her pot and chanted, "Potestatem daemonium super ortum," channeling her energy from the tiny demon gremlin she'd summoned. Did I forget to mention that?

Gigi, the demon's name, was the size of a cat with bright orange fur and large batlike ears, purple tiny horns, a short tail, a mouth filled with fish-like teeth, and abnormally large black eyes. Her four limbs ended with five taloned fingers. She was trapped in a summoning circle, her jailor, in the middle of the kitchen island. She wore a frown on her face. At the moment, Gigi was giving us the finger with both hands.

Once Iris's spell was completed, Gigi would then find Estelle Watch, kind of like a search and rescue dog, our demon GPS.

Iris continued to chant, and Gigi's fur turned yellow and then white. The demon's face was wrinkled in hatred, and I had a feeling Iris had called upon Gigi's powers more than once.

Gigi caught me staring and flipped me off again. I was starting to like this tiny demon.

The kitchen lights flickered off and on again as power soared through the room. Gigi's eyes were now closed, and her fur kept switching from orange to white, and then it turned blue.

"Veni ad nos et apud quem vocant! Veni ad nos, et habitatores hic!" cried Iris.

I felt the energy from Gigi's power flow around us like a breeze, settling around the kitchen, over the pots, the books, the piles of paper, and into every tile and cabinet until the entire area was immersed in the spell along with me and Ronin.

And then the power settled. I looked over at Gigi. Her fur was back to its orange color. "Ha'ak du rig'titu," she hissed in some guttural language I'd never heard before. And then, of course, she flipped off Iris.

But Iris never looked at the tiny demon. Her eyes were on her cauldron.

"And?" I asked, not too hopeful by the look of defeat on Iris's face.

Iris looked over at me, her bloodshot eyes a mess. "Don't worry. I'm going to do it again."

Gigi let out a cry. "Witch! Hate! Witch! Hate!" she screamed, thrashing around her circle.

I cocked a brow. "She speaks English." Gigi whipped her head around at me and flipped me off. "I think you should let her go, Iris. It's not working. And you're only making her angrier." I wasn't sure, but I had a feeling whatever power Iris was borrowing was actually hurting the little demon. I didn't like that.

"No," said Iris, sniffing and briskly swiping at her eyes. "I'm not giving up. You said it yourself. We can't give up. Giving up is giving up on Ruth."

"I'm not giving up," I told her. "But I think Ronin's right." I moved my gaze to the half-vampire who was looking at Iris with a pained expression, the affection in his eyes for her undeniable. I couldn't believe the words that were coming out of my mouth. "Maybe Estelle Watch is a dead end. Maybe we're looking in the wrong direction." Maybe it had never been Estelle…

"Then which direction should we be looking?" asked Iris, frustrated. I didn't blame her. I was frustrated too. Tired and angry, I felt like Gigi, locked in some supernatural barrier and unable to break free and save Ruth.

Defeat was not an option. Defeat was a death sentence for Ruth. She would not survive the witch prison—not at her age.

A hiss pulled my attention back to Gigi. The demon was bent over, showing her backside to Iris and moving up and down in a very rude manner.

"Is Gigi gyrating?" laughed Ronin.

"Yup. But I don't think that's what she's intending."

In a brisk motion, Iris moved to the kitchen island, muttered a few Latin words, and with a pop of displaced air, Gigi vanished.

Not before I heard her laugh and got a glimpse of her flipping us off.

If I wasn't so down in the crapper, I would have clapped. I was going to miss that feisty demon. Maybe I'd call on her sometime.

Silence fell in the kitchen. I didn't have to look at my friends to feel their despair. I took a sip of water from my glass, forcing it down, as it nearly turned to acid in my stomach. I hadn't had anything to eat since a bagel this morning. I couldn't keep anything down. Water was the only thing that didn't threaten to come back up.

My stomach cramped and I scrubbed a hand across my face. We had less than eleven minutes left to help Ruth, and we had absolutely nothing.

It was over. I'd failed.

Failing as a Merlin didn't bother me. I could survive, go on living without being a Merlin. But I'd failed Ruth…

Ronin closed his laptop. "What now? We've got about ten minutes. What do you want us to do?"

The ribbon of tension around my chest squeezed, and it was hard just to breathe. Without anything else to go on, it was over.

Guilt mixed with fear, and I sighed, shaking inside, as a feeling of melancholy slipped over me. "We pray to the goddess for a miracle—"

The kitchen's back door flew open.

"It's Patricia Townsend!" Marcus rushed into the kitchen, his face flushed. Snow speckled his dark hair, and his boots left a trail of wet, dirty snow on the hardwood floors.

I jumped to my feet. "When you ask the goddess for a miracle…"

"Huh?" Marcus looked confused for a moment. "The goddess?" His wet snowy boot prints disappeared from the floor in sweeps, like an invisible mop had just wiped them up.

"Listen," said the Chief, a smile crinkling on his handsome face as he came around to face me. "It's Patricia Townsend."

"Is this Patricia Townsend the new girl you're banging?" asked Ronin. "Who the hell is Patricia Townsend?"

I shrugged. "No idea." I glanced at Marcus, tempted to pick the snow from his fantastic hair. "Is that name supposed to mean something?"

Marcus panted as he stood, an excited grin blossoming on his face. "Patricia Townsend *is* Estelle Watch."

My jaw fell to the floor around my feet. "Holy crap. She changed her name?" My world shifted with a nauseating spin as things added up.

"She did," said Marcus. "It's why I could never find her. But I knew I had heard that name before… and then it hit me. I remembered a couple of years ago there was a mix-up with the deed of sale with the building that is Bernard's Bakery now. Gilbert was acting all, well, you know how he can get."

"Crazy? Delusional? Like a five-year-old?" I said, my heart pounding with excitement. "And?"

"He came to me for my opinion," continued the chief. "Worried that it might be a problem.

Because she'd signed a *different* name than on her ID on file. She'd signed her real name—Estelle Watch—by mistake. She'd crossed it out and put Patricia Townsend."

"Who's Patricia Townsend?" I asked.

Marcus let out a sigh. "Patricia Townsend is Bernard Townsend's wife. The baker's wife."

"Holy boiling cauldron!" I shouted, holding on to my head as though my brain was about to explode. "She poisoned her husband? Can she be that sick?"

"Apparently," replied Marcus. "She's also a witch."

My heart was about to explode like a grenade. This was it. We'd figured it out. And not a moment too soon.

I glanced at my phone. 11:51 p.m.

Damn. "Where is she now? Do you know where she is?" It didn't matter if she was in Australia right now. With the ley lines… she was toast.

Marcus nodded. "Probably sleeping in her bed. In Hollow Cove," he added with a knowing grin. "96 Mystic Road, on the corner of Charms Avenue. The house is sage green with—"

"A red door," I answered. "I know the house." I nodded.

"You're going to bend a ley line. Aren't you?" asked Iris, her excitement showing on her face as she shifted from foot to foot.

My newfound talent was proving very useful at the moment. I didn't care that it might be an anomaly—that *I* might be the anomaly. I needed it.

Though I did wonder about that man I'd seen in the ley line back in the castle's labyrinth. Would he show up again? I couldn't worry about him right now.

I had an ass to kick.

I flashed her a smile, my heart hammering away. "I am. I'll be there in a few seconds. Imagine her surprise when I magically appear in her bedroom with my boot pressed on her throat." Now that I knew I could bend ley lines at will, moving one over to her house would be easy. I rocked into motion and grabbed my jacket from the rack on the wall.

Marcus was next to me in a flash. "You're not going alone. She's a killer. And a witch. She killed her husband. She's capable of anything."

I smiled wickedly. "So am I. She messed with my family. It's my time to return the favor."

Iris let out a happy shriek of glee and clapped her hands. "We could drain her blood and boil her bones and feed the rest to the Baluba demon. I owe him."

Yeah... Not going to happen. "I have a better idea," I told them. Like haul her ass to Greta's castle.

But I needed a confession. And I had just the thing to make her confess.

"What about your aunts?" asked Ronin.

I shook my head. "They're in no shape to come with me." My gaze flicked to Iris. "Will you stay with them? Watch over them for me until I get back?" I was worried Ruth might do something drastic.

"Of course, I will." Iris squeezed my arm. "They're my family now too."

My chest swelled with gratitude. "Thank you."

"I'll stay here too," informed Ronin as he came around the table. "You do what you gotta do. Don't worry about your aunts. We'll take care of them."

"Thanks, Ronin."

"Kick her ass, Tessa," said Iris.

I pulled my arms through my jacket and wrapped my bag over my head and shoulder. "You betcha." And a few *other* things.

"I'm coming with you," announced Marcus, which was more like an order than a request, his eyes holding mine. He looked so sexy and incredibly hot just now, standing tall, his hard chest muscles barely hidden under his shirt. He stood in the kitchen, his fists on his hips like a power ranger. If I wasn't so turned on at the moment, I might have laughed.

I'd taken Willis with me in a ley line, but he was a witch, with some of the same demon

DNA in his veins like mine. But Marcus was a wereape, a shifter, and I didn't want to risk hurting him or worse, killing him if he ever stepped into a line.

But he was a wereape, and a magnificent one at that. "How fast can you run?"

Marcus flashed me a smile that nearly had me rip off his clothes. "Really fast."

CHAPTER
28

I soared in the ley line like a speeding bullet. So fast, I barely registered my body leaving Davenport House as images sped by, blurred and barely recognizable.

Though, I did catch a glimpse of a large, silverback gorilla tearing up the street as he pushed his body forward with his muscular legs at an impossible speed. He was magnificent.

I blinked and he was gone. Not him. Me. Because, well, let's face it, my ley line was much faster. Like driving a Maserati next to a scooter.

Bending slightly forward, I laughed—or maybe I howled, I wasn't sure—letting it spill from me as my hearing was assaulted by the rushing wind. It was exhilarating. I felt alive, so alive, as though I was feeling every nerve in my body for the first time.

Riding ley lines was both thrilling and terrifying. But bending them to your will was, well, that was magical.

I figured I had about nine minutes, to grab Estelle or Patricia—whatever her name was—drag her butt with me in a ley line to Montevalley Castle and get her to confess to the murder of her husband in front of Greta.

Easy peasy, right?

We'd see.

Images blurred as I sped forward in the ley line in a wail of wind and colors. Moving this fast was exhilarating. I felt like I was Superwoman, a new superhero. Did I put my body in a superhero flying pose? You bet I did. I had to clamp my mouth shut as to not scream in delight. The last thing I wanted was to alert Estelle.

I was getting really good at bending the lines. Hell, I was a freaking pro.

Take that, Greta.

Energy rushed through my head, my body, my nerves, everywhere. Houses, streets, roads, and trees blurred past me like I was on a speeding train—more like I was riding a jet. A ley line jet.

Focusing, I willed the ley line to go slower, so I could find Estelle's house. I did not want to miss it at this speed.

A moment later, my eyes found a small sage-colored cottage with a red door, sitting peacefully between two massive leafless oak trees. Black windows stared back at me. Straining, I bent my ley line to go through her house to the second floor, moving from bedroom to bedroom until I found what I was looking for.

A woman, a witch who looked to be in her early seventies slept comfortably in a large king-size bed under a lavender comforter. She lay in the middle of the bed, her limbs all spread out like a queen, like nothing could touch her. The faint snores told me she was sleeping.

You're mine.

I pulled myself forward, gauging the distance, ready to jump out from the ley line and into her bedroom.

Steadily, I yanked myself out—

And let out a howl of pain as agony stretched inside me, strained to the breaking point.

The ley line's magic severed.

A string of pain in me snapped like a broken twig. Holy hell it hurt. My breath escaped me as I was thrown back. Darkness churned, sucking the power out of me and driving it deeper away. The ley line's magic streamed out of me in a flood of pain until there was nothing left but a dull throb.

I hit solid ground with a thud. "Ow," I choked out. "Where did that come from?"

Blinking through the tears, I took a breath of cold air. *Cold air?* I looked around. I was outside, lying on my side in the front yard, my face half-buried in the snow. I pushed myself up, my head throbbing from the sudden ley line smackdown. "Definitely not inside the bedroom."

Okay, so this wasn't as easy as I thought.

I blinked, rubbing my head and my eyes found the problem. On her front red door, barely visible under the porch light, was a diamond-shaped symbol with three squiggly lines drawn across it.

A ward. I wasn't a ward connoisseur, but I recognized it from my studying. It was a trespassing ward, one against magic, sort of a "do not enter with the use of magic" kind of ward.

Okay, so she wasn't *that* stupid.

But neither was I.

I pulled my head up and took a breath, my ribs protesting like someone had taken a two-by-four and played racquetball on my chest. I glanced over my shoulder down the dark street. Marcus wasn't here yet, but I couldn't waste any more time waiting for him.

I yanked out my phone and glanced at the screen. 11:53 p.m.

She might have put a ward up against using magic to get inside her house, but the idiot forgot to add the use of any *physical* means to get in.

"Let's do this." I walked over to the snow removal driveway stakes, hauled one out of the hard-cold earth, and stepped up to the front door.

Holding the snow removal stake like a spear, I aimed it at the glass window in the middle of the door. Of course, once I broke the glass, she'd wake up and I'd only have a few seconds before she would react, possibly with a spell.

I needed to make every second count.

Holding my breath, I raised the stake—

"Let me do that," said Marcus's voice behind me, making me flinch.

I whirled around and gasped.

There was Marcus, standing on the front porch next to me with steam rolling off his body like a freshly baked potato. And yes. He was butt naked.

He stood there, unashamed, golden, and muscled like a Roman statue. Such a pretty, pretty statue.

"Nice," I said before I could stop myself.

Marcus grinned. "I know."

I laughed. "Mmmkay," I said and turned around. "You going to help me with that or are you just going to stand there all naked and muscled… and did I mention naked?"

"I've got this." Marcus stepped next to me, completely unconcerned with his lack of clothes, which I couldn't complain about. He looked at me and said, "Get ready. She's going to be pissed."

I let out a breath. "Ready."

I knew there was a one percent chance Estelle *hadn't* poisoned her husband, and we were about to commit a crime, but I was holding on to the ninety-nine percent. I was right. I had to be.

Marcus exploded into motion and kicked down the front door with a powerful hit. Estelle's front door burst open and slammed into an adjacent side wall with a thundering crash. Yup, Estelle would have heard that. The whole damn town would too.

But I was already moving.

I hit the stairs two at a time, ignoring the pain in my ribs, head, legs, everywhere. I could worry about the pain tomorrow. Marcus's heavy footsteps thudded right behind me.

Panting, I reached the landing. I'd seen where she was, so I made for the master bedroom opposite the stairs.

The door was open, and I shot through.

Only Estelle wasn't lying in her bed anymore. In fact, she was standing next to it, not stooped with age, but straight and strong. Her long white hair floated around her in an invisible breeze. She eyed me with glittering hazel eyes full of hate from within a weathered but rosy face. She wore a long flowery nightgown that brushed the top of her toes and a murderous expression on her wrinkled face. With her arms outstretched before her, a dark curse spilled from her lips—

"Duck!" I yelled and threw myself on the ground, grabbing Marcus's arm and bringing him down with me, just as whatever spell Estelle shot at us hit the doorframe.

The frame exploded in a shower of wood splinters, dust, and drywall. A steaming black stain covered the spot where it had been and part of the wall, and a sour, bitter stench filled the air.

A Dark curse, a killing one at that.

She'd just tried to kill us. Yes, I was a stranger to her, but she knew Marcus. Yeah, she was guilty.

The little old lady had some serious magic skills. But so did I.

Pissed, I gathered my will, rolled to my knees, pulled on the elements around me, and shouted, "Stagno!"

A kinetic force smacked the witch in the chest. She staggered back, her eyes widened in fear, and then she stiffened like a statue and keeled over.

"Well, then," I hauled myself to my feet and wiped the hair from my eyes. "You've been a naughty little grandma. Haven't you?" I said as I stepped next to the fallen witch. Her face twitched in fury, but nothing else moved.

"Impressive," said Marcus as he stood next to me, still in his nakedness. I tried to keep my eyes on the witch, but it was damn near impossible with him looking like *that*.

"Thanks. It's a new power word I learned recently. It immobilizes your enemy. Just enough to keep them from trying to kill you."

"Can she speak?" Marcus watched the old witch with curiosity.

"Oh, yeah. She can speak." Total lie, since I had no idea, this being the first time I'd tried it. Well, I was going to find out.

"Hi, Patricia, or should I say… Estelle," I said, seeing her eyes widen at the mention of her real name. "Yeah. I know about that. I also know you killed your husband and let Ruth take the blame for it. Thought you'd get away with it. Didn't you? Well, I'm here to tell you that you didn't."

She looked more like a nice old grandma who spent her time baking cookies for her grandkids rather than a black widow.

I waited for her to speak but she didn't say anything.

"Her voice doesn't work," said Marcus. "Maybe your spell hit her too hard."

My gaze fell back on her face. She was looking rather smug for a witch statue. She had the look of someone who'd done something terrible and knew she had gotten away with it.

I checked my phone and cursed.

"What time is it?" asked Marcus.

My tension made all my muscles stiffen. "It's 11:55 p.m. I've got five minutes for her to talk. Looks like I'll have to torture her."

"You can torture me all you want," said Estelle, her voice raspy and hard. "You have no proof I killed my husband."

"She speaks." I looked down at her, smiling. "I have proof that you bought the black belladonna."

Estelle snorted. "That proves nothing."

"Maybe not. But a confession will. And you will confess to his murder. Because I'm going to *make* you."

"I won't." She flashed me a contemptuous smile. "I'm not afraid of you. See. I'm old. I'm not afraid of some pain. It goes with age. So, go ahead. Do your worst."

I strained to resist kicking her. I had five minutes. I'd never tortured anyone before, but I was pretty sure it took a lot longer than five minutes. And by then, it'd be too late.

Marcus leaned over. "What do you want to do? We don't have much time." The concern in his voice only made my tension rise to new heights.

My thoughts rambled, and panic rose, making it hard to concentrate. Five minutes. What could I do in less than five minutes?

"No, we don't." Something occurred to me. "But if she won't talk to me, I know who'll make her talk."

The chief's face wrinkled in a frown. "Really? Who?"

"I have an idea," I said, my veins pumping with adrenaline. I looked at the chief. "Wait for me at Davenport House. I'll see you later."

Marcus flashed me a smile. "I'll be waiting." He stared at me with those damn fine eyes of his. It was so, so easy just to stand here and get lost in them.

But I had other plans.

Grabbing Estelle by the foot, I yanked her forward out of her bedroom, down the stairs (you bet I did), and out the front door.

"You'll pay for that!" she hissed as I dropped her in the snow just as Marcus joined us in the front yard.

"Sure. Whatever you say."

Thrusting out my will, I reached out to the nearest ley line. It answered. I pulled it to me, bending it with my mind, willing it forward until it was right there with me.

A sudden blast of wind shuddered around us, unleashing a flow of energies that pulsed in the air, ley line power.

And I held it, a screaming storm of power. Me.

With one last look at Marcus, I reached down, grabbed the old witch by the front of her nightgown, and dragged her to her feet. "Let's go, Grandma."

And then I jumped into the ley line, hauling Estelle with me.

CHAPTER

29

"**Y**ou could have killed me!" howled Estelle.

Her face paled or was it a shade of green? Hard to tell in the dim light as she rushed over to a large rubber tree flowerpot and heaved. My power word's hold on Estelle had vanished the moment we'd stepped into the ley line. Interesting.

"It was nothing," I mused. I think I laughed a little too. "And here I thought you were made of stronger stuff." *You murdering hag*.

Estelle let out another hurl. "I'm dying. You've killed me. My insides are on fire! Make it stop! Make it—" she vomited again.

I rolled my eyes. "You're overreacting. I love jumping the lines. Like riding a really fast car on a really narrow road next to a cliff. One little mishap, and whoops—there you go. Down, down, down, the cliff. That's what makes it so exciting. Don't you think?"

She hurled again.

Keeping Estelle at arm's length, and spell length, I looked around. The common room in Montevalley Castle was fitted with comfy sofas and chairs, two tucked into a nook lined with built-in bookshelves, and a large stone fireplace, which was without a fire at the moment. The hardwood floors were broken up by occasional Persian rugs that probably cost more than a down payment of a house.

The room was dark, dim and lost in shadow. A couple of floor lamps provided the only light, which wasn't much but enough not to walk into a chair or a wall.

But I wasn't here to discuss the décor, though lovely.

"Greta!" I howled, my voice loud over Estelle's continuous stomach failure. "Greta! I'm here. Hello?"

I waited, but only silence greeted me. Damn it. Was I too late?

"I hate you," rasped Estelle as she bent over and hurled yet again.

"Right back at you," I spat. "Would you stop already? How much food can your tiny body carry anyway?"

Estelle made a rude gesture with her finger and then bent down and vomited again.

My chest tightened. I glanced at my phone. 11:57 p.m.

Crap. Crap. Crap.

"Greta!" I shouted. "I've got her. I've solved my case." Technically no, not without a confession, but close. "Where the hell are you? You said I had until midnight?"

I had no idea where the old witch lived. But she had told everyone that we needed to bring our cases to her. I figured that had meant the castle. Now, seeing it so gloomy and silent, I wasn't so sure anymore.

11:58 p.m.

I felt sick. I was about to join Estelle in the vomit brigade.

I was too late…

"Hello, Tessa," said a voice, and Greta stepped out of the shadows of the common room. She was dressed in a long black skirt suit with a white blouse. Paired with flat shoes, she looked like she was off to some important meeting.

Greta snapped her fingers and a raging fire roared into life from the enormous fireplace, lighting up the place as well as a few table lamps. The room suddenly was blanketed in a golden glow.

I grabbed Estelle by the back of her nightgown and hurled her out of the flowerpot and out in the open. Okay, a bit harsh, but this witch had killed her husband and had let Ruth take the fall for it.

"This is Estelle Watch. She changed her name to Patricia Townsend. It's why we couldn't find her. She's Bernard Townsend's wife. And she killed him. Poisoned him and let Ruth take the blame." I spoke fast not knowing if my time was up. I just kept going. "She tried to kill me too tonight, but she failed." I took a deep breath. "She's the one."

Greta looked down at Estelle as the other witch kept vomiting, now all over the clean polished floors with a few spills on the expensive rug.

"Hope you have a good carpet cleaner," I said.

Greta eyed the other old witch with a cold stare. "Is this true? Did you kill your husband, Bernard Townsend?"

Estelle lifted her head at Greta. "Please. Make it stop. It's killing me."

"Confess your crime and I'll make it stop," said Greta.

Estelle hacked up another volley of vomit. "Yes," she glowered, and I was surprised how easily that came out. "I did it."

"Why?" I couldn't help myself.

Her eyes found me. "Because he cheated on me with Viola Biddle. That whore. So, I poisoned him," she declared proudly.

I shook my head. "You could have just asked for a divorce, you stupid, stupid, bitch."

Estelle winced in pain as she hurled again. "You promised," she pointed a trembling finger at Greta. "Make it stop. I'm dying."

Greta moved her eyes over to me. "I gather you… jumped a ley line to get here."

"I did."

"And moved it to this very spot?"

I nodded. "Yes."

Greta's face was unreadable as she looked down at Estelle, who was now convulsing. "Ley lines. Some witches just can't stomach them." She moved her hand in Estelle's direction and said, "Utal dimlivic."

I felt a surge of power rush past me. Estelle's eyes went wide and then rolled into the back of her head as the witch's body went limp. For a second I thought she was dead, but the heavy snoring said otherwise.

But I still didn't know. "Did I pass?" I felt like I was about to hurl myself. "Did I make it?"

And for the first time, Greta smiled. She smiled at me. "Thank you, Tessa. If anyone could have helped Ruth, I knew it would be you. I knew you could do it. Congratulations."

"Huh?" I said stupidly. Did that mean she cared about my Aunt Ruth? "What's going to happen to Ruth?"

Greta hadn't lost her smile as she said, "Ruth will be fine." She tugged on the front of her blazer. "I'm on my way to speak to the Gray Council to have all the charges dropped. I'll be visiting Ruth too."

My eyes went on instant burn. I couldn't help it. The tears just started and didn't stop until I was practically sobbing in joy. "So, it's over? It's really over? She's going to be okay?" I asked, trembling and tasting the salt from my tears in my mouth.

Greta's dark eyes met mine. "It's over. She's going to be just fine."

My knees buckled and I nearly fell to the ground, but it was covered in Estelle's puke, so I opted to stay upright.

Ruth, my Ruth was going to be okay. It was the best outcome possible. I felt like doing cartwheels.

"This is for you." From the folds of her blazer, Greta pulled out a rolled piece of parchment secured by a red ribbon.

With my pulse pounding in my ears, I took it and ripped off the ribbon. I stared at a legal-looking, stamped piece of paper. It read:

The undersigned hereby confer this
MERLIN LICENSE
To: Tessa Davenport

For successfully completing the three Witch Trials, as provided and proscribed by the undersigned officers of the Merlin Witch Trials Training Division.

Signed by Course Director: Greta Trickle

I beamed. I was a Merlin again.

CHAPTER
30

I stepped out of the ley line and landed in Davenport House's hallway.

I kicked off my boots and let my toes, my newly reelected Merlin toes, feel the warmth of the hardwood floors. It was a glorious feeling.

"Ruth!" I yelled as I sprinted down to the kitchen. "Dolores? Beverly? Iris? Where is everyone?" I called with excitement bubbling into my voice.

Upstairs. Yes of course. It was just after midnight.

Smiling, I spun around and vaulted back into the hallway. I ran up to the second floor and burst into Ruth's bedroom.

It was empty.

So was Beverly's and Dolores's and Iris's.

Confusion quickly replaced my elated bubble. Where was my family?

"They left to Wicked Witch & Handsome Devil Pub to celebrate," said a familiar voice.

I jumped in surprise, thinking it was just me and my thoughts to keep me company. I turned to find Marcus standing in my bedroom doorway wearing nothing but my bathrobe.

My eyebrows rose. "They did? But…"

"Ruth got a phone call," he informed me, and I remembered Greta saying as much. She must have called Ruth as soon as she left the common room. "I'd just gotten here…"

"Naked," I said.

"Naked," he answered, still unabashed. "Dolores gave me a coat, but I liked your bathrobe better," he added with a grin. "Smells like you."

I have no idea why, but that comment really turned me on.

I stepped toward him. "And then?"

Marcus shifted his weight. "Then," he said, looking at me through his thick, black lashes. "They left. You just missed them."

I exhaled, letting out all the adrenaline from before. "Well. That's fine. After all of this, they deserve to have a little fun."

"You did it, Tessa." Marcus reached out and pulled me to him. "You saved Ruth."

"You helped," I answered staring at his lips as a torrent of heat flowed through my core.

"I helped," he purred, his eyes glimmering in amusement. "What do I get for it?"

"I have a few things in mind," I answered as I yanked the robe off of him in one swift pull, revealing his once again naked body that I liked *very* much.

Yes, I was forward. Blame my large lady balls for that. But I was tired of waiting for what I wanted. And I wanted this sexy-as-sin chief.

Marcus leaned forward, his breath warm against my cheek. "You mean celebrating... like this?" he said and dipped his head to kiss me.

Even though this wasn't the first time we'd kissed, the taste of him still had me growling like an animal. His kiss wasn't gentle. It was fierce and possessive, and I melted into it. His tongue brushed mine, eager and hot, and I kissed him back just as fiercely, again and again. Then I pulled back and kissed his neck, nibbling his ear, and biting it.

He groaned, and it sent my core on fire.

"How much celebrating are we talking about?" he asked as he pulled away.

Grinning like an idiot, I pushed him back into my bedroom playfully. Then I pulled off my coat and tossed it to the floor. "I'm thinking..." I said as I removed my shirt and started to pull off my jeans. "The kind that lasts all night long." I stepped out of my jeans. "And repeats… over and over again."

I removed my bra, wiggled out of my underwear, and just stood there, bold in my own nakedness. Okay, getting my Merlin license had perhaps made me a little rash.

Yet, somehow I wasn't embarrassed. My eyes grazed down at his hard and extremely obvious desire for me. Nothing was more ego-boosting than seeing that. To hell with my cellulite. Damn my saggy, sausage arms. Screw my average breasts.

He thought I was hot.

That's it. I was going to go all primeval on his ass.

Marcus's eyes sparkled with obvious lust. "You're beautiful."

Take off!

I tackled him like a linebacker and we both laughed as we stumbled onto the bed in a tangle of naked limbs.

Marcus grabbed me and pulled me beneath him. The feeling of his weight on top of me, the weight of a man, triggered something feral in me and I pressed tighter to him. His rough, callused hands slid over my body, caressing me and sending shivers through me. I'd felt so empty for so long, and now I wanted to be full of him. I ran my hands over the cords of muscles on his back, pulling him to me.

My eyes moved to my open bedroom door. Whoops. I did not want my aunts or Iris to walk in on us. Not because I was embarrassed, but because I didn't want it to stop.

"House," I called, as heat shot through me, making me hyper and impatient. "Shut my door and lock it, please."

And with a flash of energy, my bedroom door shut with a thud and I heard the sliding of metal as the bolt shut into place.

There. Now I was ready to celebrate. Celebrate all night long with a man I cared about who thought I was hot.

And for the first time in my life, I didn't want the lights off. I wanted them on.

Hello, lady balls.

CHAPTER
31

I used to think waking up to the smell of Ruth's pancakes was the best thing in this world. But now seeing this sexy naked man with the body of a Greek god sleeping next to me in *my* bed, well, I was at a loss for words.

Perhaps Ruth's pancakes came in at a close second. Hmmm. Perhaps… not.

Marcus, the chief of Hollow Cove, that glorious, kind man, was in my bed. *My* bed. I nearly started jumping on it the moment I woke. I was so excited. But that might freak him out. Yeah. Too early to start showing him that side of me. Way too soon.

I was sitting up in my bed, and like a stalker, I was watching him sleep.

Thank the cauldron he wasn't a snorer. His handsome face was smooth and peaceful, his breathing low and rhythmic. I was so tempted to brush my fingers along his brow or rake them through his luscious black locks, but that would surely wake him up.

I stared out the window at the bright blue morning sky. There wasn't a cloud in sight. Grinning, I took a deep breath and let it out through my nose. Nothing would take the smile off of my face today, nothing. I'd never felt happier. Complete. And the feeling was dangerously infectious.

Ruth was free. All charges were dropped. Marcus was in my bed.

Hell, I could feel a song coming along.

I knew it would be a glorious day just by the intoxicating scent of Ruth's famous buttermilk pancakes. She hadn't made breakfast for months. It was good to have her back.

"Why are you smiling?"

I spun my head around and stared at a wideawake Marcus. "You're awake?" I said, my heart racing a little more at the sight of those fine gray eyes.

"I am," said Marcus lazily. "You been up long?"

"No," I lied. I'd been staring at him sleep for over an hour.

I gazed at his face, his lips, and I wanted to kiss him. But I was very aware of the thing called *morning breath*. No one wanted that, and it was way too soon in the relationship to go there. I needed some quality time with my friend Colgate.

Relationship. Is that what this was? I would have to talk to him about that later, after I brushed my teeth.

"How did you sleep?"

A wicked grin spread over his face as he folded an arm under his head. "Incredibly well," he purred, and the way his eyes fixed on me sent a wave of heat all the way to my core. Damn.

"That's good. We did… umm… *celebrate* quite a bit last night." Try three times. It had been the best sex I'd ever had. But there was no reason to let him know that.

But he looked so good, so tempting, so stupidly gorgeous, I had to restrain from jumping him right here and now. *Boy, I'm in trouble.*

With his other hand, Marcus reached out and took my hand in his. "Did *you* sleep okay?"

"Like a baby." I rubbed my thumb over his hand. "Best sleep I've had in weeks." Which was the truth. "I'm just so happy the charges were dropped. Ruth can be herself again. My family is whole again. We can finally go back to living our lives."

"Is that her cooking downstairs?" he asked as he breathed in. "I'm surprised she's up so early. They came home around four this morning."

"You heard them?" I asked, surprised that I hadn't. But I had been exhausted. I couldn't keep my eyes open after our *third* celebration.

Marcus met my eyes. "I did. You were sleeping. You're beautiful when you sleep."

I cocked a brow. "Were you watching me sleep, Chief? That is all kinds of pervy." I was such a hypocrite.

"I couldn't resist," he said around his laugh. "Guess that makes me a perve." His eyes flicked to my lips and my breath caught.

"There's something I've been meaning to ask you for a long time," I blurted, trying to control my raging hormones. I wasn't a sex-craved lunatic. Or maybe I was?

Marcus looked surprised. "Really? What?"

"What the hell is in that blue vial that Ruth prepares for you?"

Marcus let out a really loud laugh. If Iris and my other aunts weren't already up, this would have definitely woken them.

"That's what you wanted to know?" he asked, clearly stunned. "Not how many women I've been with or if I have any kids out in the world?"

I shook my head. "Nope. Just that. Whoa— wait. How many women have you been with?

329

Should I be concerned?" I teased, realizing I didn't harbor any jealous or insecure feelings. That's what lady balls do.

Marcus's eyes glinted with amusement. "It's for my allergies. I've got bad seasonal allergies and Ruth's tonic is the only thing that helps."

"That's it?" I said, a little disappointed. "You've got allergies? It's not some super-duper beast suppressor? Some superpower enhancement? An invisibility potion?"

The chief shook his head, his smile crinkling his eyes. "Sorry to disappoint you. It's for my allergies," he repeated, laughing harder, which of course made me laugh with him.

I cleared my throat and tried to look serious. "While I have you talking… I have something else to ask."

Marcus wrapped both arms behind his head. "Shoot."

I peeled my eyes from his washboard abs and looked at his face. "But you need to promise you won't get mad. Promise?"

"I promise," he laughed. "Go on. What else do you want to know? I have no secrets. I'm an open book."

My eyes grazed along his golden chest, my fingers itching to rub all over him. "Okay, so, when I broke into your office—"

Marcus jerked up. "You *broke* into my office."

Oh, crap. "You said you weren't going to get mad," I reminded him, my pulse thumping faster as heat rushed to my face.

The chief's face twisted into a smile. "I know you broke in. And I know you were with Ronin when you did." He settled back down on the pillow. "Go on. Ask your question."

My mouth fell open. "As I was saying… I saw something on one of your reports."

"Like what?"

"You crossed out my father's name, Sean Sanderson, and put a question mark. Why's that? Do you know something I don't?"

Okay, some clarification is needed. Yes, my father's surname was Sanderson. But, with witches, it wasn't uncommon to carry their mother's surname. Especially if your family name was an ancient one and powerful. Davenport happened to be one of those last names.

Marcus stared at the ceiling for a while before answering. "It's something your mother had said once, when she was here. She was helping us on a case. I can't remember why we were talking about you, but we were."

He went quiet, and I knew he was thinking of his best friend. He'd been working a case with my mommy dearest. They'd been partnered up. But she'd abandoned him to go to my father and left him alone and exposed. He was killed by a demon that night.

I swallowed hard. "What did she say?" My relationship with my mother was a complicated one, to say the least, one I didn't really want to bring up.

Marcus's eyes narrowed as he thought about it. "She said… she said, 'Her father's not her father.'"

"What the hell does that mean?" Emotions spiraled through me and not in a good way.

The chief looked at me. "It could mean a lot of things." He searched my face. "Why don't you ask her? She's your mother."

Right. It was too early to have this conversation. I'd rather jump in a steaming hot tub filled with cow manure than speak to her right now.

Though if my father wasn't my biological father, it explained a lot.

"You know what?" I said, plastering on a smile that I didn't feel. "I'm starving. And you must be starving too after all that… you know… stuff you did to me."

Marcus flashed his teeth. "I'm ready for round four if you want."

I laughed, my body tingling with heat. "Don't tempt me." I stared at him for a moment and then swung my legs off the bed. I grabbed my bathrobe that still smelled like Marcus and tightened it around me.

My phone beeped with a message, and I grabbed it from my nightstand. "It's a message from Willis."

"Who's Willis?"

"One of the witches from the witch trials— oh, my god! He made it. He passed. He's a Merlin." Little mousy Willis had done it. He'd solved whatever case Greta had given him and had passed the third trial. Lucky number thirteen.

"I'm happy for him," said Marcus.

A well of emotions bubbled up. "Me too. You have no idea how much he deserved it." Guess Willis and Wilma had done some celebrating of their own last night.

Feeling like I owned the world, I put my phone back on the nightstand. I looked at Marcus and said, "I'll be back with some breakfast and coffee." I closed my bedroom door behind me and rushed down the stairs.

I hit the bottom and turned to the kitchen. Making my way, I could see Ruth at the stove, smiling as she whisked another batch of her pancakes. Dolores and Beverly were seated at the kitchen table laughing. They were laughing, not crying.

The goddess was good to us.

Dolores and Beverly looked up as I approached. I moved into the kitchen and made a beeline for Ruth. I squeezed my little aunt into my arms, taking in her smell of soap and lavender.

Ruth let out a tiny shriek. "You're going to get some batter on you, silly," she laughed as I let her go and stepped back.

"I don't care." I sighed. Relief washed over me as I saw her pretty pink cheeks. Her color had returned. I had my Ruth back, and all was right in the world again.

"We tried to keep it down," said Dolores as she set her coffee mug down. "Did we wake you?"

"Oh, no. I've been up for hours."

"Doing all kinds of naughty things for hours. Weren't you?" taunted Beverly, her face fresh and her makeup flawless as usual.

Oh, dear. "Uh… I was hoping to get some breakfast to take up to my room," I said, feeling a flush attack my face. I didn't know why I should be embarrassed. I was a grown-ass woman. Having a man like Marcus waiting for me in my bed should have had me doing backflips.

Dolores eyed me over her coffee mug. "What kind of things? The trials are over, Tessa. Greta told us all about it. We're all very proud of you." Her face stretched into a smile. "I always knew you could do it."

"Thanks."

"She's got a man in her bed. That's what," informed Beverly before I had a chance to explain.

The kitchen went silent.

Ruth twisted around, sending clumps of pancake batter all over the kitchen island and floor. Her wide eyes matched her smile. "You've got a man in your bed!" she said happily, like I'd just won the lottery, like the chance of me having a man in my bed was slim. I wasn't sure how to take that.

"Uh… right… umm… yeah, about that." I took a breath. "You see…"

The doorbell rang.

"I got it." I spun around so fast I nearly smashed into the wall.

My bare feet slapped against the wood floors as I hurried down the hallway, wondering who it could be this early in the morning. Iris had a set of keys so it couldn't be her.

Maybe it was Gilbert. He'd finally found out we had his exotic herbs inventory notebook and wanted it back.

Holding back a laugh, I grabbed the doorknob and pulled open the front door.

My smile vanished.

A pretty fifty-year-old woman with dark hair and matching eyes stood in the doorway.

"Well, don't just stand there," she said, sounding annoyed. "Come and give your mother a hug."

Cauldron be damned.

My mother was here.

Don't miss the next book in The Witches of Hollow Cove series!

ABOUT THE AUTHOR

Kim Richardson is a USA Today bestselling and award-winning author of urban fantasy, fantasy, and young adult books. She lives in the eastern part of Canada with her husband, two dogs and a very old cat. Kim's books are available in print editions, and translations are available in over 7 languages.

To learn more about the author, please visit:

www.kimrichardsonbooks.com

Printed in Great Britain
by Amazon